mafia toy

Syndicate of Sin

emilia rose

Cover by: The Book Brander

Editor: Jovana Shirley, Unforeseen Editing, www.unforeseenediting.com

Emilia Rose

emiliarosewriting@gmail.com

1

laila

"IF YOU KEEP GRINDING on my thigh like this, doll, you'll ruin my suit pants."

I pulled my gaze away from the beautiful woman across the bar at The Syndicate, who kept throwing glances at me, and looked back at my husband, not even realizing that the woman had gotten me this horny.

"I didn't tell you to stop, did I?" Constantino pulled me further onto his lap, my ass against the throbbing bulge in his pants, then pushed some hair behind my shoulder. "Ruin them for me. I want all my men to see how wet your pussy gets for me and *only me*." He chuckled darkly and followed my gaze. "And maybe some hot chick across the bar too?"

"Sorry," I whispered, tearing my gaze away from her again. "I know I shouldn't …"

"You want to know how I feel about my wife getting off on some woman at my club?" Constantino murmured in my ear as I pressed my aching cunt against his thigh. He seized my waist with one of his large hands, pulled my skirt up enough, then sat me down right on his bulge. "You feel that, doll?"

Whimpering, I sipped on my drink and nodded. "Mmhmm."

"Words," he growled.

"Yes, I do."

"How does it feel against that aching pussy of yours?"

"Good." I ground myself on him. "Really good."

Constantino slid his rough fingers up the insides of my thighs, pushing my short skirt with them and sending goose bumps down my legs. I sucked in a sharp breath and grasped on to the bar in front of me, my nipples aching.

"I should fuck you right here in front of her." His facial hair pricked my bare neck. "I know how sexy you are when you moan. Do you think I can get you to moan loud enough so she notices us?"

"Constantino," I scolded, though his fingers were already moving in circles around my swollen, aching clit. I furrowed my brow and stared at the pretty girl who sat alone at the bar.

"Hover over me for a second, doll."

When I hovered over him, he reached between us and undid the zipper on his pants. Before I could move away and tell him not to because we were out in public, where any of my friends could see, he grabbed my hips and pulled me down onto him, filling me all the way up.

I slapped a hand over my mouth to suppress a moan and clamped my pussy down on his cock—hard. My feet were inches off the ground, my entire body weight pressed on him.

He started pumping into me slowly, filling me up and leaving me empty. I squeezed his dick even harder and peeked over at the woman, who glanced back over at us.

Constantino eyed her from over my shoulder. "Do you think she can tell that you're full with my cock? She can't stop looking over here and at you. You should go talk to her when I'm finished with you."

"I-I can't."

Constantino bounced me on his cock, slight enough to not make it noticeable unless someone was really staring over here. And I didn't doubt that some people were. Constantino was the boss of The Syndicate and of the mob.

The woman looked over at us again, her eyes lingering longer than they had before. She glanced behind me at my husband, then back to me, her pale cheeks flushing pink. She sipped her drink, eyes curious.

"Doll, she *wants* you," Constantino whispered, tucking some hair behind my ear.

I tightened around my husband's cock and whimpered, the pressure building up inside me. I dug my fingertips into the bar top until they turned white and sucked in a sharp breath.

"Show her how you ride me, how desperate you really are."

"Constantino," I breathed, warning him to stop.

"Don't make me ask again."

Whimpering softly, I kept my gaze on her and moved my hips up and down on his cock, trying not to draw any attention to us in this crowded Mafia-run bar. But Constantino was so freaking big.

My pussy tightened around him, and I furrowed my brow. "Oh God …"

"Clench your pussy and keep riding my cock," he growled, gazing over my shoulder at her. "And tell me what you'd do to her if we brought her home tonight. Tell me all those dirty fantasies you have about sleeping with another woman."

"I …" My breath caught in the back of my throat as I tensed harder. "I want to touch her, want my fingers inside her to see how she'll tighten around me. I want her cunt on my mouth and for her to ride my face."

I wanted Constantino to force her to ride my face, for him to fuck her pouty little mouth as she did, for him to fuck her pussy until her juices covered his cock, and then for him to shove himself into me, pushing her juices deep inside me.

Constantino grabbed my hips, leaned back, and drove his hips up hard and fast. I gripped the bar top harder, crying out into one of my hands. He reached around my body to cup my breast, then seized and tugged on my nipple.

Pleasure surged through my core, pushing me higher and closer to the edge.

"Go chat with her about what we talked about the other night," Constantino said.

"I can't go over to her and ask her," I said. "What if she says no?"

"Nobody could say no to you," Constantino purred against my cheek, his thick Italian accent making me warm in all the right places. He slid his hands up my body and grabbed my waist. "I mean, look at you."

"You're only saying that because you're my husband."

He chuckled darkly. "Go see for yourself."

"Can you ask her?" I shifted in his arms and batted my lashes at him. "Please?"

"You can do it by yourself, doll. She won't say no."

"But ..."

"You *do* want this, don't you? Want to see how another woman feels? Want to"—he slipped his fingers between my pussy lips and into me too, sinking them deep inside and curling them against my G-spot—"feel how tight she clenches around your fingers?"

My core tightened as my breath hitched. "Y-yes," I whispered, my voice coming out smaller than it had the first night I mentioned to Constantino that I sorta, kinda had a thing for girls too.

I had never mentioned it to anyone else because the last time I had shown mere interest in another girl in middle school, the popular girls had bullied me so badly that I spent the rest of my lunches in the crappy restroom.

And when the volunteers at the youth home had found out about that on top of everything *else* ... they had nearly kicked me out of the place.

I didn't want that to happen ever again.

I'd thought for sure that Constantino would immediately ask me for a divorce the next morning.

"I would love to have another woman in the bedroom with you, doll," he said, his stubble brushing against the sensitive part of my neck. "But only if you want it."

I slid my shot glass across the bar. "Another one, please."

"Another one?" Constantino asked, slipping a third finger inside me. He pumped his fingers in and out of me, faster and harder and deeper. "Needy tonight, aren't we, doll?"

"Constantino," I whimpered.

"And for you, boss?" the bartender asked, sliding a shot my way.

"I already have enough to taste tonight."

With his husky voice in my ear, I shuddered against him and desperately tried to keep my legs from trembling. I was so close—so freaking close—to coming for him. But he pulled his fingers out of me and away from my clit completely, as if he knew.

"You get to come when you ask her." He gently nibbled on my neck and pulled his dick out of me too. "No sooner."

"Constantino," I whined. "Please."

He swept the hair off my shoulders and took it in his fist, pulling it back. "Have some confidence in yourself, doll. Go ask her what we agreed upon. She won't say no to you, I promise."

Once I swallowed my shot, I peeked back over at her. My pussy ached from the sudden emptiness, the desperation lingering inside me. Constantino wouldn't let me come until I talked to her, until I offered her one million dollars to be our toy.

2

sage

DATELESS AND NEARLY PENNILESS, I sat at the bar in a club rumored to be run by the Mafia and took a sip of the only good thing I had going for me tonight—alcohol. Austin had left me nearly thirty minutes ago, and I couldn't get myself to go home alone.

Gaze drifting around the packed club, I spotted *her* for the seventh time tonight.

Chocolate-colored hair. Huge *fuck me* brown eyes. Pouty, full raspberry-colored lips.

She sat on a man's lap and kept stealing glances at me all night. A silky pink dress clung to her curves with a necklace dipped between her cleavage, drawing my—and probably everyone else's—attention to it. The woman was Instagram influencer perfect, but without the filters and the Photoshop.

I hadn't ever been with a woman. God, I'd be *way* too anxious for something like that. I was bad enough as it was with guys. *Ahem, Austin.* But I'd gotten off to the thought of being with one.

Never one as beautiful as her.

She was with her boyfriend.

When she slid her shot glass across the bar for the third time tonight, I spotted a large diamond ring on her finger and a wedding band glimmering under the dim club lighting. A long, disappointed sigh escaped my mouth.

Nope, definitely her husband.

Figures.

After averting my gaze back to my drink, I took one last sip of it and stared emptily at the bar top. I should've never come out tonight. Not only had I gotten to witness Austin flirting with every petite, prettier-than-perfect girl at The Syndicate, but he had left me here.

Left me here!

Who the hell did that to anyone? I would never invite a boyfriend out and leave him alone at a club without a way to get home and with a crazy-high bar tab. But I guessed he didn't give a fuck. It wasn't like we had ever been exclusive.

"Hi," someone said to my right.

I snapped my head up and my gaze over to the pretty *married* woman, who scooted onto the barstool next to me. My breath caught in my throat. *What is she doing over here?*

"What are you drinking?" she asked.

My cheeks burned. I glanced to my left to see who she was talking to because it definitely wasn't me. It couldn't be me. Why would she come chat with me out of all these people here? She had a husband.

Unless … she thought I had been staring at her husband and not her.

"I'm talking to you," she said, giving me a soft smile. "What're you drinking?"

"I, um …"

She was smiling at me a bit too sweetly. *What is going on?*

Darting my gaze around the room, I spotted large Italian guards posted at almost every door, walking around the club, lingering near the back offices. Those rumors about the mob had to be true.

If she was with them—which she seemed to be—then maybe she

was going to ask me to go for a little chat in the back hallway for staring in her direction and then blow my freaking head off.

Damn Austin. Why'd he leave me?

"Amalfi Coast cocktail mixed with Afterglow," the bartender who had been serving me all night said.

"Can we get two more?" she asked.

I grabbed my purse, knowing that I had just spent the last of my money, trying to forget Austin, with a couple of drinks of alcohol and loud, blaring music. "I actually don't have any more cash on me."

God, this is embarrassing.

Glancing down, I gulped. "I should probably get going anyway."

"Nonsense," she said, her hand on my thigh to keep me seated. "My husband owns the club. It's fine. I was going to buy you a drink anyway." When the bartender slid the drinks toward her, she thanked him and told him to put *all* the rest of my drinks tonight on her tab.

"You ... you really don't have to do that," I whispered.

"You've been here all night. Alone."

"Yeah, I, um ..." I sipped my drink. "My date left."

"He left you at a crowded club, all alone? Doesn't sound like a winner."

"He's not," I admitted, leaving out that part where I had only been seeing him because he had a huge dick and loved taking me to fancy places—something I'd never see otherwise. "But he takes care of me ... sometimes."

"Sweetheart," she murmured, inching closer and leaning against the bar. Tequila lingered on her breath, her eyes a bit hazy, as if she'd had a bit too much to drink tonight. But if she really was the mob boss's wife, they wouldn't cut her off. She brushed her fingers against my forearm. "If he cared about you, he'd bring you home. Not leave you in a club, where strangers like me could come flirt with you."

Almost as if she realized what she had said, she widened her eyes and stiffened.

Warmth exploded through me as my heart raced inside my chest. I swallowed my pride, my insecurities, everything, thanks to the liquid courage I had drunk tonight, and smiled back. "So, that's what you're doing here? Flirting with me?" I asked playfully.

She dropped her hand to my knee again, her fingers lingering on my bare flesh. Instead of moving her hand up my thigh, like I'd suspected her husband had been doing to her earlier while she stared over at me, she held it there, face softening.

"Is that too forward?" She giggled.

I glanced down at her hand on my knee and pressed my thighs together slightly to suppress the ache between them. When I looked back up at her, she dropped her gaze to my thighs.

"Maybe not forward enough?" she offered, fingers moving an inch higher. "Hmm?"

After pressing my lips together, I clutched my glass tightly and stared into her playful eyes. Slowly, she slithered her fingers up my thigh and underneath my skirt, and I didn't stop her. I let her touch me, tease me, taunt me with her fingers.

When she reached my panties, she stiffened, sucked in a breath, and gnawed on the inside of her cheek. "God, you're wetter than I am," she murmured, which only made my pussy ache even more.

I sucked in a sharp breath, too, and spread my legs a bit wider. "Still … not forward enough," I said, caught in the moment.

Her pink-painted lips twitched into a small smirk, and she gently touched my clit, rubbing it in circles underneath the bar top so nobody could see. Still, I peered around to make sure everyone had busied themselves with someone or something else.

If anyone saw this, saw us …

"What's your name?" she whispered.

"Sage," I said in a breath as she massaged my clit. "Wh-what's yours?"

"Laila," she said, gaze dropping to my lips. "Say it."

"Laila," I repeated.

"One night …" she said, smirking. "One night, you'll be moaning it."

Another wave of pleasure rushed through me, nearly pushing me to the edge already.

"I've wanted to talk to you all night."

"But your husband …"

"Is okay with this," she finished. "He even suggested it."

"Are you … serious?" I whispered, unable to believe this was real.

She was either dead serious or had had a few too many drinks or a combination of both.

She took my hand. "Let me show you."

"Show me what?"

"How serious I am." She pulled my hand up her dress and placed it over her panties, which were completely soaked through.

Warmth rushed through my core, and I clenched.

This couldn't be happening. This really couldn't be happening.

I glanced around to ensure nobody was watching us, then couldn't stop myself from drawing my thumb over her swollen clit. I furrowed my brow and whimpered to myself, the heat growing inside me.

Laila softly moaned, staring at me with huge *fuck me* eyes that no woman had ever given me before. I had been the one to deal those out to Austin every night for the past few months.

And while I knew I should be getting away from this place and going home, I couldn't stop myself from rubbing my thumb faster against her clit. My hand was buried underneath her skirt, and heat was coming off her in waves.

"Do you want to come meet my husband? We have a *proposition* for you," she asked suddenly, still rubbing my clit.

"What kind of proposition?" I asked, heart pounding.

"One million dollars in exchange for you being our toy."

3

sage

WH-WHAT DID SHE JUST SAY? *She wants me to be their toy in exchange for money? She wants her husband to use me, touch me, thrust himself inside me? And she wants to grind her pussy against me while he does?*

After pulling her hand from my skirt, Laila grabbed my hand and led me through the dancing crowd, then through a dimly lit back hallway. I stared down at the marble tiles, heart pounding inside my chest when I spotted two large bodyguards standing in front of the last door.

This has to be a joke. Or more like a death sentence.

Intertwining her fingers with mine and squeezing, Laila pulled me toward her until her breasts brushed against my arm. Warmth exploded through my core, my pussy pounding already, and she hadn't really touched me yet.

When we reached the guards, I stopped Laila. "Are you sure this is okay?"

She giggled, the sound making me tighten, and nodded to the guards anyway. They glanced briefly at me, and then one opened the door into the large luxury office. A white fur rug. A black marble desk. And the mobster with a handsome face and devilish smirk.

With dark brown hair slicked back, a black Rolex clasped around his wrist, and a tailored suit that hugged his muscular body, he gazed across the desk at me and pressed his full pink lips together.

Once the door shut, Laila dropped my hand and walked to her husband. "This is Constantino."

"H-hi," I squeaked out, nerves nipping at my insides. "I'm Sage."

"I know," he said, voice deep and gruff.

"Y-you know?"

"I know everyone who comes into my club more than once." Constantino walked around the desk so he stood in front of it, then leaned back and didn't say another word, his hooded eyes terrifyingly dark.

Laila stood next to him, her left breast pressed against his chest.

I stood next to the couch and stared at them through wide eyes, my core warming. This ... this really couldn't be happening right now. Maybe she was testing me, seeing if I'd touch her husband with her so she could ... kill me. Was that what the Mafia did?

"Come here," she said, reaching for me.

Gulping, I stepped toward her and looked between the married couple.

She dropped her hand and placed it on the front of her husband's suit pants, stroking the bulge. Wetness pooled between my thighs. I ground my legs together, trying to ease the ache between them.

"Share my husband's cock with me," Laila purred.

Dropping to her knees in front of him, she undid his belt, unzipped the front of his pants, then pulled them down. His cock was hard, long, and so thick through his briefs, and I'd bet it was throbbing, like my pussy was.

I peered up at him, my entire body hot.

But he didn't say anything, just leaned back and gently drew a finger down the side of her cheek. When he looked back up at me, his eyes were dark and hooded again, making him look like the man of all those rumors, about the man who ran The Syndicate, the man who killed for his wife.

Laila curled her slim, manicured fingers around the waistband of his briefs and slowly pulled them down, revealing his huge cock inch by inch until Constantino's dick sprang out of them.

She held it by the base and pressed her full lips on the tip, her tongue traveling around his head to lick up Constantino's pre-cum. I swallowed hard, unable to pull my gaze away from her as she took him into her mouth and stared at me.

After bobbing her head on him a couple of times, she came up for air, strands of spit dangling from her mouth to his cock. "If you don't like it, you don't have to accept any offer we give you," she murmured, unbuttoning the top button of her dress to reveal even more cleavage.

My gaze dropped to her tits, and I whimpered softly, desperately wanting to see them.

"Order my wife to take off her dress," Constantino said to me.

Heat grew between my legs. "T-take off your top."

Laila undid the rest of the buttons and let her dress slide off her slim shoulders, leaving her top half in nothing but a lacy bra that I would've sworn was a push-up bra before she took it all off.

"And her bra," Constantino continued. "Tell her you want to see her tits."

I ground my thighs together, watching Laila suck on the head of her husband's cock while he ordered me to tell her what to do. I swallowed hard, desperately needing someone to touch me, and whimpered.

"Take off your bra too. I want to see your tits."

With his cock in her mouth, Laila unfastened her bra and let her tits bounce out. While her frame was small—not quite petite, but tinier than mine—her tits lay heavy on her chest, not perky, like I'd expected them to be.

But, fuck, they were even sexier than I'd imagined. I wanted to run my mouth all over them, feel them against mine, feel her nipples glide against my chest as her husband pounded into her from behind.

Laila bobbed her head faster on her husband's throbbing cock, her tits bouncing around. I clenched and found myself dropping to my knees next to her. She took all of Constantino into her mouth until her lips met the base of his cock and stared over at me with hot tears in her eyes. After gargling on him for a moment, she pulled away and held his dick out toward me.

I stared at her, my stomach bubbling with nerves.

"Share it," Constantino said to Laila.

She pulled me closer to her and nodded at me, as if to say it was okay for me to touch her husband. Constantino pushed himself between us, and our lips traveled up and down his shaft. At first, it was just his cock on my lips, but then I felt Laila's lips on mine too.

With the head of his cock between us, Laila moved her raspberry-stained lips against mine. Warmth exploded through my core, and I hungrily kissed her back, swirling my tongue around his head and against hers.

Instead of thrusting his dick between us again, Constantino gently pulled himself away so the only thing Laila and I had left to kiss was each other. She shifted closer to me, her lips moving against mine and her hesitant hands resting on my knees.

I wanted her to touch me more. I wanted her hands all over my body.

When I finally pulled away for air, I spotted Constantino leaning against his desk and stroking his hard cock. His gaze drifted from his wife to me and back, lips parted slightly, but his stare was still harsh.

"Don't stop, doll," he ordered.

Laila glanced over at me and furrowed her brow, her drunken haze becoming clearer.

"Touch her, doll. Then, tell me how she feels."

Goose bumps rose on my skin, the anticipation growing inside me.

Laila leaned closer to me again and pressed her lips against mine, her hand sinking between my thighs. I found myself spreading my knees to give her better access as she rubbed my clit in small, torturous circles.

"Laila," I moaned against her lips.

She moved her fingers faster and crawled toward me, straddling one of my legs and rubbing her cunt against my thigh. When she moaned into my mouth, I tilted my head back and spread my legs wider, the pressure building up higher inside me.

"How does she feel, doll?" Constantino asked her.

"God," Laila murmured, her breath catching and her mouth hungrily back on mine. She bucked her hips faster and harder against my thigh, getting herself off. "She feels so good. So fucking good. I don't wanna stop."

"Please," I whispered against her mouth, "don't."

As she continued to grind her cunt against me, she rubbed her fingers against my sensitive clit. She moved even closer, her breasts bouncing against my collarbone. She wrapped her free hand around the front of my throat, forced me to look up at her, and kissed me hard on the mouth.

When she slipped her tongue into my mouth, I fucking lost it. I moaned into her, legs trembling and pleasure rushing through me. Laila rubbed me even harder and giggled into our kiss, her hips still moving against my thigh.

"Fuck, doll," Constantino grunted, pushing himself off the desk and moving toward us. His hand was tightly wrapped around his cock, stroking it back and forth quickly. He cupped her chin. "Open your mouth and share my cum with her."

As Laila opened her mouth and stared up at her husband, she continued to rub my clit and grind her pussy against my thigh. Constantino pressed the head of his swollen cock on her tongue and came into her mouth.

My pussy pounded as the pressure rose higher inside me. Laila took all of his cum in her mouth, licked her lips clean, then leaned over to kiss me. I parted my lips and swapped spit and cum with her, tasting her husband.

Wave after wave of pleasure exploded through me again. I threw my head back and moaned loudly, my pussy pulsing with delight. Strings of her husband's cum hung between our mouths. My entire body tingled.

Laila stared at me through hazy eyes and moved her pussy higher up my thigh, closer to my cunt. She bucked her hips back and forth a few more times and cried out in pleasure, coming all over my leg.

Once I finally came down from the high, I leaned back against Constantino's desk and took a deep breath. Laila crawled off me and tugged on her dress, watching me carefully, as if the alcohol had worn off. Or maybe it was the lust.

Constantino stuffed himself back into his pants and walked around his desk, pulling a manila folder out of one of his drawers. He handed it to me, and I flipped it open to find a contract for their proposition.

Laila smiled worriedly at me. "Think about it, Sage. Please."

4

sage

IN EXCHANGE *for one million dollars, Sage Stonewell agrees to be a plaything for Laila and Constantino Buratti for the term of one year. She must acclimate to the Burattis' lifestyle of travel and luxury during the term of this agreement.*

I sucked in a sharp breath and continued reading the lengthy contract that detailed everything that I would have to do as their toy, including a list of kinks that each of them wanted to explore with me or that they would be participating in with each other.

On the last page, they had left space for me to write my kinks.

Swallowing hard, I glanced around the office and inched closer to my desk. It was ten in the morning on Friday, and I had already finished my work for this week, which meant that I had the next six hours to stare at this contract.

Like I had been doing for the past week.

But I had been way too nervous. I hadn't even returned any of Austin's phone calls. Not that I even wanted to get back together with him after he left me to fend for myself at the club on Friday. He had just wanted some pussy.

I continued down the page.

Shared Kinks: weapon play, domination, oral, anal, toys, BDSM of all kinds (with the exception of watersports or scat play), name-calling, degrada—

"Sage?" my boss called, peering out of his office.

After quickly hiding the contract in the hundreds of papers on my desk, I grabbed my iPad with the designs on it for the upcoming project and hurried to his office. I had been working all week on creating the best artwork for an upcoming animated streaming romance series.

But it had been hard to focus. So hard.

Once I stepped into the office, the balding man stood behind his desk and nodded to the door. I closed it behind me and walked to the chair in front of him, placing the iPad on my thighs and remembering how it had felt when Laila put her hands there.

We sat in silence for a couple of moments until he sat down and sighed.

"There's no easy way to say this, Sage. I know we just hired you a few of months ago, but"—my boss grimaced and shook his head—"the company ordered me to lay off people on the design team."

My eyes widened. "Wh-what?"

This had been my dream job. I had spent over a hundred thousand dollars in college to perfect my art skills and get a degree so a studio of this scale would even recognize my work in a sea of amazing artists.

Everyone had called me stupid for going to art school, but it had landed me a job here.

What would I tell my family? That I was now hundreds of thousands of dollars in debt with no job, only to hear them say, *I told you so*?

"Please pack up your desk and hand in your iPad by the end of the workday."

Tears forming in my eyes, I gave him the iPad and stood. My chest tightened.

Why? Why is this happening?

I walked out of his office with a shattered heart and moved

aimlessly toward my desk, feeling so numb. Once I made it to the small cubicle, which really hindered all sense of creativity, I gathered my belongings.

No way would I wait until the end of the day.

If they were firing me, then I would leave now. I grabbed all the things that I had brought to work over the course of the last month —all the papers and pictures of my family, the cute knickknacks sitting in the cubicle corner.

And then ... I grabbed the manila folder with the contract.

I peered down at it and swallowed hard.

One million dollars per year.

That was how much the Mafia boss and his wife had offered me to be their toy. They wanted me to live in their home, sleep in their bed, and submit to them on my hands and knees at a moment's notice. The deal was to do whatever they wanted sexually and nothing more.

But no strings attached never worked out.

It would be enough to pay back my student loans, not default on any money owed to the bank. I would be able to finally buy an iPad of my own and draw all day long without the need to sell my soul to some studio.

Of course, the money wasn't legal, and the job came with countless cons. If anyone found out about me, I'd be harassed by the cops, targeted by rival families, and seen as nothing more than a filthy, easy slut by the Buratti relatives.

But I'd be under Constantino's protection. And Constantino didn't take anyone's shit.

5

laila

"SO ..." Bethany hummed over brunch mimosas. She tossed some blonde hair behind her ear and gently pressed a napkin to the corner of her glossy pink lips. "Federica said she saw you talking with a new girl at the club last Friday. Is she a dancer?"

I swallowed hard, glanced down at my food, and took a sip of my Afterglow. "Federica, uh … said that?"

Nobody was supposed to see me with Sage, never mind see me bringing her into the back room with Constantino. I didn't know if she'd ever even message us back about the agreement—it had already been a week—but I couldn't let the girls find out.

Bethany would think that I liked her and totally toss me to the side, just like my parents had. And that could never ever happen again. I had worked so hard to get to this place, to feel happy and comfortable again.

When I placed the glass down, a waiter grabbed it from me and poured me a new drink.

I smiled at Bethany and shook my head. "We're thinking about bringing her on as a maid. Definitely not a dancer. I don't need Constantino staring at her all day. She's way too pretty for that."

Bethany slid her knife into her chicken and popped a piece into her mouth. "You know what I'd do to him if he ever cheated on you, Laila. And, plus, you're hotter than any of those bitches at the club."

Lips curling into a half-smile, I peered down at my food. "I know. I know."

God, I hated lying.

But I had to keep up the act with her, or they'd kick me out of their little clique. And she and the girls were the closest damn thing I had to sisters. Especially in this family and in this life, I needed them.

From the corner of my eye, I spotted a couple glancing our way and whispering. My stomach twisted, my food suddenly unappetizing. When they saw me staring at them, they quickly looked away.

FBI.

I turned back to Bethany and acted as if nothing were wrong. I didn't want to worry her or alert the FBI that I had recognized them. Like I had said, I needed Bethany and the other girls, especially when the FBI was following Constantino.

More than usual these days.

Our informants within the police department had told us they were building a case against our family. And if Constantino went to prison, I would fucking lose it. I would have no one, except Bethany.

"I booked us mani-pedis for tomorrow at Clouds," Bethany said, tugging out her phone and glancing through her calendar. "I wanted to get my lips filled again, but all her appointments were booked for this weekend." She peered over at me, her green eyes filled with excitement. "You should definitely tag along next time I go."

I drew my tongue across my bottom lip. "You think?"

She grabbed my hand from across the table. "Once you do it one time, you're not going to want to stop. Same with eyelash extensions. Do you remember how long it took me to convince you to get your lashes done?"

Laughing softly, I took a bite of my food. "Forever."

"You should come with me and try it out. Get those pouty lips for Constantino."

"I don't want them to fuck it up," I said. "Besides—"

Someone wrapped their arm around my shoulders. I glanced up to see Constantino leaning down to kiss me on the lips.

Once he pulled away, he peered toward Bethany. "I'm going to steal my wife away for a couple of minutes, Bethany."

"Hey!" she said to him. "Not for too long. It's a girls' day."

Constantino grabbed my hand and pulled me to my feet, guiding me past the suspicious couple and toward the front of the restaurant. I intertwined my fingers with his and let out a breath I had been holding since Bethany had brought up Sage.

"What're you doing here?" I asked.

Once we slipped out the exit, Constantino walked with me to our black Mercedes with tinted windows, but didn't push me inside the way he usually did when he didn't want anyone to hear our conversation.

"I wanted to see my wife," Constantino said.

"Have you heard anything from Sage?"

"She's all that pretty mind thinks about, isn't she?"

My cheeks burned, and I glanced at the pavement. "Sorry."

He cupped my chin, lifted my face, and chuckled. "I already told you that I don't mind, doll. If she doesn't return to the club tonight, I'll find her. We'll get your horny ass a response either way."

"Don't pressure her," I whispered, heart swelling. "Please."

While I might've been his wife for years now and might've witnessed more than just him forcing someone to do something, I didn't want him hurting Sage in any way. I wanted her to want this the way we did.

I sure hoped she wanted this.

Because I hadn't been able to erase her from my mind. Her body. That kiss.

I had touched myself every night this week while Constantino was working, just thinking about the way she'd feel against me. I wanted to kiss her again, to touch her again, to play with her anytime I wanted.

"FBI's here," he said. "Vincent called me."

Looking back into the restaurant, I caught Vincent—my bodyguard—standing by our table, pissed off as Bethany gossiped to him about something. I stifled a laugh and watched the undercover couple walk out of the restaurant.

They didn't look our way once, but I knew they had been watching.

They were always watching.

I gripped Constantino's hand. "Do you think they have something?"

With his sharp jaw clenched, he shook his head. "They have a lot of shit, but nothing that can put me away. Or else they would've arrested me already." He turned back to me and gently took my face in his hands, kissing me on the forehead. "I have to go take care of something, but I'll see you tonight, doll."

After he ushered me back into the restaurant, I glanced through the large window as he slipped into his car. Every time he left me, I feared that it'd be the last time I saw him, the last time I touched him.

Being the wife to the most wanted mobster had never been easy.

6

constantino

I STROLLED around the basement of The Syndicate, holding a chef's knife in my hand. Blood dripped from its edge onto the cobblestone floor as harmonic screams drifted through my ears.

"I'm going to ask you again," I said, turning toward the man and placing the tip of my knife right over his heart. "And if you don't answer me"—I trailed the knife down the center of his abdomen—"I'm going to finish taking those fucking fingers of yours and then cut off your dick."

Holding up the knife, I tilted my head and let him watch his own blood drip off its edges. "It won't be a clean and easy cut with a knife like this. So, why don't you open your fucking mouth and tell me who snitched?"

"I don't know!" he shouted.

Sighing through my nose, I grabbed his hand and chopped off one finger. He gargled in pain as the blood leaked out of his wounds now. Three fingers gone, and this fucker still didn't want to talk.

"The hell do you mean, you don't know?!" I growled. "We have the fucking FBI looking into us because someone opened their big fucking mouth. And, Flavio, you seem to have the biggest mouth in the family. Don't know when to close it."

"I didn't do it!"

Another finger.

"Please!"

His thumb.

He wailed out in pain. "I didn't mean it!"

I pulled my knife away from his second hand and tilted my head. "Ah, there we go. Finally want to start telling me the truth, don't you? So, fucking spill it before I cut off your cock."

"I-it was a girl I brought home. She got me drunk, and—you're right; I talk too much when I have some drinks in me." He chuckled half-heartedly. "You know how it is, right? With those women and—"

I slammed my knife into the side of his throat and left it there, watching the light fade from his eyes. After ordering some men to clean it up, I walked to the bathroom to wash the blood off my hands, then headed back upstairs.

I had better things to do than listen to the man who had betrayed our family.

Amid flashing lights and grinding bodies, I walked through the Buratti family club toward the back offices, where my men were stationed in black suits. After nodding to them, I stepped into my office and closed the door behind me.

When I made it to the desk, one of my men knocked twice on the door. "Boss, Sage is here to see you."

"Sage?" I asked, mind flickering to Laila. "Send her in."

Staring down at her feet, she scurried into the room and sat down in front of me on one of the two leather chairs, chewing on the inside of her lip. When the door clicked closed, she sucked in a breath and peeked a glance up at me.

Awaiting her answer, I sat back in my chair, tapped my finger on the armrest, and glanced down at the contract in her shaky hands. "I see that you've come to a decision."

"Yes," she whispered.

"Speak up when you talk to me," I growled, remembering how timid Laila had been when I first met her.

"Yes," she said a bit louder, obviously trying to fake confidence.

"And?" I asked, unable to read her.

"And I ..." She fumbled with the contract and slid it across the desk. "I want to do it."

The corner of my lips twitched up as I grabbed the contract from her. "Do what?"

"I want to be your toy."

After a couple of moments of staring at her intensely, I flipped to the last page of the contract, spotted her signature, and smirked. "Abele!" I shouted to my men.

The security guard opened the door and stuck his head into the room. "Yes, sir?"

"Bring the car around the back."

When Abele disappeared, I stood and held out my hand for her to take. "You will start tonight. Laila will be surprised. She's been waiting for your reply since last Friday, Sage."

Hesitantly, she grabbed my hand. "And you?" she asked. "How do you feel about it?"

Guiding her toward the door, I chuckled. "This might've been Laila's idea, but I've been waiting for your response almost as much as she has. After seeing how excited my wife was when she saw you last weekend, I can't wait to tie you up and have my way with both of you."

Not only because it made Laila happy, but because if this worked out, then Laila would have someone there for her if the FBI found something incriminating on us and hauled me off to prison. I didn't trust any men with Laila, but Sage ...

I had looked into her history the first night that Laila glanced over at her and found that they had a lot of the same interests before I married Laila. The girls in the family had changed my wife, and I wanted her to find love in her art projects again.

Sage shifted slightly and rubbed her thighs together while we walked down the hall, opposite of the club and to a back door.

Abele opened the door for us, glancing briefly at her hand in mine, then handed me the keys.

"Don't call me for the night," I said to Abele, glancing at Sage. "Laila and I will be busy."

After curtly nodding at me, Abele shut the back door. I slid into the driver's seat and peered at Sage, who pressed her hands to her thighs in an attempt to stop them from bouncing.

Once I drove about ten blocks down, I pulled into the underground parking lot of my luxury skyrise building. Nervously, she shuffled out of the car and walked with me to the elevators as I tapped on my phone to send her the first half of the payment.

"You will get half now," I said, pressing the top button in the elevator. "Half once this year is complete. All your expenses will be paid, and you'll live in this building, a couple of floors down from us. We already have a place set out for you."

Sage's phone buzzed, and my payment popped up on her screen. A deposit of $500,000.

When the elevator doors opened, I grabbed her hand. "Come. We're going to see my wife."

7

sage

ONCE CONSTANTINO PRESSED his finger to the door pad and tapped a couple of buttons on his lock, the door swung open, and I was hit with a shit ton of nerves. Yet, instead of moving back like I usually did, I stepped into their penthouse and gulped.

It smelled just like her in here, the air doused in her rosy perfume.

"Laila," Constantino called, his usual demanding voice calm now.

"In here!" Laila shouted from inside the home. "I've been waiting all day for you."

He placed a hand on my lower back and guided me down the hallway, toward a back room. A soft moan drifted down the hall, and I swallowed hard, the heat gathering between my legs.

What will Laila do once she finds me here? Does she even know I am coming?

When we reached the last door, I stopped in my tracks. Laila was lying back on the bed in the sexiest pair of maroon lingerie I had ever seen, her eyes closed, her breasts barely covered, and her fingers dragging along her lacy panties that didn't hide anything.

"Look who I brought home for us, doll."

Laila opened her intense brown eyes and froze, sucking in sharply. For a moment, I thought she wanted to pull her hand away, but when her lips curled into a small smirk, she continued playing with her wet folds, the sight making me clench.

"What do you think?" Constantino asked, grabbing my hand and twirling me around like I was an object—I guessed that was what I was to them now. The Mafia's toy. To use. To play with. To pleasure themselves with.

"I love her," Laila murmured, biting her lower lip. "She's so sexy."

Constantino gently pulled me in front of him, one arm curling around my waist, his other hand dipping between my legs to touch me under my skirt. I yelped in surprise, my heart pounding against my rib cage. He massaged my clit from behind, his other hand trailing up my body to grasp my breast through my top.

"Take it off of her," Laila said. "I've been waiting to finally see her again."

With one of his hands still buried between my legs, Constantino pulled my shirt over my head and swiftly undid my bra, and my breasts bounced out of it. Laila spread her legs a bit further, hooking one finger around her panties and pulling it to the side so we could see everything as she rubbed herself.

After popping all of the buttons on my skirt, Constantino let it fall to the ground and left me in just my underwear. He continued to rub my pussy, the pressure building higher and higher in my core.

"Does my wife turn you on?" Constantino murmured in my ear.

"Yes," I breathed, watching as Laila's head fell back as she moaned.

"Do you want to eat her pussy?"

A wave of heat rushed through me. "Yes."

Constantino slipped his fingers into my underwear and pulled apart my folds, teasing my pussy harder and faster until my legs started trembling. "She's wanted to eat yours all week, kept asking me what you'd taste like."

After he pushed me a bit closer to the bed, I placed my knees on the edge and let him continue.

He gazed over my body at her and gently kissed my shoulder. "Come over here, doll." He held out his wet fingers toward her. "Have a taste."

Laila crawled over to us, grabbed Constantino's wrist, and tugged his fingers into her mouth, wrapping her pink-painted lips around them. Like how she'd sucked his cock, she bobbed her head back and forth slightly. Heat gathered between my legs as she moaned.

Moving even closer to me, Laila placed her knees on either side of my thigh, sat her sopping pussy against my leg, and ground herself against me as she leaned over my shoulder to kiss her husband, her breasts near my face.

My breath caught in my throat, nerves zipping through me. I had never been with a woman like this before, but I had wanted to try it for so long. It wasn't a phase or taboo or even something impulsive.

Pushing my nerves to the side, I leaned forward and placed my mouth just above the hem of her lacy bra, kissing her softly at first. Laila set her hand behind my head and pulled me closer to her, moaning into her husband's mouth and continuing to grind her pussy against my thigh.

Constantino shoved his fingers back into my panties, and Laila followed, her fingers moving just as quickly as his. The sensation from two pairs of hands all over me drove me wild. I sucked harder on Laila's breast, tugging down her lacy bra and taking her nipple between my teeth.

"Fuck," Laila murmured, pulling away.

For a moment, I thought I had fucked up or done something wrong. But Laila pushed me down onto the bed, my back against the mattress, and forced me to spread my legs. She and Constantino dipped their heads between my thighs and ate my pussy, each wanting to taste me for themselves.

The pressure rose in my core, my toes curling. "Oh my gosh ..."

With his callous hand gliding against my inner thigh, Constantino entered me with two fingers and pumped them in and out while his wife's tongue flicked against my swollen clit. I laced my hands into her hair, my legs trembling hard.

"I'm going to ... to ..." I threw my head back, on the verge of the most intense orgasm I had had in a while.

And when Laila said, "Come for me," and tugged on my nipple, I screamed out in pleasure.

Wave after wave of ecstasy rushed through me, my arms and legs numbing with pins and needles.

If this was what the next year would bring, I would be so happy, being their toy.

Once I finished, Laila sat back next to me. "Sit on my face," she said breathlessly, licking her bottom lip.

My brow furrowed. "A-again?"

"Yes, again."

Hesitantly, I crawled onto her with my pussy in her face and her pussy in mine before dipping my head to kiss just above her underwear line. I clenched at the mere thought of me kissing her further down, yet the nerves reappeared because I had never done this before. Ever.

Wrapping her arms around my thighs, Laila spread my legs, pulled me down closer to her, and flicked her tongue against my clit. I dipped my head again and mirrored her actions, pulling her underwear off and eating her, just how I liked.

She moaned against me, the vibration making me feel oh-so good.

Constantino watched hungrily, undoing his belt and pulling down his zipper. When he kicked off his pants and pulled out his huge cock, he walked over to us and grabbed Laila's knees, pushing them as far apart as they could go, then slowly thrust into her cunt. In and out, he pounded until I saw the juices covering his cock.

When he finally pulled out of her a couple of moments later, he grasped my chin and forced me to look up at him. "Suck my wife's juices off my cock."

Clenching, I opened my mouth wide for him to enter me. Constantino shoved his huge cock down my throat and face-fucked me until I cleaned his dick for him.

When he finally pulled away, he pushed himself back into Laila and grunted, "Fuck, you both are so tight for me."

Constantino shifted from his wife, back to me, then to his wife. Over and over again.

Once he pulled away for good, he placed his hands on my waist and lifted me up with ease, turning me around so I faced Laila. She wrapped her arms around my shoulders, pulling me down to kiss her, softly at first but then wildly, like she was desperate for it.

With one knee on the bed, Constantino pushed his bare cock into me, grabbed my hips, and started pounding away. My breasts swayed against Laila's, her hands traveling down my body to cup them.

I moaned into her mouth, the pressure immediately rising in my core. Just when I was about to tip over the edge, Constantino pulled out of me and thrust himself into his wife. She moaned and kissed me harder, pinching and tugging on my nipples.

When her body tensed, Constantino pulled out of her and pushed himself back into me, teasing us both for the next ten minutes. Desperate for a release, I ground my clit against her mound, the pressure rising higher and higher in my core.

"Oh fuck," Laila breathed against me. "Keep doing that. You're going to make me come."

Not wanting to stop, I continued to grind myself against her while Constantino fucked me from behind. He dipped his hand and pushed a couple of fingers into Laila's pussy, finger-fucking her at the same pace.

My toes curled, and I sucked on Laila's lower lip as wave after wave of pleasure rushed through me. Laila watched me come, her body tensing even harder, and then she finally threw her head back and came as Constantino stilled deep in my pussy.

When I collapsed on the bed beside Laila with her husband's cum deep in my cunt, she wrapped her arm around my waist and pulled me closer. "You're ours now, Sage. All ours."

8

constantino

"THIS IS MY APARTMENT?" Sage asked later that night, gawking at the windows that spanned from wall to wall and ceiling to floor.

Once the floors had been cleared so nobody would spot Laila and me bringing Sage here from our place, Sage moved into the living room, drawing her fingers across the marble side table next to the plush white couch.

"It's beautiful."

"I'll have some of my men pack up your belongings from your old apartment and bring them over this weekend to officially move you in. You will not leave this apartment without Riccardo, your personal bodyguard, with you," I said.

Sage glanced at Riccardo, who stood at the door, then nodded. "I understand."

Laila shuffled from foot to foot next to me, smiling at Sage, but not saying a word. While Laila seemed to want Sage to sleep with us tonight, I needed to talk to my wife alone. We had never had someone else in bed with us before, and I wanted to make sure she was still okay with it.

No matter what, the agreement with Sage would still stand. But if we were doing this, then Laila needed to trust me. And with Bethany always whispering in her ear about shit that wasn't always true, I didn't want Laila to get any ideas.

Continuing to walk through the apartment, Sage slipped into the bedroom and stared at the item I had placed on her dresser earlier this morning.

"An iPad?" Sage asked, eyes widening. She set her purse down on the bed and ran her fingers over the white box, then peered over at us. "Is this for me?"

When Laila glanced at me, I nodded. "For your art."

"How did you know that I draw?" Sage asked.

She doesn't need to know the real reason.

I wrapped my arm around my wife's waist. "I have my ways."

Laila gazed up at me, slightly arching her brow, as if she was scolding me. She had told me not to threaten Sage, and I hadn't. But that didn't mean Sage hadn't needed a little convincing to sign that contract and bring it to me.

I had killed men before for even looking at my wife wrong. I had taken care of countless people to protect her, including her own family members. I didn't have a problem giving someone a *better opportunity* than their previous job.

Sage would never find out anyway.

Her ex-boss wouldn't speak a word to her about it. He had almost shit himself when I walked into his office Thursday night, held a gun to his thick, balding head, and told him that Sage Stonewell's last day would be Friday.

Glancing at the iPad, Laila smiled nervously. "I didn't know that you draw."

Sage blushed. "Yeah, I do."

"Do you do it for fun?"

"Sorta," she said, teetering from foot to foot. "I had a job at an animation studio, but they just laid a couple of people off, including me. So, I ..." Sage looked up at me. "I really appreciate your offer and *this.*"

Fuck.

Laila cut her gaze to me and snatched my hand *hard*. She knew.

"Maybe you could show me sometime," Laila said, turning back to her.

Strands of dirty-blonde hair fell into Sage's face. She smiled softly and nodded. "Maybe."

They stared at each other for a few moments, and then Laila swallowed hard, the way she did when she didn't know what else to say. The alcohol I had smelled on her breath earlier tonight must've worn off.

"We should get going, doll," I said to save her.

"If you need anything," Laila said, "we're just a few floors up."

I gently tugged Laila to the front door. "She knows where to find us."

Once I shut the door behind us, Laila marched to the elevator with her arms crossed. She didn't speak a single word until the elevator doors slid shut. Then, she threw her hands up. "You got her fired?!"

"No," I lied.

"Oh, so it was a coincidence that the same day she decided to accept our offer, she got fired from her job?" She stared at me through wide, angry eyes. "I told you not to coerce her into joining us."

"I didn't coerce her into anything. All I did was pay her boss a visit last night."

Laila's angry expression contorted into one of sadness, her brow furrowing and her eyes getting big. "Why did you do it?" she whispered, drawing her arms tighter around herself. "What if she finds out?"

"She won't find out, doll," I said, sliding a hand around the back of her neck and tugging her forward. "I've done worse for you, and you know that. Why are you becoming so emotional about this? Do you regret what we did with her?"

Laila stayed quiet for a few moments, then pulled me tightly to her. "No, I don't regret it."

"Then, what is it?"

"I'm just nervous," she whispered. "The same way I was with you when we started seeing each other. I don't want her to find out that you had her fired just so she would accept our offer. I don't want her to be angry with me."

Laila always had this whole fear of people leaving her. She didn't want to be alone, didn't want people not to love every bit of her. I wasn't complaining, but she gave too much of herself away to other people to please them.

Like that fucking Bethany bitch.

"If we're going to do this, you need to be honest with me. Tell me if anything she does or if how I act with her bothers you." I took my wife's face in my hands and forced her to look up at me. "Do you understand?"

"Yes," she said, slightly nodding. Then, she stood on her toes and kissed me. "Thank you for this. For all of this. I don't know any man in this family who would willingly invite someone else into the bedroom and not be a total creep about it."

I tucked some hair behind her ear. "Everything I do is to make you happy."

And to protect her.

If the FBI found incriminating evidence to use against me, Laila would have someone that *I* trusted. Bethany would use her. Men in this family would fight for the spot at the top of the food chain and toss her aside like she was nothing.

Sometimes, the most trustworthy people were complete fucking strangers.

But in a couple of weeks, Sage wouldn't be a stranger anymore.

9

laila

FEET SOAKING in salts and hot water, I sat back on the caramel leather spa chair next to Bethany the following day, closed my eyes, and inhaled the essential oils drifting through the air. I hummed softly to the sounds of musical rainfall.

"What do you think about this?" Bethany asked, shoving her phone at me.

On the screen was a picture of a young woman with long blonde hair extensions that came down to her ass.

I glanced over at Bethany. "Are you sure you'll be able to manage all that hair? That'd be so much for me."

"Don't be silly," she said, reaching for her phone. "Of course I could."

After giving it back, I chewed on the inside of my cheek, picked up my phone from my lap, and scrolled to Sage's number in my Contacts. Constantino had given it to me before I left with Bethany this morning, but I didn't even know what to say to her.

I was married to a loving man who let me sleep with a girl from his club.

Can we be friends? Or is this all just a hookup type of scenario?

Still, I wanted to talk to her and needed to see her again today.

Me: Hey, this is Laila. :)

Once I sent the text, I placed my phone in my lap and closed my eyes again. Constantino had told me not to ask, to take. Sage would be paid one million dollars of dirty Mafia money for this job. I should be able to have her anytime I wanted, but it felt weird, being so up front with her about what I wanted.

But I couldn't get her body out of my head. The way she had felt last night. The way she had reacted to my touch, how she had kissed me and fondled me, teased my pussy with her own. It was the wildest night I'd ever had.

And I wanted more.

But what if she didn't get back to me?! Left me on *Read*? Thought my text was weird?

Sage: Hi! Do you need me?

I pressed my thighs together. *Yes, I fucking need her. Badly.*

Me: Sorta, ha-ha.

Sage: Do you want me to come up?

Me: I'm not at home right now, but I, um ... want to see you.

Me: Maybe, um ... send me a picture?

Fuck. Why do I feel like an awkward teenage kid, asking for nudes?

When I wasn't drunk, I didn't know the first thing about talking to a woman. The same thing had happened when Constantino introduced me to the girls in the family. I'd spend ten minutes trying to come up with a single text to them.

Sage: Okay, uh, give me a second.

Sage: I just woke up, sorry. I was up all night, drawing.

Sage: Not that you asked or anything, ha-ha.

I tapped the message bar to respond and typed out two long messages, telling her not to apologize, but then deleted them. I didn't know the first thing to say to her, especially over the phone and not when I didn't have a buzz.

Before I could say anything, an image popped up on the screen. Sage sat in front of a floor-length mirror, dressed in nothing but an oversize T-shirt that I could see right up through the reflection, her hair shielding her face.

Heat rushed to my core, and I pressed my thighs together as discreetly as I could. All I wanted to do was run my tongue across every one of her curves, between her pussy lips, and eat her tight little cunt until it was crying on me again.

"Who are you texting?" Bethany asked, sliding her phone back into her purse.

Quickly, I turned off my phone and shoved it into my purse too. I didn't want her to know yet. We had only spent one night with Sage, and I didn't want things to get weird between Bethany and me when she found out I was into women too.

"Just messaging Constantino."

"He's so needy, isn't he?" she said playfully.

I laughed, though it wasn't really funny to me, and finished getting my pedicure with her before she dragged me off to lunch down in the city, like we did almost every day.

After lunch at Mastro's Steakhouse—Bethany's favorite lunch spot—we strolled a couple of blocks down the crowded walkways toward her parked car, my bodyguard following us. I wanted to stuff my leftovers there before we continued to wherever she had planned for us next.

Once we reached the car, I glanced across the street at The Museum of Modern Art and smiled softly, tugging on Bethany's sleeve. "Do you want to do something spontaneous?" I asked, excitement bubbling in my stomach. The MoMA had a couple of new pieces that I wanted to check out.

Bethany swiped some lip gloss across her pink lips. "You know I'm always down."

"Want to check out a couple of pieces of art in the museum?"

When Bethany glanced over to the building, she frowned. "Oh, um ..." She looked down at her phone. "I actually forgot that I booked us a massage at three. We won't have time to get through that line and stroll through the entire place. Sorry, Laila."

My smile dropped, but I quickly shook my head. "No, no. It's okay. We can go some other time."

"Yeah, definitely. I'd love to go with you." She took my hand and pushed me into the passenger seat. "Come on. We'll be late." She slipped into the driver's seat, backed out of the parking spot, and drove into traffic.

As we passed the museum, I stared at the doors with a sinking feeling in my stomach.

Bethany just overbooked us for today, I reassured myself. *We'll go some other time when I plan a day for us and the girls.*

"Maybe Monday?" I suggested.

"Monday for what?"

"For the museum."

Bethany chewed on the inside of her cheek. "My brother will be in town."

"Oh, uh, no worries. You guys are talking again?" I asked.

"Yes."

Not wanting to push it because Bethany didn't like her brother, I pursed my lips and pulled my phone from my pocket. NYC traffic was no joke, and I didn't really have anything else to talk to Bethany about. I had exhausted all my talking points at the spa.

Tilting my phone away from her, I leaned my head on the window and gazed down at Sage's messages. She'd sent another picture, this time dressed in absolutely nothing but a pair of gold hoop earrings.

Sage: I hope this one is a bit better. xx

Wetness pooled between my thighs, my nipples aching. I wanted to tug on them to relieve a little stress, but Bethany was too close, too observant. I swallowed hard and ground my knees together.

When I got home tonight, I'd have her all to myself.

10

sage

I PACED AROUND the living room of my apartment that overlooked the city, nervously chewing on my inner cheek. Constantino's men had brought over all my belongings from my old place earlier, but I hadn't been able to dive into unboxing anything after Laila sent me that text.

She had wanted a picture of me, but maybe I had ... sent her something wrong.

Maybe she hadn't wanted a nude or a semi-nude.

After walking toward the window, I rested my forehead against the glass and looked down at the tiny figures hurrying down the sidewalks. It had been three hours, and she hadn't even responded to my messages. She had Read receipts turned on, and still, nothing.

Did I do something wrong? I didn't know how to act around pretty girls like her.

Do women require a different kind of sexy picture? More ass, less booby?

How does this even work?!

Deciding that I couldn't just pace around my apartment anymore, I found a mid-length green dress with white flowers in my closet and glided some nude and matte lipstick across my lips. After grabbing my new iPad and drawing pen, I stepped out of my apartment.

Standing at least six foot tall with dead eyes and slicked-back black hair, Riccardo, my bodyguard, waited outside my door with his hands crossed over his front. I smiled softly at him and locked the door.

"I'm just going up to Constantino and Laila's floor," I said.

No response.

I waited for another moment before politely nodding and walking toward the elevator. Riccardo followed a foot behind me and not any farther. I sucked in a breath and stayed quiet because I didn't really have much of a say.

As soon as I had signed that contract, I belonged to the Mafia.

No matter what, I had to follow Constantino's rules. And I was sorta, kinda glad he had assigned me a guard because I didn't want someone to gun me down because I had information about the mob boss and his wife. I didn't want to get *that* messed up with them.

When the elevator doors opened, we stepped inside. I hit the top button and glanced over at Riccardo once the doors shut.

"Do you ever get bored, just standing outside my door?" I asked. It had only been a night, but still.

How could someone stand outside a door all day and night?

"No."

"Oh," I said, awkward tension building between us. "Well, if you ever get hungry or thirsty, you can come in. I feel bad that you're stuck, standing there and going everywhere I do. I'd get so bored if I were you."

"It's my job to protect you."

I bounced on my toes and averted my gaze because Riccardo wasn't down for any type of conversation, it seemed. If he was about to spend every moment of his life with me, I surely hoped that he'd open up to me. I didn't have any friends here.

But then again, did I want to be friends with a gangbanger? I was already sleeping with two of them.

When the elevator doors opened, I hurried into the hallway and to their front door. My stomach twisted and turned as nerves bubbled inside it. I didn't know if I was overstepping by coming up here, but I wanted to see if Laila had come home.

What if she didn't like the picture I had sent? If I had sent it to a guy, he would've immediately messaged me back, asking for another or commenting on it. I didn't want the Burattis to kick me out on my first day.

Riccardo stood behind me as I lingered by their front door, trying to build enough confidence to knock. Instead of staying quiet by my side, he knocked on the damn door for me.

My eyes widened, and I jumped back. "Wait, I'm not—"

Constantino opened the door. Freshly showered with water dripping off his dark hair, he buttoned a cuff on his dress shirt, his undone tie hanging around his neck. His lips curled into a small smirk, and he opened the door wider. "Come in."

After glancing at Riccardo once, I stepped into the penthouse. Constantino closed the door behind us and walked farther into his home, gaze dropping to my dress. Nervously, I smoothed it out and teetered from foot to foot with my iPad in my hands.

"One day, I need to take you out for new clothes."

"New clothes?" I asked, shaking my head. "These are fine for me. I don't need any—"

"I already told you, *princess*, you're part of the family now. You agreed to adopt our lifestyle, which means designer clothes, luxury vacations, and anything my wife and I would like to give you." His voice was matter-of-fact, like I shouldn't argue.

But I felt bad. They had already spent half a million on me.

"Are you sure?" I asked in a whisper. "I don't want you to spend your money on me."

He paused for a long moment, an unreadable expression on his face. When he drew his tongue across his lower teeth, I thought he'd yell at me and throw the contract in my face, becoming angry with me.

But he just chuckled and continued to button his shirt.

"What?" I asked, placing my iPad on the marble countertop.

Turning away from me, he walked toward the bedroom. "You remind me of Laila when we started dating," he said. His voice was always softer when he spoke about her, like she was his everything.

I glanced at the ground. I hoped one day, I'd be that person for someone.

"Follow me," he called from the hallway.

Once I made my way to their bedroom, I gazed at the bed where I had slept with them for the first time last night. My core warmed at the thought, memories of yesterday floating through my head.

Hopefully, it was okay to be here with Laila's husband while she was gone.

He opened another door and walked into Laila's huge walk-in closet that must've been bigger than my old apartment, filled with clothes, handbags, heels, and jewelry. Eyes widening, I brushed my fingers across all the fabric.

Constantino stopped in front of a dress rack and shuffled through the articles of clothing until he finally pulled out a short, low-cut pink dress that tightened around the waist. "Try this on," he said, handing it to me.

I took it from him. "Right here?"

He leaned against the nearest wall, arms crossed and dark eyes on me. "Right here."

Warmth exploded between my legs. I swallowed hard and unzipped my dress, letting the straps fall off my shoulders and down my body. When it fell to the ground, I stepped out of it and stood in a pair of matching bra and panties—thank God—in front of him.

After unzipping the pink dress, I pulled the straps over my shoulders. Constantino guided me to a full-length mirror and grabbed the zipper, staring at me through the reflection and slowly zipping the dress up. His warm breath fanned my neck, his dark eyes all over my body.

When the dress was zipped all the way, I ran my hands down the rich fabric and stared at myself in the mirror. The dress was lower cut than what I was used to, and I'd bet that if I bent over, he'd get a view of my ass, but it didn't feel cheap, like all my other dresses.

He moved closer to me, burying his face into the crook of my neck. "You look fucking incredible," he growled into my ear. "My wife is going to soak right through her panties, just looking at you."

"You think?" I whispered, gently closing my eyes and hoping she didn't mind.

I was still worried about what she thought of my text message earlier. I didn't want her to be angry with me because Constantino had made me put on one of the dresses in her closet, which she must've filled out *way* better than I could.

"Of co—"

The closet door opened wider, and my heart leaped in my chest. Laila was home.

I glanced over my shoulder, but instead of seeing Constantino's wife, I spotted a woman with curly and bouncy blonde hair, wide green eyes, and a sneer on her lips.

She threw her manicured hands into the air. "What the fuck, Constantino?!"

11

laila

AFTER PLACING my purse down on the marble counter back at home, I spotted Sage's iPad next to it. I furrowed my brow, unsure how it had gotten here, and followed Bethany through the house to my closet. She had complained all the way back to my place because one of her buttons had come off her pants and she needed new ones.

"Laila!" she called from the closet.

Cursing to myself, I jogged into my bedroom and then into the closet, spotting Bethany staring, wide-eyed, at Sage and Constantino, who stood at my floor-length mirror.

Fuck, Sage can't be here while Bethany is.

Standing in one of my dresses that hugged her curves, Sage gulped, chewed on the inside of her cheek, and glanced over at me, cheeks red as a tomato. My breath caught in my throat as I remembered those damn pictures she had sent earlier.

I had meant to get back to her, but Bethany …

While the dress looked to be a size too small around the waist, her breasts were pressed together in the halter-top. My gaze dropped to them, and I pressed my thighs together, wanting to rip off her clothes right here and now.

"Who is this?" Bethany asked Constantino, wrapping her arm around mine.

"Our housekeeper," Constantino said. "She spilled something on her dress."

Bethany pursed her lips. "So, you let her wear your wife's skimpy clothes to clean your home? Why are you in the closet with her? That close to her?"

Constantino clenched his jaw and glared at Bethany. They had never gotten along, and I didn't want Constantino to shout at her. Out of our entire friend group, I was closest with her. She had been there since I'd joined the family.

"Bethany," I said, tugging her closer, "it's fine. She really is our housekeeper."

Sage looked away from me, her expression dropping slightly, and nodded. "Sorry, Mrs. Buratti." She bent down to pick up a green dress off the floor, her cleavage even fucking better from this angle. "I should get going."

When she walked past me, I grabbed her wrist, my fingers tingling on contact. "No, stay."

Bethany would stay for a drink, and then I'd kick her out as quickly as I could because I hadn't been able to get Sage out of my fucking head. She couldn't leave now. Those pictures and the way she looked in my dress ...

Fuck.

"Okay," Sage squeaked, then hurried out of the closet.

Constantino stared at me and tied his tie, jaw clenched. "I'm leaving for work," he said, but his eyes told me that he wanted Bethany out of here. Now. Then, he turned his gaze to Bethany. "Go to the kitchen."

"You can't do—" Bethany started.

"Go to the kitchen now, Bethany," Constantino growled at her. "Don't argue with me in my house."

Bethany gave my hand one hard squeeze—as if to tell me to really give it to him, as if he had done something wrong—and marched out of the closet to the kitchen. When the door shut, Constantino looked back at me with hard eyes.

"She can't be barging into our bedroom, Laila," he said harshly. "What if I were changing or preparing the bed for you and Sage? I know you don't want her to know about Sage, but it's going to be hard if you let her walk all over you."

"She doesn't walk all over me," I said, shaking my head and looking away. "But I'll make sure she doesn't do it again. She just needed to get a pair of pants. One of her buttons had popped off today."

After letting out a low sigh, he stepped closer to me and took my face in his hands. "I didn't mean to raise my voice at you, doll. I'm sorry. I'm trying to protect you. You know how I feel about Bethany."

"I know," I whispered, gazing up at him. "But you don't even know her that well. All she wants is the best for me."

He stared at me for a few moments, inhaled deeply, then nodded, the way he did when he didn't agree with me, but didn't want to fight.

"I have to go to work," he said, dropping his hands from my face and grabbing his suit jacket.

"Please, be careful," I whispered.

"I will, doll," he said, pecking me on the lips, and then he was out the door.

I inhaled deeply and glanced in the mirror, trying to come up with a plan to kick Bethany out as soon as possible so I could have some alone time with Sage before Constantino returned from work. I didn't know how much longer I'd be able to wait for her to sit on my face again.

When I went into the kitchen, Sage struggled to carry a huge basket of folded laundry to our bedroom. I wanted to help her or to tell her that she didn't really have to do work around here—that wasn't her job—but she kept her gaze focused on the floor as she walked by.

Bethany stood in front of the counter with two champagne

glasses. She uncorked a bottle of champagne and looked over her shoulder at me with her lips pursed. "You should put him in his place," she said to me.

"Who, Constantino?" I asked.

"He shouldn't get away with that shit just because he's the boss."

"He wasn't doing anything wrong, Beth," I said, wanting her to drop it.

She twirled around and widened her eyes. "You saw them together!"

I sat down at the counter and blew out a breath, shoulders slumping forward. "Please, Bethany," I whispered. "It was nothing, really. Let's have a drink and forget about it. I'll talk to him when he gets home."

After a couple of moments, Bethany sighed and placed a glass on the counter in front of me. "You know how pissed I get when someone tries to hurt you," she said. "I'm sorry, but you deserve better if he is cheating on you."

"It's fine."

"Promise me that if you catch him with her like that again, you'll call me so I can chop off his balls?" she asked.

A small giggle escaped my lips. "I promise."

12

sage

DRESSED in a lacy dark green lingerie set, Laila lay on the bed beside me a couple of hours later with her soft lips pressed against mine and her tongue moving rhythmically in my mouth. I shuffled my thighs together to ease the ache between them and kissed her back, my hands traveling down the curves of her body.

Constantino had been at work all day, and Laila had been eyeing me like I was some kind of prey since she and *Bethany* had gotten back to the high-rise apartment earlier to have a drink. To Bethany—and I'm assuming all of Laila's friends—I was the housekeeper.

But we both knew that I didn't clean anything around this house.

"God," Laila murmured against me, "I'm so glad that she's gone. I couldn't wait another moment to get you alone." She moved her hands down my body, undoing my bra and tugging it off me. "I haven't been able to stop thinking about you since last night with Constantino. And those pictures you sent me ... God ..."

"You liked them?" I asked, dipping my fingers down her thigh and brushing them gently over her lacy panties, feeling how soaked they were for me. I whimpered into our kiss and crawled on top of her, moving my mouth down her body until I reached the top of her panties.

"They were fucking amazing." She arched her back slightly and pulled off her underwear, tossing them over the bedside.

When I placed my mouth on her cunt, I sighed in delight, my warm breath against her clit. I flicked my tongue on the sensitive bud over and over and reached my hand between my thighs to rub myself off at the same time.

"Eat my pussy," Laila moaned, grasping my hair to hold me in place and bucking her hips back and forth to ride my face. "God, just like that, Sage. You're going to make me …" Her legs trembled around my shoulders, her pussy pulsing and moans escaping her lips. "Yes!"

Legs shaking, Laila cried out and came all over me. Then, she flipped me over onto my back and crawled on top of me, pressing her raspberry-colored lips against mine again. Her tongue slipped into my mouth, her teeth gently biting down on my lower lip. She dipped a hand between my legs and rubbed my clit, her breasts swaying against mine.

"My turn," she said, kissing down my body, then burying her face between my legs. She placed my left leg on her shoulder and pushed the other one further away against the bed to spread them. Her tongue flicked out against my clit again, making me squirm.

Closing my eyes, I sank into the mattress and moaned softly.

"What do we have here?" Constantino asked.

I sucked in a surprised breath and snapped my eyes open. Constantino walked into the room, tugging off his tie, his gaze shifting from me to Laila, who had pulled back from my cunt to look at her husband.

"Go back to eating her cunt, doll," Constantino commanded, unbuttoning his shirt, his dark eyes back on me. "I've had a long day at work. All I want to do is watch Sage squirm for you."

I lay back on the bed, my head on the pillows and my legs spread wide for Laila. She crawled closer up the bed toward me, on her hands and knees, stuck her ass up into the air, and dipped her head between my thighs. Fingers pulling my folds apart, she glided her tongue across my clit.

Constantino rested one knee on the bed behind Laila, his large hands all over her ass. He undid his pants and pulled out his cock, positioning himself at her entrance. When he pushed himself into her, she moaned against my clit.

Every time Constantino plowed into her from behind, her tits swayed against my thighs, her perky and hard nipples making me clench. I laced my hand into her hair and tugged on it to pull her closer to me, the pressure rising in my core.

"More," I whispered, arching my back.

God, I was close. So close.

"Don't come," Constantino growled, fingers curling into Laila's hips.

"Come for me," Laila dared me, her fingers stroking my G-spot and her tongue flicking my clit back and forth and back and forth at just the right rhythm. "Don't listen to my husband. Come all over my face, Sage."

"If either of you comes, I'll fucking punish you for it."

"You're getting so tight for me," Laila murmured. "I know you want to."

"Laila," Constantino growled, grabbing a fistful of her hair and pulling her off my aching pussy.

But her fingers were still inside me, thrusting in and out and vibrating the bundle of nerves that would soon make me explode.

"Are you disobeying me?" he continued, eyes hooded. "Do you need me to show Sage how I punish you to keep your filthy"—he wrapped his free hand around her chin—"little"—he stuck his fingers between her lips—"mouth in line?"

Laila stared down at me, brows drawn together in pleasure, and continued moving her slender fingers inside my tightening hole. She knew that I wouldn't last much longer, that I would come all over her fingers in a couple of moments.

"I'm going to come," she said to me, big brown eyes wide, "when you do."

Unable to stop, I threw my head back as a leg-trembling orgasm ripped through my body. My chest moved up and down, my breaths quicker by the second. I grasped the bedsheets in my fists and pulled them up. Wave after wave of pleasure shot through my body.

Laila grinned wickedly down at me, then threw her head back and came on her husband. Our moans drifted through the large high-rise apartment in the middle of the city. She pulled her fingers out of my cunt and stuck them into her mouth.

I relaxed against the mattress, ecstasy rushing through me.

"I warned you," Constantino said, pulling out of her.

Constantino tugged me up roughly with one hand and grabbed Laila in his other. With her wild hair all over the place, she shuffled beside him and glanced toward a room that neither of them had let me into since this little *thing* had started.

Constantino stopped in front of the door, pulled a key out of his pocket, and unlocked the door, pushing it open with the tip of his shoe, his cock still hard and swollen between his legs. As soon as he shoved us into the room, the dim lights turned on.

Thick chains and cuffs hung from each wall. My eyes widened slightly, taking in the toys on the dresser in the far corner of the room. Constantino brought me to one wall and locked the cuffs around my wrists and ankles, spreading me apart. Then did the same to Laila on the opposite wall.

"Your punishment will be worse than hers, doll," Constantino said. He grabbed her jaw and forced her to look up at him. "The next time we go out, *I* will dress you. No wearing those expensive clothes from Barneys. A brat like you gets fabric so cheap that all your little girlfriends will judge you for it."

To my surprise, Laila snapped her mouth shut and stared up at Constantino with wide eyes. I didn't know what had sparked her sudden change of action—I couldn't comprehend just how making Laila walk out of the house in cheaper clothes could affect her so much—but it seemed like they exchanged a few private words with just their eyes.

Either the family was extremely judgmental … or something else had happened.

"Do you understand me?" Constantino asked, sharp jaw clenched.

"Yes," Laila whispered.

"Now …" Constantino said, walking to a mahogany dresser and opening the first drawer. He pulled out two identical G-spot vibrators and walked back toward Laila, inserting one between her dripping pussy lips. "Since you both love to disobey, you'll stand here and watch each other come over and over … and over again until I think you've had enough."

After securing the vibrator inside of her, Constantino walked over to me and drew the head of the vibrator across my swollen clit and to my entrance. My pussy was so wet that the vibrator slid right into me and filled me up.

I whimpered slightly, my nipples aching to be touched and tugged, and looked up at him, desperate for him to touch them, to touch *me*, to touch any part of my body because I needed it so badly.

"Please," I whispered.

Instead of giving me what I needed, he stepped back and stuffed his hand into his pocket, and then he pulled out his phone and tapped a button on an app. My body jolted up, a strong vibration shooting through me.

Glancing over at Laila, I watched her naked body struggle against the cuffs and chains, her breasts bouncing slightly and her mouth parted in delight.

Constantino shuffled backward a few feet, then turned around and walked toward the door. "I'll be back in a few hours. Have fun, girls."

13

sage

CONSTANTINO LEFT Laila and me in his BDSM room, chained up to the walls with vibrators stuffed deep inside ourselves. I grasped the chains in my fists and clutched them tightly. We had been here for what must've been over an hour now, coming over and over again.

Every vibration from the vibrator thrust me higher and higher. I threw my head back and glanced at the wall-length mirror on the side of the room, knowing that it probably wasn't a regular mirror, but a way for Constantino to watch us while we came, to control the vibrators and give or take away pleasure anytime he wanted.

My pussy tightened, and I moaned loudly. Wave after wave of delight rushed through my body from my core, making my limbs tingle and my mind numb. And while I would've taken the vibrator away if I'd had control, the vibrations didn't stop.

In fact, every time I came, my vibrations seemed to get even faster somehow. Or maybe it just felt that way because they hadn't stopped for the longest damn time now. They had kept coming and coming, not once seizing, not once slowing down.

"He's watching us," I breathed, glancing over at the puddle of cum underneath Laila. "Isn't he?"

Instead of looking over at the mirror, she stared at me and curled her pink lips into a soft smile. "Don't look over at him, Sage. Don't give him the satisfaction. You watch me as I come, then come with me," she said, body convulsing for a moment as I listened to her vibrations become louder. "Please, come with me."

Chained to the wall on the opposite side of the room, I stared at Laila, who struggled against the restraints, and for the first time, I really had the chance to admire her body. Dark brown hair cascaded past her shoulders. Huge brown eyes watched me as I watched her. Her breasts were bigger compared to her smaller frame, bouncing slightly every time a vibration shot through each of us.

"You're so fucking sexy," I whispered, pussy tightening on the vibrator for the umpteenth time in the past couple of hours.

All I wanted was to release another orgasm, let it shoot through my body and destroy me even further, but Laila wanted me to come with her. So, I waited.

Laila intently watched my body, her eyes lingering on my swollen clit and sopping pussy.

The more she eyed me, the closer I got to having an orgasm.

I squeezed my eyes shut, praying that I wouldn't come too soon, hoping that I could hold out for just a bit longer. I clutched the chains between my fists again, legs trembling slightly. "Please, Laila, I don't know how much longer I can hold out. I'm about to come again."

"Not yet," she whispered, legs trembling. "Hold off. I'm so close, baby."

Just before Laila could give me permission to come, the door opened. Completely dressed again in his suit, Constantino stepped into the room. Instead of paying any attention to his wife, he walked over to me and pulled the vibrator out of my pussy before I had the chance to come again.

He stepped to the side of me so Laila could see everything that he was doing to me, then placed his fingers against my aching clit.

My legs jerked into the air, my pussy clenching on nothingness and feeling so empty.

"Your clit is swollen, Sage," he murmured, gently moving his fingers around my clit. He pressed his hardness against the side of my thigh and growled into my ear lowly, "We're going to try this again. You're not going to come until *I* tell you that you can." With his free hand, he captured my nipple between two fingers. "Understand?"

"Yes," I breathed, legs shaking.

"I know my wife is sexy, but I'm the boss both inside and outside this bedroom." He gently sucked on the skin underneath my ear, his scruff tickling my neck. "You come when I tell you to from now on. Not her."

Desperately trying to hold back my orgasm, I nodded. "Okay."

"Watch my wife," he murmured, tugging on my nipple and making me moan softly.

Laila was watching her husband skillfully touch my folds.

"She's going to come for me on command, and then you'll learn to do the same thing."

I swallowed hard and stared at his profile, unable to believe that I was really here with a Mafia boss and his wife. Out of all the women in the world they could've had, they'd chosen me; they *wanted* me.

He turned back to me, lips curling into a smirk. His eyes were as dark as I imagined they'd be when he was holding a gun to someone's head, threatening to pull the trigger, and killing them dead.

"Doll," Constantino called, his dark gaze still focused on me, "come."

On command, Laila threw her head back and screamed louder than I'd ever heard her. Body convulsing, she tugged on the chains and cried out in pleasure, drawing her legs together as much as she could.

Pleasure coursed through my body at the mere sight of her. My pussy tightened, and I squeezed my eyes closed, forcing myself to take steady breaths so I wouldn't explode all over Constantino's fingers.

"Please," I whispered to him. "Can I come?"

There was a moment of complete silence.

"Open your eyes and look at me."

I opened my eyes and stared into that cold and callous gaze. "Please."

"No."

Pressure rose even higher in my core. I dug my fingernails into my palm and whimpered. He stepped back from me and walked over to Laila, taking out her vibrator, undoing his belt, then pulling out his cock. Once he undid the chains around her ankles, he lifted her legs into the air and positioned himself against her entrance.

When he slipped himself inside her, I whimpered again. I didn't even have a vibrator inside me anymore, but just watching him fuck her was pushing me closer and closer to the edge, and I didn't know how much longer I would be able to last.

"Oh God," Laila moaned.

He pounded into her tight hole, his cock becoming wetter and wetter with every thrust.

"Cover my dick in your cum, doll," he commanded Laila, tucking some hair behind her ear. "So I can push it into our little toy, who's convulsing over there, and make her feel good." He grasped her jaw and forced her to look at me. "Look at her struggling, on the brink of coming."

He stuck three fingers into her mouth, the same fingers that had played with me. She sucked on them, her saliva dripping down her chin.

"Please," she begged him. "God, please, let me come. She tastes so good."

After he stuck his fingers deeper into her mouth, he whispered something into her ear that I couldn't hear. Then, she threw her head back and came while staring at me, spit rolling off her parted lips.

Once her body slowly relaxed, Constantino pulled out of her and walked over to me. He took off the chains around my ankles and grasped my hips, pulling me toward him and positioning himself at my entrance.

"Beg for my cock, covered in my wife's cum."

I stared down at Laila's thick juices covering his throbbing cock, his head centimeters from my entrance. My core tightened even more, and I whimpered again, desperate to come on him too.

"Please, give it to me, Constantino. Please, I need it."

He grasped my hips and shoved himself into me hard one time. "Come."

I parted my lips, wanting to scream out loud, but the pleasure was almost too much to bear. My legs trembled uncontrollably as I came all over his cock on the first thrust. Wave after wave of ecstasy rushed through me.

Constantino pulled out of me, unhooked his wife from her chains, and forced her to drop to her knees. "If Sage tastes so good, suck her off me," he commanded.

She wrapped her mouth around his dick and sucked me off him, cheeks drawn in tightly. He laced his hand through her hair and shoved himself as deeply as he could get. He threw his head back and grunted, hips convulsing. When he finally came, he pulled out of her and undid my restraints.

"Have you girls learned your lesson?" he asked.

My lips curled into a soft smile, and I glanced over at Laila, who had the same smirk on her face. I guessed that we hadn't, and the only thing left to do was to have him teach us again.

14

constantino

BEFORE I RELEASED Laila and Sage from the room, I walked to the master bathroom and filled the tub with warm water, scented soap, and bubbles. Like after every night that I punished Laila in our secret BDSM room, I lit the candles around the bath.

I ran a hand through my hair. After the shit day I'd had today, dealing with *another* mole in our family, I had wanted an easy night. But Laila wanted to be bratty and force Sage to come when I told her not to. Watching those girls come over and over as punishment had been more than enough to help me relax.

Once the water filled the tub up halfway, I turned it off and walked back to the room where Sage and Laila waited, sweat rolling down their trembling bodies. Laila's eyes softened when she looked at me, as if she knew I had run them a bath.

"Take Sage first," she said.

I pulled Sage's trembling body into my arms. She gripped on to my shoulders and breathed unevenly.

"Where are we going?" she asked.

Pushing the bathroom door open with my foot, I walked into the bathroom, crouched by the tub, and let Sage sink into it. Body instantly relaxing in the hot suds, she rested her head against the edge and sighed softly.

"It's so warm," she murmured, closing her eyes.

I walked back to Laila. She relaxed in my arms, like she always did after a night like tonight, and rested her head against the crook of my shoulder, sighing softly too.

"Thank you," she whispered.

"For what?"

"For this," she murmured. "For Sage."

"Anything for you, doll," I said, stepping back into the master bathroom and setting Laila into the tub, opposite Sage.

They sank down in the bubbles together, both more relaxed than I had ever seen them, especially Laila.

After disappearing into the hallway, I retrieved a bottle of After-glow wine from the wine fridge in the pantry and three glasses from the cabinet. When I reached the bathroom, I uncorked the bottle and poured two glasses for the girls.

I grabbed the bar of soap as well as Laila's favorite loofah, then soaked them into the water. When I pulled it out, suds covered the wet material. I ran it across Laila's shoulders and cleaned her body with it, washing away all the sweat.

Once I reached her neck, I gently took her chin in my hand. "When you're finished washing yourself, dry off. I need to talk to you alone ..." I growled so low that she barely heard it, "About the family."

Who were slowly betraying me to protect their own asses after I had done everything for them. Fucking everything. I bloodied my hands for them to thrive in this city, and these moles did nothing but rat me out and put my family in danger.

Laila widened her eyes and nodded. "Okay," she whispered.

She quickly washed the soap off her body and hopped out of the tub, grabbing a towel to dry herself off and then slipping into a silky black robe. When she walked out of the bathroom to find clothes, I moved to Sage.

I sat on the edge of the tub and ran the loofah across her chest. She stared up at me through wide eyes.

"Is everything okay?" she asked, glancing at the door where Laila had just exited. "Do you need me to leave?"

"No," I said quickly. "Don't go."

I needed her to stay a while longer with Laila as I handled more *business* at work tonight. Laila usually stayed alone, but I wanted her to have company. By that small smile on her face after I unlocked her restraints to her *thank you*, I could tell that Laila needed this.

Needed her.

Fuck that Bethany bitch.

Sage stayed quiet while I washed her body, just staring up at me like I was the most fascinating person ever with her huge blue eyes and an innocent smile.

"One day, you should just get in the tub and relax. You look like you need it," she whispered.

I do.

"It'll be fun," she said with a small giggle. "The tub is big enough for all three of us."

"One day," I hummed. "One day."

After I finished washing her off, I set a towel at the edge of the tub. "Stay in here for as long as you want. When you're finished, you're welcome to any of Laila's clothes," I said, heading for the bathroom door.

Laila sat at her vanity in her closet, running a brush through her wet hair and staring at me through the mirror, brow furrowed. "What happened today?" she asked, setting the brush down and turning to face me.

I ran a hand through my hair, closed my eyes, and blew out another breath. "These fucking men in the family, doll," I growled. "Men I've known all my fucking life, betraying us. These eighteen-year-old kids out here are more trustworthy than uncles and cousins."

"Who was it this time?" she asked, standing and walking toward me.

"Raul," I said, still remembering the last breath he had taken in my hands today, the way he had tensed as he sputtered out his last few words, apologizing for everything he had done, for the betrayal he had committed to our family.

"Raul?" Laila repeated, eyes widening. "He is one of your most trustworthy men."

"*Was* one of my most trustworthy. Now, he's dead."

Dead because I had killed him for putting the Buratti family in danger.

"What are we going to do?" Laila asked. "How much does the FBI know?"

"I don't know," I said, running a hand over my face. "Pietro is working on it."

Pietro, my brother, was the loudest—sometimes most infuriating —guy in the entire family, but he loved Laila like a sister and had been wanting us to have kids for months now so he could finally be an uncle. We had been trying, too, but ... Laila hadn't been able to get pregnant.

"I have to go meet him"—I peered down at my watch—"now, but please, stay safe."

"I will," she said. "Promise me you'll come back to me."

I kissed her. "I promise."

15

laila

WITH HER TABLET, Sage sat on our white velvet upholstered sofa near the floor-length windows and drew her pen across the screen a couple of hours after Constantino left. Expression soft, eyes light, fingers gliding her pen in small strokes, she hummed.

I grabbed a wineglass from the cupboard and opened the last bottle of Armand de Brignac Rosé that Constantino and I had bought on our trip to France last year. We had plans to go back in June, but with all this FBI nonsense, I didn't know if we would.

After I filled my glass halfway, I leaned back against the counter and stared over at Sage. She had that same look of awe on her face that I remembered feeling while painting years ago. But I couldn't even remember the last time I'd held a brush.

"Are you drawing?" I asked, the mere scent of Afterglow wine giving me confidence.

Earlier, I had completely screwed up over texts, asking her for a damn picture of herself. I didn't know what had come over me, but I just … I couldn't talk to Sage like I could with Bethany or any of the other girls. Sage made me nervous, and all she was doing was drawing.

Sage glanced up at me, cheeks tinting pink. "Um, yeah."

I took my glass and sat on the opposite side of the couch. "Can I see it?"

"It's, um, not that good," she said in a whisper, swallowing hard and glancing back down at the screen. She curled her fingers around the edges of it until her knuckles turned white. "I've been thinking that's the real reason why my job laid me off."

My chest tightened as guilt washed over me.

She thought she wasn't good at something she loved doing.

I closed my eyes and inhaled deeply, pushing the bad memories and feelings away from when I had thrown away my art supplies for good, when I had told myself that it just wasn't for me anymore, that I was happier being a housewife who went to brunch every day with her friends.

"Stop it," I said once I finally shook the feelings away. I crossed my legs and leaned closer to her. "That is definitely not why you were laid off from your job. I bet your art is amazing. So, think of this as a way to … do what you love now."

Sage stared at me, inhaled sharply, then pressed her nude-colored matte lips together. After another moment, she turned the tablet toward me. A colorful drawing of a woman lying in a bed, staring up at the ceiling, her breasts and torso covered with a thin sheet, glowed on the screen.

"Sage," I said in a breath. "This is amazing!"

"You think?" she asked shyly, blushing even harder.

"Yes!" I exclaimed. "We should put it in a gallery or an auction."

"A gallery?" Sage asked, shaking her head and taking the iPad back from me. "I'm definitely not *that* good. There are so many artists better than me. I can't even imagine someone would want a naked woman hanging up in their house."

"Please," I said, playfully rolling my eyes. "If you drew this on an actual canvas, I'd hang this in our bedroom."

Sage stared down at the drawing, looked back up at me, then smiled softly, changing the direction of the conversation. "You know, I'm actually sorta, kinda glad they laid me off," she whispered. "I worked for an animation studio who liked giving the females unrealistic body proportions since the content is mostly all geared toward men."

"Like everything else in this world," I said.

She frowned. "I mean, there's nothing wrong with that, but some of the characters were really getting out of hand. Like … come on. What kind of character can have boobs that big and *not* have any back pain?"

I giggled and took another sip of my wine. "When I used to paint, I was friends with—"

"Wait. Wait. Wait." Sage placed the iPad down, sat crisscross on the couch, and faced me. "*You* used to paint?"

"Yeah," I said, glancing away in embarrassment. "A long time ago."

"Let me see."

"What?"

"Oh, come on," Sage teased. "You coerced me into showing you my art. Let me see yours."

"I don't have any paintings anymore. I tossed my art and brushes out a long time ago."

Sage furrowed her brow. "Why?"

I shrugged even though I knew the exact reason. I'd wanted to fit into the luxury life of yachts, dirty money, and found family. No one else in the family drew or painted. They were into fashion and food instead.

"That's not the point," I said, waving my hand dismissively. "I used to be friends with this girl who started an online platform for sexually gratifying things for women. Last time I checked, she hosted all sorts of content on the platform, like art, audio, and animation made for women. I could see if I still have her number, if you'd like."

Sage widened her eyes. "Really? That'd be so amazing! I'd love to talk to her. I've been wanting to draw for women, but I could never really make a living off of it while I was in college."

"Well then, it's settled. I'll connect you with her if I can find her number."

Sage grinned at me from the other side of the couch, eyes wide with excitement. For a moment, she dropped her gaze to my lips and sucked in a small breath, and then she looked back up at me.

"Thank you so much," she said, then glanced out the window. "It's getting late. I should get going."

No, I want her to stay.

But how can I ask without sounding desperate?

"Um, okay," I said stupidly, standing with her and walking her to the door.

Fuck.

"See you tomorrow," Sage said, walking out with her bodyguard and down the hall.

"Are you busy tomorrow?" I asked, teetering from foot to foot by the front door.

Sage twirled around with her iPad pressed to her chest. "Constantino wanted to take me out to get new clothes, but I'm not sure what time." She paused and chewed on the inside of her lip. "I hope that's okay. Why?"

"I just …"

Fuck, how do I ask this? Last time I asked Bethany, she completely turned me down.

I glanced back into the penthouse and swallowed hard. "I'm going to the MoMA tomorrow morning to see a new exhibit." *Lie. I had no plans to go to the museum alone.* "If you're interested, you're welcome to come with me."

Eyes widening, Sage curled her lips into a half-smile. "Really?"

"Yes."

"I would love to, but …" she started, glancing down at her feet.

Well, here it comes. Rejection.

"Wouldn't it be weird that you're bringing your housekeeper along with you to a museum with your friends, especially with Bethany? I'm not sure she likes me."

"I'm not going with Bethany," I reassured her, cheeks flushing.

"Oh, who are you going with then?" she asked.

Double fuck. What do I say to her? That I don't have friends who like art, so I'm going alone? Would that make me look like a complete and utter loser? Would she think I am asking her out on a date?

"Just …" I sucked in a deep breath. "I'm going by myself."

Sage widened her eyes even more. "By yourself?"

"Yes, but it's totally fine if you're busy," I said, my words coming out quickly as panic set in. I must've looked so stupid right now in front of her, asking if she wanted to go to an art museum with me because I didn't want to go alone. "It's nothing, Sage. Forget I—"

"I would love to go," Sage said with a smile. "What time?"

This time, my eyes widened. "Wait, really? You want to go with me?"

"Of course," she said, bouncing on her toes. "I've never been."

Warmth exploded through my chest, and I desperately tried to hold back my grin. Someone actually wanted to go to the art museum with me. I had been wanting to go back for forever and didn't think I'd get a chance until Constantino was free.

"Does ten in the morning sound good?"

"It's a date!" Sage called.

"A date," I whispered, grinning like an idiot as she stepped into the elevator. "It's a date."

16

sage

"IF YOU GET BORED, we can leave," Laila said, walking into the art gallery. Dressed in a black velvet body-con dress with a sweetheart neckline and Italian heels, Laila pulled off her tinted cat-eye sunglasses and stuffed them into her small Valentino Garavani clutch. She glanced over at me and offered me a half-smile. "I mean it."

After nodding, I scurried next to her, dressed in a checkered skirt and black bodysuit that was *way* less expensive than any of her clothing. We walked into the first gallery of sculptures and statues from the twentieth and the twenty-first centuries.

"I love sculptures," Laila hummed. "We have a couple at our main house."

"Main house?" I asked.

"The family has a home about forty-five minutes outside the city," she said, walking around the statue and staring at it in awe. When she looked up at me, her eyes were wide with excitement. "We'll have to bring you there sometime."

Butterflies fluttered in my stomach. "I'd love that."

"You will!" she squealed, clutching my hand. "We have an entire art collection."

"Any of your paintings?" I mused.

She blushed and glanced over at me. "I already told you that I didn't keep any."

"That doesn't mean you can't start again," I said.

We walked toward the next sculpture.

"If I made anything again, I think I'd start with sculpting. I've only done it a couple of times. I'm quite terrible at it, but I love getting my fingers wet with clay and creating. I'm nowhere near good, but"—she giggled—"it's fun."

"You don't have to be good at something to enjoy it."

"If it's not good, then nobody will like it."

"Who cares if people like it or not?" I said. "Especially if it's what you love doing."

Laila glanced shyly at me, then looked away. "Constantino says the same thing."

I continued through the museum with her, admiring the artwork.

"We can leave anytime you'd like." Laila glanced nervously at me. "Don't feel like you have to stay because of me. I'm fine with walking around here alone ... if you have other plans for this morning."

"It's okay," I reassured her, playing with the ends of my sleeves.

Honestly, I wasn't sure why she kept telling me that we could leave. Did *she* want to go?

We walked through the tenth exhibit.

"One day, I'd love to host an art auction for charity," she said.

"An art auction?"

She glanced at me. "Do you think that's stupid?"

"No, of course not!" I smiled. "It's very sweet."

"I want to start a foundation where we do art auctions quarterly, but it's a lot of work," she said. "I don't think many people, especially in the family, would appreciate it. They're too money-hungry to donate to charity."

"I think you could do it," I said.

We walked into the twentieth exhibit of the day, it seemed. I wasn't keeping count, but we had already taken in so much art. It was incredible. While most of my art was digital, seeing these paintings and the sculptures made my little creative heart happy.

"I know this place can get kinda boring," Laila said, her black heels clattering against the floor as we walked into the next room. But she seemed interested in *everything* here. "If you want to leave, please let me know."

I furrowed my brow but kept my mouth shut. This was the third time she had asked me if I wanted to leave. It was as if she was expecting me to yawn and ask to leave, like she didn't want me to feel bad about thinking this art was boring.

"I don't want to leave," I finally said, walking past her to the next gallery.

"Okay," Laila said, almost embarrassed. "Sorry."

"Do you want to leave?" I asked, worried that *my company* was boring.

"No!" she said, eyes wide, as if I were crazy, which just made me even more confused about this all.

Why did she keep asking me if I wanted to leave?

She nodded toward a new exhibit. "They have new pieces of art up here that I've been wanting to see."

We walked through it, side by side. Laila gawked at the new exhibit, strolling from art piece to art piece and gushing about the history behind each one.

"You must come here with Bethany a lot," I said.

Laila seemed to know where every piece of art in this place was located along with each artist, the date the artist had created the piece, and the history behind it. The MoMA seemed to be her little happy place.

When Laila didn't answer me, I glanced over at her. She stared up at a large painting that had a single stroke of red paint in the center of the canvas. Her full lips were pulled into a tight line, no curve to them.

I moved closer to her until we stood shoulder to shoulder. While she had pulled her hair into a tight bun at the base of her neck earlier, two locks curled around the shape of her face, shielding her eyes from me.

I didn't know what possessed me to, but I tucked a strand behind her ear. She stared straight ahead at the painting, her big eyes filled with what looked to be hot tears. But when she blinked, they didn't fall down her cheeks.

"What's wrong?" I whispered. "Did I ... did I say something?"

After she shook her head, she plastered a fake smile on her face and briefly turned toward me. "No, it's nothing. Sorry about that." She twirled on her heel and headed toward the next painting. "Come on."

Following her, I stared at the light reflecting off her silky, dark hair. My stomach clenched.

What was that all about?

Even though I didn't like Bethany, she and Laila seemed like they were good friends. I'd go as far as to say *best friends. Do they not go out and do things together?*

"I'm sorry if I offended you," I whispered, trailing after her. "I didn't mean it."

"Sage, it's fine," she said, stopping in front of the next art piece.

Whatever it was ... it wasn't fine. She couldn't even look at me when she spoke, but I didn't want to mess with her anymore, didn't want to nag her or have her hate me. This was still so new to me.

Maybe it has to do with Constantino? Last night?

"If there is something wrong, you can talk to me," I said, lingering a couple of feet away from her while I stared up at the artwork. I hated when people were angry with me. I was a damn people pleaser to the very end. "I don't want you to be mad at me."

She snapped her head toward me. "I'm not angry with you."

I peeked over at her, heart racing, and stayed quiet. She sure seemed like it.

When I turned toward the art, she grabbed my wrist. "Sorry. That wasn't supposed to come out bitchy. I just ... I'm not used to going to see art with friends. I don't want you to be bored. Bethany doesn't like going to museums with me. She's more of a spa and mimosa girl."

Did that mean Bethany *never* went with her to museums? Did they only do things Bethany wanted? I mean, I doubted it because Laila seemed like a spa and mimosa girl too. High-maintenance. But … I mean …

"It's okay," I said.

She gripped my wrist tighter, her fingers hovering close to mine. But before she grabbed my hand completely, she glanced around at the room at the other visitors and then at our bodyguards standing at the entrance.

The guards watched us, so she released my hand and moved closer to me. She turned back to the painting, but her knuckles brushed against mine at our sides.

Her lips twitched into a small smile. "You being here means more to me than you know."

17

laila

AFTER THE MOMA, Constantino texted me to meet him at Cantu Boutique for high-end designer clothing. Tucked away on a quiet street corner in Manhattan, Cantu Boutique didn't get much traffic from the wealthy—yet. It was my and Constantino's gem of a designer clothing shop. We found all my clothes there.

I pulled up to the side of the street, finally weaving out of traffic, and parked. Rain pattered against the windshield. The guards parked the other cars in front and behind us, protecting us on either side.

A moment later, Constantino walked down the sidewalk toward us with a large umbrella in one hand and his other stuffed into his pants pocket. He walked around the car, opened my door first, and helped me out. Then, he did the same for Sage.

Especially because Bethany had already suspected something was going on between Sage and Constantino, I usually didn't want to be out in public with us all together. But Bethany wouldn't be out today as rain poured down on the sidewalks. She'd be too afraid of ruining her makeup.

Constantino held a large umbrella over us from the car to the entrance of Cantu. Before we walked into the shop, Constantino closed the umbrella and left it outside with all three of our guards.

"Laila, *dear*," Viola—one of the designers—said, hurrying over and kissing me on either cheek.

I inhaled a mouthful of her perfume.

"Beautiful as always!" When she stepped back, she gazed over at Sage and smiled tensely. "And who is this?"

My mouth dried as Sage shifted nervously at my side.

Fuck. What do I say?

Constantino stepped forward. "A family friend. We'd like for you to style her."

Viola's eyes widened in excitement. "Of course! Follow me," Viola said to Sage, marching through the store to the fitting room.

Sage followed behind her, her short legs moving quickly to keep up with Viola. I held back a giggle, knowing that Viola was about to give Sage about fifty pieces of clothing to try on, like she had the first time I met her.

After gazing over her shoulder, Sage widened her eyes, as if to say, *Help me.*

I picked up my pace to match hers. Constantino followed after us, lingering behind and picking up clothing off the rack for Sage.

Once Viola ushered Sage into a large fitting room, I sat on a blue velvet couch in the same area.

Constantino walked over with four pieces of clothing hanging off his forearm and handed them to Viola. "Have her try on these."

Viola nodded, opened Sage's door—earning a squeal from Sage, who was probably in the middle of undressing—and handed her the clothes. "Oh, I see women naked all the time, dear. Don't worry about it. We all have the same parts."

My lips curled into a small smile, and I crossed my legs, excited to see Sage in something that Constantino had picked out. He might've had Viola style me when we started dating, but he picked out most of the clothes I liked wearing now.

When Constantino sat next to me, a man in a white button-up and gray suit jacket walked over to us with two glasses of champagne. "Champagne while you wait?" he asked, holding out the glasses for us.

I took a glass and sipped.

"Make sure you come out here once you finish putting on each piece of clothing, dear," Viola said to Sage, then walked out of her fitting room and closed the door. "What kind of clothing are we looking for, Mr. Buratti?"

"Clothing for every occasion," Constantino said.

A moment later, Viola disappeared into the clothing store on a mission to find Sage clothes for every occasion, like Constantino had requested. I took another sip of champagne and smiled to myself, butterflies erupting through my stomach as I thought about this morning.

We had walked through the entire museum together today, and she hadn't wanted to leave once. Even though she enjoyed art, I'd expected her to get bored at some point. Bethany had been so excited the first time that she came with me, but a quarter of the way through, she had asked to leave.

Hell, even Constantino had walked through it all with me, but hadn't particularly enjoyed it.

I hadn't wanted Sage to feel bad, but she hadn't wanted to leave today. She had actually seemed like ... she wanted to be there.

Sage walked out of the room, dressed in black leather pants and an oversize black blazer that tied around the waist, nothing underneath. With her shoulders slumped forward, she stepped in front of the mirror and scrunched her nose.

She looked so sex—

"I look so frumpy."

Constantino stood and walked over to her, resting one hand on her shoulder and tugging it back so she stood up straight. "You can't slouch when you wear clothes like this," he said, lifting her chin so she wasn't staring down. "Chin up."

"This feels so weird," Sage said, chewing on the inside of her cheek. "What do you think, Laila?"

"What do *I* think?" I asked, standing and walking over to her. "You look so sexy."

Cheeks flaming red, Sage glanced away and walked back to the fitting room. "Okay, I guess I'll try the next one on then."

Fifteen outfits later, Viola waited outside Sage's room and tapped her shoe. "Sage!"

"It's not zipping. I think I need a bigger size," Sage called from inside the room.

"Nonsense," Viola muttered, walking into the room without an invitation.

Sage yipped again and closed the door.

After some rummaging around, Viola cleared her throat. "Suck in."

"I'm sucking," Sage said. "It's too tight."

"We can make it fit."

"Ow," Sage whimpered, followed by the sound of zipping.

"Voilà!" Viola clapped her hands. "Beautiful!"

The door swung open, and Sage scurried out of the room in a skintight, silky black dress with silver snakes that hugged the curves of her breasts, dipping between them, their forked tongues reaching out for the other.

"Fuck," I murmured to Constantino, warmth exploding between my legs.

Sage stood in front of the mirror and ran her fingers over the smooth material, swallowing hard. "I don't think I'd ever even have an occasion for when I'd wear this dress," she said. "This looks so …"

God, I hope she doesn't say frumpy again.

"So fancy."

"We're getting it," Constantino said without room to argue.

Sage's mouth dropped open, and she glanced at the tag. "But it's—"

"We're getting it."

Viola ushered her back into the fitting room and closed the door, helping her take it off.

"I'll be right back," Viola said, stepping out of Sage's room and walking into the store.

Half-naked, Sage stuck her head out the door and stared at us through wide eyes. "Please don't tell me she's bringing me more clothes to try on," she whisper-yelled. "I must've tried on half the clothes in the store!"

"Oh, Sage!" Viola called, walking back toward us. "You're not done yet."

Please, help me! Sage mouthed to us, eyes growing wider as Viola handed her more clothes.

Constantino chuckled next to me, lips pulled into a soft smile. He rested a hand on my knee as Viola pushed Sage back into the fitting room to try on a skirt and gently dug his fingers into my thigh. "Do you remember when that was you?"

"I wish I didn't." I giggled.

When Viola came out of the fitting room, Constantino stood.

"Leave us," Constantino said to Viola, glancing at the other customers in the store. "You have other guests to attend to. I can help style Sage from here. Thank you for your help. You're always a pleasure, Viola."

Viola nodded. "Of course, Mr. Buratti."

Once she walked away, Constantino wrapped his hand around the front of my throat and shoved me into the room with Sage. "You girls," he growled softly, shutting the door and locking it behind us, "are driving me crazy."

18

constantino

BEFORE SAGE COULD CONTINUE to fiddle with her clothes, I took her by the throat and pressed her and Laila against the door. My cock throbbed inside my pants. Seeing Sage in that dress ... made me hard as hell.

"Stay," I ordered, releasing their throats and trailing my hands down their bodies.

They both stared up at me through wide eyes, sucking in a collective breath when I brushed my fingers against the front of their short little dresses. Laila grabbed Sage's hand and intertwined their fingers, like a good girl.

When they held hands while I touched them, when they kissed each other around my cock, when they used each other to get off ... God, it did something fucking terrible to me. It made me into a monster, hungry for their pussies.

"You'd better keep quiet," I murmured, gazing from Laila to Sage.

I slipped my fingers underneath the hem of their clothes and trailed my index fingers up their inner thighs. Laila spread her legs for me, like I had taught her to these past few years, while Sage pressed hers together, restricting my access.

"Laila," I said softly, stepping closer to them so I didn't have to raise my voice in here, and I glanced over at Sage, as if telling Laila to look, "tell our toy what she should be doing."

"Spread your legs," Laila whispered to Sage. "Or he'll … punish us."

"Isn't that what you wanted yesterday?" Sage whispered back to her.

A dark chuckle escaped my lips, and I rested my forehead against Sage's. "Princess, I thought my wife had been corrupting your pretty little mind yesterday. But you like to backtalk too, don't you?"

She sucked in a breath and swallowed hard. "N-no."

"Spread your legs, Sage," Laila whispered, tilting her head toward Sage's ear, her nose brushing against it. "Or else he will punish us here. In public. In front of everyone. And he has enough money to … make sure nobody says a word about it to anyone."

"Do you want to be humiliated, Sage?" I murmured. "Do you want me to fuck you in the middle of the store, make you scream so loud that all the passersby peer through the glass windows and see your naked body getting railed by my huge cock?"

Sage widened her eyes and inched her legs apart. "N-no, sir."

But when I cupped her cunt, her pussy was soaked.

"Your pussy says otherwise," I hummed, dipping my hand between Laila's thighs too. I pulled a couple of inches away from Sage and peered over at my wife. "I know you'd love watching me fuck our little toy in front of everyone."

"No," Laila whispered, but when I slipped two fingers into her, she tightened around me.

"You're a bad liar," I said, pushing my fingers into Sage.

They both clenched around me, gripping each other's hand harder. I growled and gritted my teeth, my cock throbbing against my tightening suit pants. I pushed my fingers in and out of them, listening to their wetness get stuffed over and over.

Laila was used to me touching—*taunting*—her in public like this. After hundreds of times, she had learned to muffle her moans. I usually had to work hard to get her to whimper out loud for me, but Sage couldn't hold herself back.

"Fuck staying quiet, Sage," I said to her, my gaze on Laila. "I want you to be louder."

"N-no," Laila whimpered, pussy tight around my fingers. "She c-can't. We're in public."

Laila had wanted to taunt me with Sage last night. It was my turn.

"Louder, *princess*." I egged on Sage, thrusting my fingers deeper and faster. "You can moan louder for me."

Laila stared over at Sage, eyes growing wide as her pussy grew tighter. "S-Sage," she whispered.

They both tightened around me, as if they couldn't hold back, as if staying quiet made them even hornier.

And when I knew I had caught Sage, when I knew she wouldn't be able to hold back her moans any longer, when she was right about to scream out in pleasure for me, Laila pressed her mouth against Sage's.

Sage jerked against the wall, thrust her tongue into my wife's mouth, and came undone. "Fuck," Sage whimpered, lips parted.

Laila kissed Sage harder, muffling her moans, their breasts brushing together. My dick twitched.

Laila suddenly tightened around my fingers, her body jerking next to Sage's as she came. Sage gripped her hand tighter and kissed her, their breaths becoming jagged and raspy together in this small changing room.

"Doll," I grunted quietly, "I want to watch you eat her pussy again."

"R-right here?" she asked.

"Right here," I said, pulling her off the wall. "While I fuck you from behind."

Sage stumbled into a plush, small accent chair in the corner of the room, lying back and resting her legs over each armrest, her dress riding up her thighs and her creamed pussy glistening underneath the bright light above.

I bent Laila over in front of Sage, seizing my wife's hips and yanking them closer to me. After pulling out my cock, I rubbed it against her pussy and plunged it right into her, unable to control myself anymore.

Grabbing a fistful of her hair, I pushed her head down to Sage's cunt and watched my wife eat our toy's quivering little pussy. She lapped at her clit as I pounded into her, wanting them both to come undone again.

After tightening my grip on her hair, I shoved her down further, wanting her face to be covered in Sage's juices, wanting my wife to look and feel like a dirty little slut by the time I finished with them. Laila fucking loved it.

I had promised her that, one day, I'd take her to a city we'd never been to before, cover her face in my cum, and make her walk down the street, looking like a whore, like a slut, like my pretty little pet while everyone stared at her.

And I planned to keep that promise.

If I had two pretty girls covered in my cum, walking down the street, hand in hand …

"Fuck," I grunted, slamming into Laila one last time, my cum spilling into her cunt.

She gripped Sage's thighs until her fingertips turned white and buried her face deeper between her legs, lips clasped around her clit to muffle her moans. She held a hand over Sage's mouth while they both came together with me.

19

sage

MONDAY MORNING, I grabbed my bagel from the counter of The Coffee Club, a cute two-story coffee shop tucked away in Manhattan, and waited for my iced tea. Riccardo, my bodyguard, stood stiffly beside me, staring straight ahead at the case of cookies.

"Do you want—" I started.

"No."

I pressed my lips together and bounced on my toes, waiting for my drink. I had my iPad in my purse, and I couldn't wait to start drawing today. Even after everything that'd happened so far, I still couldn't believe that this was my life.

Instead of having my soul sucked out of me by the old art studio, I now got paid to have sex and draw whenever I wanted. What else could I ask for in my life?! Maybe a boyfriend … or girlfriend?

"Iced tea for Sage," the cute guy with puppy-dog eyes said behind the counter.

Once I grabbed my tea, I headed toward the stairs to find a place to sit.

"Do you want to sit with me?" I asked, walking up the steps to the open second floor.

"No."

When we reached the top of the stairs, Riccardo walked across the room and sat at a table alone, his jaw clenched and his gaze focused on me. I scrunched my nose and hoped that he'd open up to me one day. Or at least, let me sit *with him*.

After humming to myself, I gazed around to find another seat. The second floor had a balcony that overlooked the first floor. A great place to people-watch and find inspiration for my art today. Because most of the single tables had been taken, I sat at a large collaborative table that nobody had taken yet.

I pulled out my tablet and my drawing pen, opening a new canvas to work on. As I drew, I could feel Riccardo's hard stare boring into the side of my face. I lifted my eyes to meet his intense, angry ones.

He had eyed the freshly baked M&M cookies in the display downstairs.

Maybe a cookie would make him less grumpy. It always worked for me.

Grabbing my purse, I walked downstairs to the counter. Riccardo glanced over the balcony and eyed me the entire damn time I ordered two large cookies for us. Once the cashier handed me a plate, I strolled back up the stairs and to his table.

I set the plate down in front of him and grabbed my cookie, stuffing it into my mouth and walking away before he could refuse a sweet. When I reached my table, I grabbed my tablet and looked over at Riccardo, who hadn't even touched the damn thing.

The warm cookie still sat on the pink plate in front of him, just waiting to be eaten.

Concluding that he hated his job as my bodyguard—*because who could turn down a cookie?!*—I turned my tablet back on and opened up the project that I had been working on yesterday—one beautiful female embracing another.

I had decided to add the second female at the last minute, but it was one hundred percent worth it. I finally had the freedom to draw what I wanted to draw instead of some unrealistic bust-to-waist-to-hip ratio that my old studio had wanted me to draw.

This was authentic.

When I glanced up from my tablet, Riccardo now peered around the coffee shop with half the cookie in his hand while he chewed on the other half. The tenseness in his face faded, his jaw finally slack for once.

I smiled. *Nobody can turn down a fresh cookie.*

"Excuse me," a young woman with short, curly red hair said, leaning over the table toward me, her cheeks flushed. "Sorry, I don't mean to come off as rude for looking at your work, but your art is amazing!"

Warmth spread across my face, and I smiled shyly at her. "Thank you."

She giggled and walked to the other side of the empty table. "Do you mind if I sit here with you? This place gets kinda packed during lunchtime." She glanced over her shoulder. "And that family just took the table I wanted."

"Oh, yeah. Of course."

After I moved my purse out of the way, I returned back to my tablet and continued drawing the curves of the women's bodies. Warmth spread through my core, my heart racing at the sight, at the *thought* of how intimate I had been with Laila.

A couple of weeks ago, I hadn't known the first thing about being with another woman. I hadn't known if they kissed the same, touched the same, made each other feel good the same way as a man did.

But, hell, I was so happy that she had approached me that Friday night.

Continuing to create small strokes on the screen, I finished with the first woman's long hair that covered her breasts and started on the second woman, who was a bit bigger than the first. With a belly and smaller breasts, legs that weren't smooth and perfect.

My lips curled into a small smile. God, I loved art so much.

"Did you go to school for art?" the lady asked me suddenly.

I snapped my gaze up to her, cheeks flushing. "Yeah, at Charter A University."

"No way," she said, fingertips on the table. "I went to Charter A for psychology."

"You're kidding," I said, placing my tablet down and inching forward. "Really?"

"Graduated three years ago. I swore you looked so familiar."

"I just graduated last year!" I twirled my pen and smiled. "I can't believe this."

She crunched on a chip. "Me neither. What's your name, by the way?"

"Sage."

"I'm Poppy." She held out her hand for me to shake. "What're you doing in New York?"

Charter A University was the newest university in the northeastern US, located in the most northern part of Maine. Not many people attended, and those who did usually stayed local because their families lived around the area.

"I came to work at an animation studio, but I'm ... taking some time off," I said.

It was against my contract to even speak about Laila and Constantino to anyone, so I didn't know exactly what kind of excuse I would need to come up with. But ... I would need to find something believable.

20

constantino

MONDAY AFTERNOON, I walked with Pietro from lunch back to The Syndicate, where we had business to finalize about shipments. A slight breeze blew toward us, my tie pressing against my chest.

An eerie feeling washed over me.

While Pietro gossiped about the latest woman he had picked up from the club, I paused for a brief moment and scanned the street. Something didn't feel right. And I swore to God, if it was another family member getting it on with an FBI—

When I spotted the black SUV with tinted windows that I didn't recognize about half a block down from the entrance to the club, I gritted my teeth. A female sat behind the wheel, typing on her phone but gazing at us.

Hands balling into fists, I grabbed Pietro by the collar and stormed into the building with him in tow. After I slammed and locked the door, I released him and growled to myself.

Fuck the fucking police. The FBI. All of them.

Fuck!

I drew a hand across my face and stepped farther into the empty club. The lights blared overhead, the room completely silent, except for the padding of footsteps across the floor. I inhaled a waft of perfume someone must've fucking doused my leather bar stools in last night.

"I want them fucking out of here," I growled to Pietro. "They're too close."

"They're not close enough," Pietro said. "You see that one out there? I'd bend her—"

"I don't have fucking time for this shit." I ran a hand through my hair. "Get rid of her. She's stressing me out. Vincent told me that he and Riccardo spotted the FBI when they took Laila and her ... *friend* ... to the museum the other day."

"Friend?" Pietro asked. "Hot girl for me?"

"Pietro," I scolded, wishing that our parents had dropped him on his fucking head when we were babies so I wouldn't have to do it now if he didn't shut the fuck up and take this seriously. "If they find anything else on us—"

"Relax," my brother said, placing his hands on my shoulders. "Relax. I'll take care of it."

"Good," I grumbled, turning toward my office.

But Pietro stopped me. "On one condition."

I rolled my eyes, knowing that he was about to crack a fucking joke that I really couldn't take right now. All I could think about was how to keep Laila safe, to keep her out of this mess. She hadn't done shit, but those fuckers would try to charge her with something.

"You get your ass home and get Laila pregnant," Pietro said. "I want to be an uncle."

While I wanted Laila pregnant even *more* than he wanted to be an uncle, I couldn't tell him that we had already tried. Multiple times. Multiple positions. Multiple ways. And I hadn't been able to put a baby inside her.

I felt like a fucking failure as a man.

If I told Pietro, he wouldn't let me live it fucking down. Half the family would know by noon, which was—I glanced down at my watch—in twenty minutes. I trusted him more than anyone in this family, but he had a loud mouth.

"Constantino!" Laila called from somewhere in the empty club, her voice traveling.

"In here!" Pietro called, smirking wickedly at me as we walked into the office.

"Laila," Pietro cooed, wrapping his arms around my wife and throwing me a wink. "I told Constantino to take you home, make you *rest* for the day."

Laila playfully pushed him away and arched a brow at me. "He's bad."

Pietro grinned like a fool. "Only for you, Laila."

"And about a hundred different girls at the club every Friday night," Laila shot back.

"Ooh," Pietro said, murmuring Italian to himself and backing out of the room. He threw me a smirk. "She has some punch in her today, Constantino. You'd better watch you back before she snaps at you like that."

When my brother finally left and shut the door behind himself, Laila walked over to my desk, placed her purse on top of it, and climbed into my lap. She rested her head on my shoulder and wrapped her arms around my body.

"We need to find him a girlfriend." Laila giggled, her warm breath fanning my neck.

He needed more than that.

"He's still too immature for a girlfriend," I said. "Give him a couple of years."

"Or you know," Laila suggested, "we could just cut down his ego a bit. Hire a pretty girl to tease him and then shut him down every time he tried to put a move on her, unlike every other girl in this entire world would."

I chuckled and placed my hand on her knee.

It was a plausible idea, but I didn't even know if that'd work on him.

"So, what is it, doll?" I asked, dragging my hand up her bare thigh. "Why are you here?"

"Do you want to … maybe go to the store with me?"

"What do you need? I need to finish up some work."

"I wanted to get some supplies to start sculpting."

My eyes widened. "Sculpting?"

She wants to start creating art again? What happened? For years, she had been adamant about not wanting to paint or draw or even sketch. She thought that being part of the family meant that she had to give up that part of herself.

"Do you think it's a bad idea?" she asked, glancing down at her lap. "I mean, I don't—"

"I think it's a great idea," I said, sinking my fingers into her thigh. "Let's go."

"Right now?" she asked, eyes wide. "I thought you had work."

"I can make time for you," I murmured against her lips, sucking her bottom lip into my mouth and gently tugging on it. "But why the sudden change of heart about it all? I thought that you didn't want to do art anymore."

"Yeah, but …" She glanced toward the window and smiled to herself. "Sage and I were talking while we went to the museum, and I sorta mentioned that I'd be interested in sculpting. And she thought I should try it out. So, I'm going to. Is that weird?"

Heat surged through my body, my lips curling into a smile. Sage had done this.

I would have to plan something nice for her later.

"No, of course it's not weird," I said. After scooping my wife's hand in mine, I tucked my gun into my waistband and walked with her to the office door. "Follow me, doll. We're going to get you those art supplies so you can create something amazing."

21

sage

CONSTANTINO: **Can you make sure Laila eats tonight?**

After turning off my tablet, I slid it into my purse and grabbed my phone from off the wooden table at the coffee shop. I had been here for hours, and Mr. Riccardo the Bodyguard looked pissed off that I hadn't bought him another cookie.

Me: Sure! Does she like anything specific?

Constantino: Nothing specific.

Constantino: She's sculpting at our place. When she used to paint, she'd forget all about the time.

My eyes widened. *Laila is sculpting?* I almost couldn't believe it. When we had gone to the museum, she had seemed like she'd never pick up art again, like she desperately wanted to start back up but feared what everyone would think of her.

Constantino: Thank you for that, by the way.

What is he thanking me for?

Me: For what?

Constantino: For urging her to pursue art again.

Warmth spread throughout my body, and I couldn't stop the grin that spread across my face. *Did I inspire Laila to buy a bunch of art*

92

supplies and start working on her next piece? Does she really value my opinion that much?

"Maybe I'll see you around?" Poppy asked when I stood.

I smiled. "Yeah, definitely. I'll probably be here tomorrow too!"

"Great." She beamed. "I'll see you then."

Once I grabbed my iced tea from the wooden table and wiped the wet residue off with a napkin, I took my purse and nodded to Riccardo, who stood with his empty cookie plate. He followed me down the stairs and to the exit, licking his lips.

"Do you want another one?" I asked before we left.

"Another what?"

"Cookie."

"No."

After rolling my eyes at him—because who could turn down a second free cookie?—I walked out of the café and toward a black SUV with tinted windows parked on the side of the road. I slipped into the backseat while Riccardo got in up front with the driver.

"Where are we off to?" the driver asked.

"Burgerland," I said, gazing out the window at the New York streets.

———

An hour later, I stood in front of Laila's door with a greasy bag of burgers and fries. I knocked and bounced on my toes, waiting for her to answer. After some shuffling through the house, Laila pulled the door open a couple of inches and glanced outside.

When she spotted me, she widened her eyes and opened the door completely. "Sage," she said, pulling off her dirty apron. "I thought you were out today." With the back of her clay-covered hand, she pushed a couple of strands of hair off her forehead. "If I had known you were coming over, I would've showered."

My cheeks warmed. "You don't have to do that for me. I'm just here to deliver dinner."

Laila washed her hands in the kitchen sink and glanced over her shoulder at the bag of fast food in my hands. "Burgerland?" she asked, inhaling deeply as a huge grin broke out on her face. "God, it smells delicious."

"It's probably not the kind of food you normally have, but it's my favorite."

"I haven't had a burger in forever." She giggled. "I'm excited."

I set it on the counter and headed toward the bathroom. "I'm going to use the bathroom."

It had been a long day at the coffee shop, and I hadn't wanted to lose my seat to use the restroom. But that iced tea had *really* gotten to me and settled in my tummy these past few hours. And then sitting in all that traffic!

After I shut the door and made a run for the toilet before I peed myself, I slumped my shoulders forward and blew out a deep breath. From inside the bathroom, I listened to two pairs of feet shuffling around the house.

Shit! Is Constantino back? I had only gotten food for Laila and me.

Once I finished my business, I hurried back into the living room and spotted Bethany dragging Laila toward the front door.

"Come on," she called. "I made a reservation for dinner at seven tonight with the girls."

I stopped in my tracks and sucked in a quiet breath. *Oh, definitely not Constantino.*

"Beth," Laila said, "I really don't think—"

Bethany glanced over her shoulder at Laila, but spotted me and dropped Laila's hand, pausing at the door. "Why are you here?" she asked me, then gazed at the paper bag with a grease stain at the bottom. "Did you bring that over for dinner?" She turned to Laila. "She's a housekeeper, but doesn't cook?"

"Bethany, please," Laila said, standing up straight and fiddling with her fingers. "We—I ..."

"I'm here to ... clean up before Constantino gets home," I said, not wanting Laila to have to tell Bethany about me. I knew deep down that she didn't want anyone to know. I glanced at the bag from Burgerland and hurried over to it. "This is just … my dinner for tonight."

"You shouldn't eat while you work," Bethany said, pursing her pink lips together. She pushed past Laila to the counter, grabbed the bag of food, and dumped it upside down in the trash. "If you're working for Constantino, at least respect his wife."

"S-sorry, Mrs. Buratti," I stuttered. My stomach growled. "I-it won't happen again."

"It'd better not," Bethany growled, seizing Laila's hand.

"I don't think that was necessary," Laila said to Bethany, not moving.

After turning toward Laila, Bethany scowled. "She's fucking your husband."

"N-no, she's not," Laila stuttered, mouth opening and closing, as if she didn't know what else to say to her supposed *best friend*. "She's our housekeeper and nothing more. I-I planned to have dinner here tonight any—"

"You don't want to come out to dinner with us?" Bethany asked, frowning. "Come on, Laila. We are heading to your favorite place, and the girls haven't seen you in, like, over a week now."

Laila stared at me through sorrowful eyes. She didn't want to let Bethany down.

And it freaking killed me on the inside.

But it wasn't my place to say anything. My chest tightened. I was her toy. *Nothing more.*

"Go," I said to her.

"She doesn't need your permission." Bethany dragged her out of the penthouse.

Laila gazed back at me, hurt spread across her face, brows drawn together, raspberry-painted lips tugged down. "Sage, I'll order you something. I …"

Bethany pulled the door closed just as Laila mouthed the words, *I'm sorry,* to me.

22

laila

AFTER SEARCHING through the App Store, I found Uber Eats and downloaded it. I had never used one of these apps, but I needed to buy something for Sage to eat tonight after Bethany completely trashed her dinner.

"Okay," the waiter said, setting down plates of appetizers on our table. "Caprese and caviar and another bottle of champagne for the table." He set a bottle of champagne, sitting in an ice bucket, on the center of the table. "Enjoy."

I lifted my gaze while the girls each took some. "Thank you."

Instead of grabbing some myself, I peered back down at my phone and frowned. A selection of restaurants popped up on the screen, and I scrolled through them.

Where did Sage buy those burgers from again?

Burger ... World?

When no results appeared on the screen, I furrowed my brow and continued searching. I should've stayed home with her tonight. My chest tightened. *Why the hell didn't I? Why did I let Bethany drag me away?*

"Come on, Laila." Gigi giggled. "Get off your phone. You can text Constantino later."

"One second," I said, desperately searching through all the places that had burgers in New York City. I could buy her anything, but I wanted to send her something that she'd like, something she had gotten me.

Fuck, where is it?

Burger House.

Burgerside.

Burgerland.

After scrolling past it, I scrolled back up and clicked Burgerland. About a hundred different burgers popped up, all with different flavors, different types of meat. I didn't know what Sage liked, so I opted for a regular cheeseburger.

She would like that, right?

Once I checked out and paid with Apple Pay, I gazed at the delivery time.

An hour and a half. *The food won't make it back to the skyrise for an hour and a half?!* Sage hadn't answered my texts that I sent her on the way to dinner, and she had seemed so hungry when I left.

She would starve. Or maybe she wasn't even at our home anymore. *What if she went out to get her own food, pissed off at me for leaving her?* My heart pounded against my rib cage, and I shook my head.

Me: I'm sorry.

Me: Please don't be angry.

Me: I ordered your food to be delivered to the penthouse.

No response.

I pressed my lips together, feeling so much hurt because of my own decisions, and slipped my phone into my purse. I stared out the window at the traffic and frowned. Rain had begun to fall as we arrived, and now, it was pouring outside. Vincent sat in the car just outside the restaurant.

I had stopped listening to the gossip between the girls a while ago, only catching snippets of their conversation here and there. All

I could think about was the awful look Sage had had on her face when she walked out of the bathroom to see Bethany pulling me out the door. The sadness that had spread across her face when Bethany dumped her food in the trash, the food she had willingly picked out and brought over for me to eat.

God, why the hell did I leave her? Why the fuck did I come out here tonight? I didn't want Sage to feel like she didn't matter. I knew how that felt, had grown up like that for so many years. I hated hurting people close to me.

My eyes widened slightly. *Is Sage close to me?*

"Your tits *are* pretty small, Laila." Bethany giggled.

Snapping out of my thoughts, I glanced over at Bethany. "What?"

"Have you not been listening?" Gigi said with a playful smile. "Too busy thinking about Constantino?"

"Maybe," I said, cheeks flushing.

Marcie sipped on her champagne. "We were talking about what guys in the family like."

I glanced over at Bethany. "My tits are the topic of conversation?"

She smiled and playfully shoved her shoulder into mine. "They are."

"You know the men in this family." Gigi giggled. "All they see is tits, and they're sold."

"Constantino doesn't seem like that," Marcie said. "Refreshing for once."

"Who knows though?" Bethany said. "He might be, but just doesn't want to hurt Laila."

"You think my tits are that small?" I asked, brow furrowing.

"Of course they are." Bethany giggled.

They are?

Obviously, I didn't have natural F-cups, like she did, but … I liked my Ds. I thought they were a manageable size, and as far as I knew, Constantino liked them too. But he didn't say anything negative about my body—*ever*. Maybe he thought I could be even sexier for him.

"That isn't a bad thing, but don't you wanna keep Constantino's gaze from ... straying?" Bethany hinted at Sage catching Constantino's eyes.

The girls suddenly became quiet, and I cleared my throat. I didn't know what to say because, lately, *my* gaze had been straying. I had brought Sage into our relationship, and I wanted her to stay as my plaything too. It wasn't only Constantino, but I didn't want to tell her that.

"I need to use the restroom," I said, excusing myself from the table as the waiter brought our entrées out.

Once I made it to the luxurious bathroom with a marble sink, I stared at myself in the mirror, the dim lights barely brightening the room. My gaze dropped to my breasts in my oversize shirt. If I had known Bethany wanted to go out, I would've put on something nicer, a push-up bra maybe.

My stomach tightened, and I held back tears. *Do I look that bad? Is that what Constantino wants? What about Sage? Will she like me more if I have bigger tits, like Bethany suggests? Guys in this family sure like them, but ... do I have to do that?*

After pushing back the tears, I set my shoulders back, plastered a fake smile on my face, and walked back out to dinner with my friends. I wanted to leave and go home to see Sage and Constantino, who should be back by now, but I couldn't leave in the middle of the entrées.

Bethany wanted the best for me and Constantino—that was why she had dragged me out to dinner tonight; that was why she had kept bringing Sage into the conversation. That was all. They were looking out for me. That was what friends did, right?

23

constantino

"FUCK," I growled, standing on the elevator and running a hand through my hair.

Those FBI fuckers hadn't left my club the entire night, had waited for me to leave and then followed me. We had lost them about ten blocks down through the traffic, but they were getting too close and way too ballsy.

When I reached my floor, the elevator opened. Riccardo stood outside the door, leaning against the wall, but Vincent wasn't anywhere in sight. I pressed my lips together and nodded to Riccardo, wondering what the hell was going on.

After stepping into my home, I placed my jacket down on an island stool. Two wrapped and untouched burgers sat in the trash, along with a couple boxes of fries and a paper bag from a place called Burgerland. I furrowed my brow and walked farther into the penthouse, my home silent, except for a couple of sniffles coming from the living room.

Sage sat on the windowsill, staring out the wall-length windows at the city below us, with her arms wrapped around her knees. She rested the side of her forehead against the large window.

"Sage?" I called.

As if she hadn't heard me walk into the penthouse, she snapped her head in my direction and wiped tears from her cheeks. I furrowed my brow.

Why is she sitting in my house alone, crying? Where the hell is Laila?

"S-sorry," Sage said, sliding off the windowsill and hurrying past me. "I probably should've left a while ago when Laila left." She glanced at the unopened food in the garbage. "I'll get out of your hair."

Before she could make it another foot, I snapped my hand around her upper arm and stopped her. "Where did Laila go? She just left you here?"

Sage stared at the ground and shrugged her shoulders, tensing. I snatched her chin and forced her to look up at me. She stared for a few moments before more tears filled her eyes. She shook her head and suddenly wrapped her arms around me.

"I'm sorry," she whispered. "I don't even know why I'm crying."

Slowly, I settled my arms around her shoulders. Laila had been the only woman to hug me like this in years, and I ... wasn't sure how to react to her. *Do I hold her back? Do I ask her what is wrong?* She wasn't my wife.

"Where is Laila?" I asked again.

She pulled away from me and wiped the tears from her cheeks again, shoulders heaving. "I'm sorry for crying. I-I brought her dinner, just like you had asked, but she left with Bethany before we could eat."

I stiffened and balled my fists. "Bethany?"

Of course, Bethany had come over to snatch Laila away. I hated that fucking bitch. I had told Laila too many times to stop hanging out with her, and I could've fucking stopped it myself, too, by offing her, but Laila would hate me.

Bethany had been Laila's first *friend* when she joined the family.

"Why are you crying? Did Bethany hurt you?" I asked because if she had ... then I wouldn't care *what* I did to her. Laila would understand.

"No," Sage said. "I'm sorry. I'm just tired and hungry."

"Don't lie to me," I demanded.

She snapped her head up and shook it. "I-I'm not."

"You are."

After a couple of moments, she pursed her matte-colored lips and gazed out the windows again. "I don't mean to overstep. I know that I'm ... that I'm only your toy to play with, but Bethany doesn't seem like a good friend to Laila."

"She's not."

"It makes me sad," Sage whispered. "Laila is so sweet."

Once I let out a low sigh, I drew my tongue across my teeth. Despite everything that Laila had been through in her life, she was one of the sweetest women I knew. That was one of the reasons I had married her. But this family was slowly corrupting her.

Sage's stomach rumbled, and she quickly clutched it. "I should go back home."

"What happened to the food?" I asked. "Why is it in the trash?"

Sage opened and closed her mouth without answering. Laila did the same thing when she didn't want to tell me the truth or when she didn't want to disappoint me.

"Don't lie to me," I ordered.

"I don't want to get anyone in trouble," she murmured.

"If you don't want to get in trouble, you'll tell me."

She eyed the trash. "Bethany dumped my food into the garbage."

"She what?" I said between clenched teeth.

Sage walked over to the can. "They're still edible, so it doesn't matter. I should've eaten it earlier, but I wasn't thinking straight."

She reached for one of the unopened burgers, but I seized her hand before she could touch it.

"You're not eating food from the trash."

"It's okay, Constantino." She attempted to release herself from my hold. "Really."

I tightened my grip. "Where was Laila when this happened?"

Instead of struggling to escape, Sage lifted her gaze to mine, pressed her lips together, and widened her eyes. "S-she was ... in the other, um, room. She didn't see." She stumbled over her words, which only made me fucking angrier.

"She watched the whole thing happen, didn't she?" I growled.

Sage clutched my shirt in her tiny fists. "Please, I don't want her to get in trouble."

"Fuck!" I growled, ripping myself away from her and turning around.

Laila was sweet, but not when she was with Bethany. She had literally *watched* Bethany dump Sage's food into the trash and hadn't done anything to stop it? She hadn't ordered another dinner for her and stayed here with Sage? How could she do such a thing?

"Please, Constantino," Sage pleaded, "don't be mad at her."

"I'm not mad." *I am fucking furious.*

"Constantino, please, I—"

"Come on." I grabbed her hand. "I'm taking you to dinner."

"Dinner?" she asked, eyes widening. "You don't have to. Really."

"Don't fucking fight me on this, Sage. I'm already pissed off."

Sage snapped her mouth closed and shuffled along after me to the front door. I walked out of the house with her hand in mine and three guards in tow behind us. Unlike Laila, I didn't care who saw us. Right now, I would kill anyone in the family who said shit about Sage.

24

sage

A MAFIA BOSS in a suit sat across from me in Burgerland.

I stifled a giggle at how silly Constantino looked in a fast-food joint and popped a fry into my mouth, burning the sensitive skin of my palate. Constantino belonged in a high-end restaurant with five-hundred-dollar plates. Not sitting in a colorful plastic booth.

But he didn't seem like he minded *that* much.

"I could've taken you somewhere nicer," he said, scarfing down his burger.

"This is fine for me," I said. "This was my favorite food, growing up."

He chuckled. "Burgers and fries?"

"Hey, don't make fun of me." I giggled. "My family was low-income, so it was a treat to eat out at a restaurant like this. It ... brings me back. My parents might not have had a lot, but they tried for me."

When he didn't say much—not that I wanted him to because I was definitely oversharing now—I cleared my throat. "I don't mean to be rude," I started, chewing a mouthful of my food and setting my fries down, "but I have a question about Laila."

Constantino wiped his mouth with a white paper napkin. "Go ahead."

I chewed on the inside of my cheek and frowned. I didn't know if it was okay to ask him this about her, but he didn't seem to like Bethany either. "Why does she let Bethany push her around?"

After tensing slightly, Constantino straightened himself out. "Don't tell her I told you," Constantino said. "Nobody in the family knows, except me."

"I won't say anything," I promised.

"Laila was in foster care since she was three. She stayed with … probably around twenty families until she turned eighteen. Some— not all—were abusive to her. More verbally and emotionally than physically."

My eyes widened. "That's terrible."

"She moved around so much that she never really formed any friendships," he said. "So, since we started dating, she has tried to please all the girls in the family by doing anything that they want. She's desperate to be accepted and loved by them."

I frowned, tears building in my eyes. "She doesn't like saying no."

"She can't," Constantino said. "She's terrified that they'll all end up hating her and she'll be left with nobody."

"But she has you," I said.

Constantino paused.

"Right?" I asked.

"Sage," Constantino said, leaning forward and lowering his voice, "of course she has me, but I have the FBI breathing down my neck. If another person squeals to them about our family, they'll put me in prison for decades."

"D-decades?" I whispered, unable to believe it. "But that … that can't happen."

"I'm not going to prison without a fight, but if something happens to me, I need *you* to be there for Laila. I don't want her in the middle of the mayhem that will follow once they sentence me. This family will do everything in their power to hurt her so they can become the head of this family, especially because we don't have a child."

"A child?" I asked. "Would that stop it?"

"Probably not, but it'd be someone for Laila to care for so she doesn't get wrapped up in the drama those girls she calls friends bring her," he said, then paused. He glanced around once more and then dropped his gaze to our table and let out a breath. "We've been trying."

"You have?" I asked softly, hearing how fragile his words sounded.

"For months."

My lips curled into a frown. "If anything happens, I promise to help Laila."

He held out his hand, and I reluctantly set my hand in his. His expression softened more than I had ever seen it, the lines in his face disappearing.

Then, he chuckled. "I was going to ask for your phone."

Cheeks reddening in embarrassment, I pulled my hand out of his and stuffed my hand into my purse for my phone. *God, what is wrong with me? Why did I think he wanted to hold my hand? He just held it out there and expected me not to take it?!*

When I placed my phone in his palm, he snatched my hand, too, and squeezed, throwing me a breathtaking smile. Not one of his smirks or those harsh eyes he'd had the first night with me. A genuine smile.

"I didn't mean to make you embarrassed."

"I'm not embarrassed," I lied.

For some reason, his smile softened even more. I swallowed and smiled back, warmth exploding through my chest. God, his smile … and those eyes. He might've killed people for a living, but, damn, he was so sweet.

Once he finally released my hand, he typed something into my phone and handed it back. "I saved a contact in your phone. His name is Vito Ferrara. He's a family friend. If anything happens and you're in trouble, contact him."

After nodding, I placed the phone into my purse.

"And thank you for talking Laila back into art," he said, smiling genuinely to himself again, his eyes lighting up when he talked about her. He leaned back in his seat and finished off the last of his burger. "I haven't seen her that excited and happy in a long time."

My smile faltered just a bit, but I quickly recovered and nodded. "Of course."

Stupid Sage.

He had only brought me out because of Laila. Of course he wouldn't bring me out for any reason other than his wife and the gratitude he had for me being with her and maybe because of the way she had left me earlier too. I had been contracted to be their toy. Nothing more.

First, it was Laila ditching me for dinner. Now, this? These feelings had to stop.

So, I brushed them all off, and after dinner, I followed Constantino out of the restaurant toward the tinted SUVs that were parked on the side of the road.

"Boss," a middle-aged man called, jogging across the street toward us.

Constantino didn't drop my hand, like Laila would've. Instead, he held it tighter.

"Giulio," Constantino said.

Giulio gazed at our hands, then smirked at Constantino. *"The man."*

I averted my eyes and pressed myself closer to Constantino, not liking the way that he looked at me. Constantino squeezed my hand tighter and stared at the man, refusing to back down from his curious gaze, unlike me.

"Who is this?" Giulio asked, peering at me.

"None of your business."

"The housekeeper?" Giulio asked, smirk widening. "Bethany has mentioned her."

"Don't ask questions," Constantino growled, grabbing him by his shirt collar and yanking him closer to him. After staring him down for a few moments, he shoved him away. "You don't speak of this to anyone."

"Don't worry, boss," Giulio called, staggering away. "Your secret is safe with me."

My stomach twisted into knots. *Fuck, this isn't good.*

Besides our bodyguards, nobody but Bethany knew much about us. And of course, Bethany *had to have* a big mouth and blab it to the entire family, it seemed. I hoped that Constantino could keep it under control.

But I had a bad feeling that things were about to spiral.

25

sage

"YOU'VE HAD A LONG DAY," I said once we made it back to his penthouse. I assumed because he hadn't clicked the elevator button for my floor that he wanted *something* from me. "Do you want me to run a bath for you?"

He paused and lifted his suddenly dark gaze, taking my hand and walking toward the bathroom. When we made it inside, I started the warm water and added bubbles as Constantino began undressing while watching me. Once the bath was full, I shut off the water.

"Take off your clothes," he ordered.

My eyes widened slightly. "A-are you sure?"

"Take off your clothes."

I pulled off my clothes and stepped into the bathtub with him, the warm water relaxing me after everything that had happened tonight.

Before I could stop him, he seized my waist with his rough hands, shoved me against the side of the tub, still in the water, and moved between my legs. Pressing his hot mouth against mine, he sank his hand between my thighs.

"You're Laila's toy," he said against my mouth. "But Laila isn't here to play with you."

I gripped on to his round shoulders, fingers sinking into the muscle, and clenched.

God, I had been thinking about this all night.

He moved his fingers in tortuous, small circles around my clit, then slipped them right into me. "And I can't send you back down without taking care of this first," he murmured, suds covering his tattooed chest as he pumped his fingers in and out of my wet pussy. "Have you been this wet all night?"

"Constantino," I moaned, leaning back against the tub and accidentally sloshing water and bubbles over the edge. I spread my legs in the large bath and whimpered, the pressure building and building inside me.

With his thumb, he rubbed my clit.

I sucked in a sharp breath, whined, and gripped the edge of the bath. "God-d-d. You feel amazing." I used my grip to buck my hips and ride his thick fingers, my pussy clutching down on him, aching for his cock.

More. I wanted more.

"Just like that, princess," he growled. "Ride my fucking fingers like a slut."

Tightening around him, I began bouncing up and down on his fingers. I used my grip on the tub to pull myself up further until I could seize his shoulders again and gain steady footing in the water. When I did, I wrapped my arms around him and thrust up and down on his fingers. Pressure rose in my core.

"Call me a slut again," I whimpered. "Please."

"You're a filthy slut," Constantino said, thumb rubbing my clit and driving me wild.

"P-please, don't stop," I cried. "It feels so good."

"Tell me what you want," he said, wrapping his free arm around my waist to hold me closer. "Tell me what my dirty little slut wants."

"She wants to come. Please, let me come!"

Constantino pulled his thumb off my clit and his fingers out of my pussy, stuffing them into my mouth. I hungrily wrapped my lips around them and sucked off the wetness, my pussy pulsing in the water, aching to be filled by his huge cock.

"Please," I mumbled on his fingers, my words muffled. "Please, fuck me."

"You want me to fuck your little whore hole?" he asked, pulling me on top of him so his dick lined up with my entrance. "You want me to fill you all the way up until your pussy milks out every last drop of my cum?"

"Y-yes," I begged.

Constantino slammed his cock into me, hands on my hips to hold me down so every single inch of him would fit. A moan escaped my lips, the heat rising in my core.

I dug my fingers into his muscular shoulders and whimpered into his ear. "God, yes!"

A wave of pleasure rushed over me, and I clenched. He grabbed a fistful of my hair, tugged it to the side, and placed his hot mouth all over the column of my neck. I bounced up and down on his cock, tightened each time I did, moans escaping my mouth.

"God, sluts like you ride dick so fucking well," he growled against me. "Beg for my cum."

"Please, give me it," I whimpered, about to explode around him. "Please, Constantino, fill up my tight hole. I need it so badly."

"Fuck," Constantino grunted, slamming my hips down on his cock and forcing me still.

I whined and dug my fingers into his shoulders. "P-please … don't stop. I want your cum in my pussy!"

He popped his thumb into my mouth for me to suck. "I think I'd rather decorate your face with it and make you even prettier."

I clenched around him.

"Your desperate little pussy seems to like that."

"Please, cover my face," I whimpered. "All over. My eyes, nose, mouth. Make me pretty."

"Make you pretty?" he grunted, pulling out of me and shuffling around in the water. He stood up in the bathtub, the water and suds rolling down his muscular body. He wrapped his hand around his cock. "Come here. Open that whore mouth of yours."

I moved closer to him until my breasts pressed against his thighs, and then I opened my mouth. He gripped a handful of my hair to keep me in place. I stuck out my tongue, flicking it against his balls and making him groan.

"Play with that desperate pussy," he ordered.

Dropping a hand between my thighs, I rubbed my clit. Pressure rose in my core. I massaged it over and over and over, brow furrowing and thighs beginning to tremble underneath the water. I needed it so badly.

"You come when I come. Understand?" he asked. "No sooner."

"Yes, I understand," I heaved out, breath hitching. "Please, I'm so close."

"I don't care where my cum lands on your face," he said. "Keep your eyes open the entire time. Sluts like you should know how to take it. You *are* my dirty little slut, aren't you?"

"Y-yes," I moaned, pussy tight. "Please. I'll keep my eyes open."

"Fuck," he grunted, gaze dropping to my mouth. "God, look at you with your tongue out, as if you deserve to drink my cum. You're getting it all over your fucking face, like a whore, Sage. Call yourself a whore for me."

"I'm a whore," I said. "I'm a whore. I'm a whore. I'm a wh—"

Constantino's cum sprayed all over my face, across my mouth, my nose, even my eyes. It hung heavily on my lashes, and I had the urge to blink it away, but I kept my eyes open and screamed out in pleasure. Ecstasy surged through my body.

"I'm a whore!" I continued. "I'm a whore! I'm your dirty fucking whore!"

After dropping his dick from his hand, he shuffled out of the tub and grabbed his phone sitting on the counter. He snapped a picture of me sitting in his tub, naked and covered in his cum. And when he placed his phone down, he kissed me right on the mouth.

"Let's clean you up."

26

laila

WHEN I FINALLY MADE IT home after dinner with Bethany, I walked into the penthouse and dumped my purse onto the island countertop, next to Constantino's keys and … Sage's purse.

Did she stay here the entire time? I had been gone for *hours*.

Tiptoeing through the house—because it was nearly one in the morning—I walked into the master bedroom and flicked on a lamp. Dim light scattered across the room, and I spotted Sage curled up against Constantino's naked chest.

My heart leaped, and I couldn't tell if it was from jealousy.

Am I jealous? Of Sage or of Constantino?

I quickly pushed the thought away, slipped into my walk-in closet, and found a pair of thin, silky red PJs to wear to sleep. Once I finished washing the makeup off my face, I scurried back into the bedroom and slipped underneath the blankets of our California king-size bed, behind Sage.

My body molded to her naked one. I wrapped an arm around her waist and snuggled my nose into her neck, breathing in the scent of her strawberry shampoo. It reminded me of the night

Constantino had convinced me to talk to her, the night I had kissed her for the first time.

While I desperately wanted to fall asleep, I found myself rubbing soothing circles across her stomach, the way Constantino did to me when he had something on his mind. I opened my eyes and gazed out the large ceiling-to-floor windows, eyes filling with tears.

"I'm sorry," I whispered, though I wasn't sure I'd be able to say it to her face. "I'm so sorry."

She mumbled something in her sleep and scooted closer to Constantino.

God, I wish she were still awake.

I wanted to see her, wanted to make up for leaving, wanted to ensure she wasn't angry with me for what I had done earlier tonight. It was so wrong, and I should've come home sooner. But I hoped she had actually eaten the food I had sent here. I hoped she hadn't fallen asleep, starving.

"We need to talk," Constantino suddenly said, jolting me up.

Glancing over Sage's body, I spotted him staring up at the ceiling with a hard, unreadable expression on his face. He looked over at me through dark eyes, the dim light of the city making his face glow.

"Now."

"It's almost one in the morning," I whispered.

"Should've thought about that before you stayed out all night with Bethany," he scolded.

Fuck, he is angry. Really angry.

After nodding, I shuffled out of the bed, careful not to wake Sage, and walked to my closet to give us more privacy. I didn't want him to wake Sage either, and I felt a nasty fight brewing between us. Constantino rarely raised his voice at me, but tonight, he was pissed.

Once he walked into the room, he closed the door behind himself and ran his tongue across his teeth. I crossed my arms, hating the way he looked at me, and swallowed hard.

"What is it, Constantino?" I asked. "Sage is—"

"You ditched her for Bethany," Constantino said.

"Bethany is my friend."

"Bethany is not your friend!" he shouted, then shut his eyes and blew out an angry breath. He turned around and paced the room, running a hand through his hair. "Sorry for raising my voice. But I can't stand that bitch."

"Why?" I asked. "You always say that, but you never tell me why you do."

"Because she manipulates you. She lies to you. She's disrespectful of our space. She convinces you that you need to do shit that you have never once been interested in doing."

"Like what?"

"Lip fillers. Botox. Fucking chin lipo!"

"She didn't convince me to do any of those things. I make my own decisions."

Constantino pursed his lips together. "Laila, come on."

"What?!" I exclaimed. "When Bethany suggests things, she doesn't force me to do them. She's just being honest with me about what she's doing and if she thinks I should too. That's what friends do."

"Friends shouldn't make you feel like you need to quit your passion to be accepted."

I had been prepared to go on and on about why he was blowing this way out of proportion, about why he was wrong about Bethany and the girls, but as soon as he shot back about my art, I didn't know what to say.

I must've opened and closed my mouth five times, no words coming out.

"You know what else friends don't do, Laila?" Constantino said between gritted teeth. "They don't watch someone dump their friend's dinner into the trash without saying and doing something about it."

"I did say something," I defended.

"And then you went to dinner with Bethany!"

"It shouldn't matter," I said, though it did matter. A lot. "Sage is our toy. Nothing more."

Lie. Lie. Lie. Lie. Lie.

Sage was my friend.

At least, I considered her so.

But I couldn't stand how my husband was attacking me over her, making me feel even more like shit than I already did. I had thought about Sage all night since I had left for dinner. I knew that I had hurt her really badly when I didn't say anything more to Bethany.

Still … I hated feeling so attacked.

"That is what we agreed," I said. "What, are you catching feelings for her or something?"

Because it had only been a weekend, and I … I thought I might've been. I didn't want to be alone in it. I was scared, terrified of falling for another woman. *What will everyone say about me? What will the family and my friends think?*

"No," Constantino said, shaking his head and pacing the room once more. "You're my wife, Laila. I could never love anyone the way I love you. But if it didn't matter"—Constantino pointed toward the bedroom, where Sage slept—"if she doesn't matter to you, then you wouldn't have come home and cuddled up behind her. You wouldn't hold her the way I hold you."

I glared at him, but really, it was to hold back the hot tears building in my eyes.

"Whether you're friends with Sage or not, I don't give a shit," Constantino said. "But the woman I married would *never* have been okay with letting their friend dump someone else's food into the garbage while they were hungry."

Tears welled in my eyes, and a sob escaped my throat. "I wasn't okay with it."

"Then, why did you leave?"

"B-because," I whispered.

I had been asking myself the same question over and over and over again tonight. *Why did I leave Sage before finding her something else to eat? Why did I let Bethany dump her food into the trash?* Deep down, I *had known* that Bethany would do it. I'd fucking known it, and I'd let it happen.

"Because you're not a good friend yourself," Constantino said.

"S-stop," I cried. "Please, stop."

"It's the fucking truth, Laila."

My chest tightened, and I wrapped my arms around my body. "Please, Constantino."

All I wanted was for him to hold me, to tell me that everything would be okay, that I wasn't a bad friend. I had dedicated the last few years to being the best person and friend I could to the girls. *Years!*

Constantino's phone buzzed in his hand. He growled and gazed down at the screen, scowling. "I have to go clean something up," he said, walking through the closet to find a suit. "Think about what you've done tonight."

And when he stormed out of the closet and shut the door, I collapsed to my knees and curled into a ball on the cold floor. Tears raced down my cheeks, and I sobbed into my hands.

Why am I so stupid? I had hurt her so badly.

The sadness on her face when Bethany had dumped her food … I couldn't erase it from my head.

This was my fault, and I didn't know how to fix it. Someone was bound to get hurt.

And that someone would be me.

When I walked back into the bedroom, desperately wanting to hold Sage again, the bed was completely empty.

27

constantino

I SPED through the relatively quiet streets of New York City, racing toward our external warehouse, where a shipment of drugs was supposed to land tomorrow night. When I spotted a police cruiser lurking at a street corner, I slowed and gripped the steering wheel, unable to stop thinking about what Laila had said tonight.

She was right.

According to our agreement, we used Sage as a toy. Nothing more. We could come and go as we pleased and could request her service at any time. What Laila had done didn't break the agreement in the slightest.

Sage was our plaything—more specifically, *Laila's* plaything—the girl I had bought in case something went wrong with the FBI and Laila was left alone without a baby and with Bethany the Bitch. We didn't have to be Sage's friend, and she had to deal with it.

So, why the fuck had I felt like shit when I found her crying? I was the fucking boss of this family, had killed and tortured more men than I could count. Why did a sex toy's tears anger me? We were to use her and be done with it.

I growled underneath my breath and shook my head to clear my mind. I didn't know what the fuck I was even going on about anymore. I shouldn't have brought her out to dinner, shouldn't have held her hand. All I should've done was bend her over the living room couch and fucked her tears away.

Deciding on taking the long way through the city—so the police didn't track me—I finally drove down a deserted road to the warehouse that was based on the river. Pietro's car was parked out front, the engine still on, as if he had jumped out of the car in a hurry.

Once I cut the engine, I yanked the key out of the ignition and hurried to the open door, spotting blood on the concrete just outside. Inside, corpses littered the room with bullet holes decorating their bodies. I walked through the men I hadn't seen before and massaged my forehead.

"The hell happened here?" I asked Pietro, who stood with a couple of other men from our family.

Antonio and Diego.

"Trying to disrupt the shipment," Pietro said, nodding to the men. "They have been lurking for a few days. I saw a boat dock a bit down the river and loaded some *goods* into our warehouse earlier this evening. Not the shipment of drugs, but some fake shit, like you had suggested, to lure these fuckers in. Turns out that someone in the family tipped them off."

I glanced at Diego. "Take care of this place." My gaze shifted to Antonio. "And find who it was."

Pietro pulled his gaze back up to me and clenched his jaw. "I need to talk to you. Privately."

Fuck.

He never wanted to talk privately, which meant something wasn't right. Maybe he suspected that the snitch was Antonio or Diego, two guys who had been in the family for fifty years now.

So, I followed him out of the warehouse and to my car. "What is it?"

"You were out with someone tonight," Pietro said. "Not Laila."

Fucking Giulio. Of course he opened his big mouth.

"She's the help," I said to him. "Laila knows I brought her out."

"The help, huh?" Pietro asked. "You hold hands with the help?"

"You're one to talk, Pietro," I said between my teeth. "You have a new girl every night."

"I don't have a wife. What're you becoming now, Dad?" He shoved me. "You remember how heartbroken Mom was every single time he came home with another woman's perfume on his collar."

"She means nothing to me, Pietro. Drop it."

"Are you fucking her because you're incapable of getting a woman pregnant? You think it's okay?"

I growled and slammed my hands hard into his chest. "Shut the fuck up."

How fucking dare he bring that up into the conversation! He knew nothing about what happened in my marriage, didn't know the first thing about what we enjoyed, how we lived, how much I wished to give Laila a baby.

This had been Laila's idea.

"You're my fucking brother," Pietro said. "I'm not going to tell Laila, but you have to fucking quit it."

"I'm not doing anything with her."

"Look me dead in the fucking face, Constantino, and tell me you're not fucking her."

"I don't have to say shit to you," I growled, shoving him away again.

He stopped me and pushed me back. "I can't believe you."

Fury rushed through me. I snatched his collar and shoved him against the car, staring him right in the eyes. "Whatever Laila and I are doing in the bedroom is none of your business, Pietro. You don't know the first thing about our preferences, so shut the fuck up."

"You talk like Laila knows about her."

Laila didn't want anyone to know. And despite us being in a bit of a fight right now, I wouldn't put Laila in harm's way like that.

"She does. She's our housekeeper," I said through gritted teeth. After hardening my glare, I set my lips into a tight line and shoved him back. "I don't have fucking time for this. It's nearly three in the morning. I need to get back home to Laila. She's waiting for me."

"You sure you don't want to stop by your maid's house on the way home?"

Deciding to ignore him, I gritted my teeth and stormed back to my SUV. Nobody in this fucking family could keep their mouth shut. And one day soon, it would get us in trouble.

28

sage

FINGERS MOVED in small circles around my clit. I slowly blinked my eyes open to adjust to the bright morning light and pushed myself back against the body behind me. For a moment, I thought Constantino was lying beside me, but Laila moaned softly into my ear. Warmth spread through my core, and I clenched.

After I had overheard Laila and Constantino's fight last night, I'd decided it'd be best to excuse myself and sleep in my own bed, which meant that Laila must've ... come down here and decided to lie with me herself sometime after I fell asleep.

She moved her fingers between my folds, back and forth over my sensitive clit. I ground my ass back against her pussy, my entire body aching for a release from her after her husband ruined me last night in the bath.

I was her toy to use. I had to remind myself of that.

No feelings involved.

"Good morning, *princess*," she whispered in my ear, pressing her breasts against my back, nipples grazing against my bare skin.

I furrowed my brow and sucked in an unsteady breath, my core growing warmer.

Princess?

That was Constantino's nickname for me, but something about the way she had said it ...

Pulling her hand away from my core, she drew it up the center of my naked body to my chin, tilting my head toward the ceiling and placing her full lips against my ear. "Lie on your back and spread your legs like a good girl for me," she purred.

I whimpered and followed her orders, spreading my legs and giving her all the access she could ever need to stuff her fingers deep into my pussy and fill me with pleasure. She drew her slim fingers down the center of my body again, and goose bumps rose on my skin.

When she reached my nipple, she drew her thumb across it, making it hard. Pressure rose in my core, and I clenched my wet pussy, glancing over at her pretty brown eyes, my heart fluttering.

I'm her toy. Her toy. Nothing more.

For a moment, she paused and gulped, her stare softening. "Spread them wider for me."

I dropped my knees to either side of the bed. She rolled her thumb around my nipple a couple more times, then trailed her fingers lower and lower and lower to my mound. When she reached my slit, she took a shaky breath.

"God, Sage," she murmured against me. "I love your body."

Glancing down between my legs, I impatiently waited for her to move her fingers lower. My pussy lips were glistening from the sunlight flooding in through the windows. And my clit ... God, my clit was aching.

"P-please," I whispered. "Touch me. That's what I'm here for."

Laila froze completely, her entire body stiffening. She opened her mouth, then shut it. Her fingers were close, so close to fluttering over my clit once more, to slipping inside me. I didn't know how much longer I could wait.

"Please," I pleaded. "Laila, I need—"

Laila pressed her fingers to my clit. Heat exploded in my core. I rested against the pillows, feeling her press her breasts against my arm, and then I spread my legs even wider. Her fingers moved in a steady rhythm around my sensitive bundle of nerves between my legs.

After dropping her hand even lower, she slipped two fingers into my entrance. I grasped the bedsheets in my fists and arched my back, a moan escaping my lips. Almost immediately, she found my G-spot and curled her fingers.

"Is this okay?" she said almost shyly.

"G-G-God," I moaned. "Don't stop."

Laila must've done this many times with many different women to have found my G-spot so quickly. Every night I spent with her just got better and better. I wasn't sure if I wanted to know how many other women she'd had as her toy.

Curling her fingers against my G-spot faster, she ground the heel of her hand against my clit. I tilted my head toward her and captured one of her nipples in my mouth, gently latching my teeth around it and tugging slightly.

Laila moaned and lay back on the bed herself, pulling me on top of her so I straddled her waist. She stuffed three fingers into my core once more and began massaging my G-spot quicker this time.

I placed my hands on her tits to hold myself up and gently squeezed, her nipples hard against my palms. She arched her back, lips parted, and stared up at me through hazy eyes.

"I wanna buy us a toy to use together," she murmured.

"Yeah?" I asked breathlessly as I bucked my hips against her hand.

"One to stuff inside both of us at the same time."

Wetness pooled between my thighs, and I moaned. "Please," I whispered.

"Would you like that?"

I skimmed my fingers up around her breasts and captured her nipples between my fingers, pulling on her tits. She threw her head back and moaned, eyes rolling back. Pleasure rushed through me.

"Would you like that?" I asked her.

"I would love it," she whispered, squirming under me. "Don't stop."

I rolled her nipples around between my index fingers and thumbs, then tugged. She continued to pound her fingers into my pussy, the heel of her palm smacking against my clit once more and driving me fucking insane.

Breath hitching, I pulled on her nipples harder, listening to her cry out.

"Grind your pussy against mine," she pleaded, dropping her hand from my pussy. She had gotten me so close to the edge—so close—but didn't tip me over. "Please, Sage. I'm so close, and you've barely touched me. I need it."

Shifting my weight, I gently pressed my body against hers, barely moving. She moaned into my mouth and sucked my lower lip between her teeth.

"Come with me …" She brushed her thumbs over my aching nipples. "Please."

I rested my forehead against hers and stared down at her, ecstasy ripping through my body. I parted my lips and cried out, my legs trembling. Eyes rolling back into her head, she came undone underneath me.

29

laila

NIPPLES TAUT, Sage collapsed onto the bed beside me, breathing heavily and staring up at the ceiling. She swallowed and peered over at me for only a moment, and then she glanced away from me and toward the window.

I wanted to apologize to her for what Bethany had done, but I … I didn't know what to say or how to say it. I didn't want Sage to hate me, didn't want her to decide that the last half of the million dollars wasn't worth staying around for.

When I had found our bed empty last night, I had been so devastated, so heartbroken and worried that I'd screwed everything up. So, I gathered the courage to come to Sage's place and apologize. But she had been sleeping then, and now … I couldn't find the right words.

"Is there anything else you need today, Laila?" Sage asked, rolling out of bed and walking to her closet to find a silk robe that I had picked out for her the other day while we shopped with Constantino. She wrapped the tie around her waist and hurried to the kitchen.

Sitting up in the bed, I leaned against the headboard and

pulled up the blankets to cover my chest, Bethany's words from last night lingering. I chewed on the inside of my cheek, gazed through the bedroom door and into the kitchen, and watched her boil water.

We had spent time alone together before this morning, but something felt … different.

Did Sage love it? Enjoy it? Even like it in the slightest? Should I have stayed in the penthouse and come to her later instead of weirdly waking her up with my fingers buried between her pussy lips and my body pressed against hers?

Sage wandered around the kitchen and grabbed a green tea bag from the cupboard. "Do you want tea?" she asked, taking out two cups and setting them on the black marble countertop. "I have green and black. Coffee too."

I stood and pulled on my clothes. "Coffee would be nice, but I don't want to bother you."

Pausing, Sage sucked in a deep breath and then shook her head and continued, "You're not bothering me. You're welcome to come over whenever you'd like. You're paying me after all …"

Something about the way she had said it … put me off. Something wasn't right.

She couldn't even … look at me.

"I'm sorry about Bethany," I said.

I had screwed up. So badly. But how could I make this better? Maybe Bethany wasn't even what Sage was angry about. Maybe I had overstepped this morning. Maybe I should've asked her before I came over. Maybe she just wasn't as attracted to me as she was to Constantino. The best sex happened when we were all together, not with just me.

It had been lousy this morning—on my part. I should've done more, made her feel better, made her come over and over instead of getting too horny, just lying next to her and asking her if she wanted to come with me.

"It's fine," Sage said, jerking me out of my thoughts.

"No, it's not."

"It's not my place," Sage said, pouring my coffee. "You don't have to apologize for her."

"I do," I said. "She's my friend."

Sage stiffened again, carefully set down the coffeepot, and pursed her lips. Then, she finally turned around and shook her head. "You don't have to apologize. You didn't do anything. I'm here for *you*, not the other way around."

"Are you angry with me?" I asked, brow furrowed.

She paused. "No."

"Sage," I whispered, moving closer to her.

My chest tightened. I didn't want her to hate me. She couldn't hate me. I needed her to like me, to *love* me. I hated when people were angry with me because … when they were angry with me, they left.

And when they left, they didn't come back.

"I'm sorry," I said. "I'm so sorry. Please, don't hate me."

Teacup halfway to her mouth, Sage widened her eyes. "Hate you?"

"I'm sorry," I repeated. "I didn't mean—"

"Relax, Laila," Sage said, smiling and handing me the coffee mug. "I don't hate you."

I grasped the cup. "You don't?"

She sipped her tea and walked into the living room, gazing out the large windows. "Of course not. Why would you think that?"

"Because you seem … off this morning," I whispered and took a gulp of coffee.

"There is nothing wrong," she said, though she still couldn't look at me. "I just didn't get much sleep last night. We got home fairly late, and then …" She paused, cheeks flushing. "Never mind."

But there was some—

My phone that I had left on the counter last night buzzed. I took one last look at Sage and walked over to it, reading Constantino's name on the screen. When I tapped the message, there was an image of Sage sitting in our bathtub with Constantino's cum covering her face.

Constantino: A good-morning gift for you, doll.

Constantino: Hope you're enjoying your morning with Bethany.

Though something about the tone of text made me feel like he was still a bit pissed at me about last night. And then to find our bedroom empty when he came home from business … of course, he thought I was with Bethany. I was with her all the time.

Constantino: You missed the fun last night.

I glanced over at an innocent-looking Sage as she curled up next to the window and stared out of it, the teacup near her lips as she blew the heat off it. Maybe that was why she felt weird. Was that the first time they had spent time alone together?

Constantino: We need to talk today.

Me: About Bethany?

Constantino: About the family. Meet me at the club.

Constantino: We have problems.

After blowing out a breath, I held my phone between my hands and stepped closer to Sage. "Do you want to come down to the club with me this morning? You don't have to. I know I woke you up early."

Sage rubbed her nude and matte lips together. "Is it okay if I stay back? I wanted to head to the coffee shop."

Excitement dropping, I forced a smile on my face. "Yeah, don't worry about it."

After smiling awkwardly at Sage, I excused myself and walked out of her apartment.

I had hoped she'd say she would come with me. I had made sure not to have plans with Bethany today, and I hated being alone. But I guessed that this was how it had felt for Sage yesterday when I skipped our dinner plans.

Like shit.

30

constantino

"BOSS," Abele said, peering into the office and around it, "your wife is here."

I eyed him for a moment, wondering why the fuck he hadn't let her in and why he was warning me. But as he scanned the room, I fucking knew he was looking for Sage. I fucking knew that he was warning me to hide her if I wanted.

"Send her in," I growled.

A couple of moments later, Laila walked into my office, dressed in a pink plaid dress that hugged her breasts. She held her purse tightly to her chest and gave a strained smile to Abele. "The FBI is sitting outside."

"I know," I said, peering at Abele. "Leave."

After a moment, he walked out and shut the door behind her. I finally slumped my shoulders forward and blew out a deep breath. If they didn't already, this entire family would know by the end of the day. We needed to figure this out now because I didn't want Laila getting hurt in the midst of all this. If she wanted to still keep it quiet, she'd endure the entire family thinking I'd cheated on her.

That I *was* cheating on her.

Knowing Laila, she'd become an insecure mess over it if she began thinking I was sneaking around with anyone other than Sage. And if more and more people started talking about it all the time, especially Bethany, we would have more than just a problem.

"What did you want to talk about?" Laila asked, placing her purse down on the desk.

"One of my men saw me with Sage last night."

Laila pressed her lips together. "Everyone knows," she whispered. "The girls were talking about it last night. They think you're cheating on me and won't stop commenting on it. I … I don't know what to say."

"Don't let them get into your head," I said. "Please."

"T-they won't."

But I could hardly believe that.

"Do you still want to keep it a secret?" I asked.

Laila snapped her head up to me. "Yes. I-I don't want Bethany knowing."

I clenched my jaw. I would rather Bethany know so she would leave Laila the fuck alone.

"You know I love you, right?" I whispered.

Laila stayed quiet for a few moments, then nodded. "Yeah, I know."

"Why'd you pause?"

She chewed on the inside of her cheek. "I-I didn't."

I grimaced and balled my hands into fists. I'd bet Bethany had had something to do with that. If I found out that bitch had been putting those thoughts into my wife's head—that I didn't love her and that I was cheating on her or some fucking shit like that—I would end her.

"Why'd you ask?" Laila asked, changing the subject.

"Because you missed out last night," I said, humming.

If any other man had sent an image of another naked woman, covered in his cum, to his wife, he'd be in the shithouse for the rest of his life. But the other night, after our time in the changing room, Laila had gushed about how much she actually wanted it to happen.

How she wanted to see Sage as our little cumslut.

"If you were trying to make me jealous with that picture of Sage" —she giggled and playfully crossed her arms—"it didn't work. I had Sage trembling in her bed this morning, her cum all over my fingers."

"So, you weren't out with Bethany?" I asked, brows raised.

She sat on my lap and peered over her shoulder at me. "No."

I pulled her higher up my lap and sank my fingers between her legs, pushing up her skirt enough for me to see her glistening pussy against my thigh. "What'd you do to her, doll? I want the details."

"I want the details of last night first," Laila said.

Stuffing my fingers inside her, I kissed her neck. "Ahh, doll, I just fucked her pretty pussy like you did with your fingers this morning. That's all. Do you want to watch us next time?"

Laila blushed and looked away.

"Next time you're with her, call Sage a slut," I said. "She loves it."

"Sage?" Laila asked, eyes widening. "Really?"

"You couldn't tell by the way she happily posed for a picture with my cum?"

I moved my fingers in and out of her, gently rubbing my thumb against her swollen clit. She whimpered on me and spread her legs like a good girl, her hand finding the front of my pants. She stroked me back and forth until my dick was throbbing inside my suit pants.

"I'm going to take you girls on a vacation," I announced.

After last night, I had decided that we needed to pause all jobs for the next couple of weeks. Between the FBI and whoever the fuck had interrupted business at the warehouse, we needed to let things cool off.

"I'm going to bring you to a place we've never been before and decorate *both* of you with my cum, take you to an exclusive club, make you sit at the bar with my cum on your face, let everyone see what sluts you girls are. Would you like that? Being publicly humiliated?"

Her pussy suddenly soaked my fingers. She reached into my pants and began stroking my dick faster. "Y-yes."

I pushed my fingers in and out of her tightening cunt. "Then, I'll make you girls play together in front of everyone. Let them watch you get each other off, swap my cum, and eat each other out."

She whimpered and nodded. "P-please."

Sinking my face into her neck, I gently sucked on her skin. My cock throbbed in her hand as she stroked it faster and faster, breath hitching and small moans escaping her pretty mouth. She stiffened and held her breath, the way she did moments before she came undone.

"I want to get us a toy," she said in a breathy whisper. "One we can use together." She stroked me faster, pushing both of us closer to the edge. "I want to make her a crying, whimpering mess, the way you make me. To both be full at once …" Her legs began shaking. "You could fuck both our mouths, stuff us with your c-c-cum …"

I grunted, balls heavy.

She tossed her head back. "Oh God. Oh God. Oh God."

When she came around my fingers, I grabbed her pussy and closed my eyes, my cum pumping into her tiny hand. Pleasure surged through my body, and I finally relaxed against the chair.

"We leave this week," I said because there was no way I could wait any longer for our little fantasy to come true.

31

sage

"TWO COOKIES, PLEASE," I said to the barista at The Coffee Club. "And a hot green tea."

When the barista walked away, I glanced up at Riccardo, who stood still as a statue by my side, face pointed straight ahead but eyes focused intently on the cookies in the case in front of me. I stifled a giggle.

"Do you want any—"

"No."

"Okay," I hummed as the barista handed me two cookies and a tea. "More for me."

Riccardo's face dropped for a mere moment, but when I handed him the cookie, the blank expression on his face returned. He took it and walked up the stairs with me to the second floor, sneaking a bite into his mouth.

"You're welcome," I said, earning me an eye roll.

Yes, an *eye roll* from the stoic bodyguard.

When we reached the top, Riccardo walked off with his cookie to sit across the room. I collapsed at a table and pulled out my tablet and pen to begin a new sketch, occasionally sipping my tea.

My pen glided against the tablet, strokes and curves forming a female's body.

Laila's body.

After spending time with Laila this morning, I had refused to go with her to see Constantino for my own sanity. If I had accompanied her to The Syndicate, followed by lunch and seeing art with her, I feared that I'd have fallen for her more than I already had. And I couldn't let that happen.

I am a toy.

But my stupid heart wouldn't stop wishing for more.

Once I saved this sketch, I opened a new canvas and vowed that I wouldn't turn back to Laila's portrait. I couldn't. Because every damn time I looked at her, thought about her, fantasized about her, it got worse.

"Thought I'd see you here," Poppy said, appearing at my table with a cup of soda that she couldn't have gotten here. She gestured behind her toward the exit of The Coffee Club. "There is an art festival a couple of blocks down. Wanna go?"

My eyes widened. "There is?"

She giggled. "Wasn't sure if you saw it or not. It's a bunch of street vendors."

I clutched my iPad to my chest and sat up, wanting to buy a couple of paintings for my place. Constantino's style was heavily chic and overwhelmingly boring with sleek blacks, grays, and whites. Some colorful pieces of the city would really spice things up and make it finally start to feel like me.

"Let's do it!" I said, leaping up and stuffing my iPad into my purse.

Halfway to the stairs, I paused and glanced back at Riccardo, who was now closing the distance between us. I wondered what Poppy would think of him. *Do I have to explain why he is with me? What good excuse will she believe?*

Swallowing hard, I continued to follow her and hoped that she either didn't notice or didn't say anything about him because I wasn't prepared. This entire year, I hadn't planned on making friends, especially not this early. Everyone I had met in the city was too selfish, like my stupid ex. Maybe I had been hanging out with the wrong people.

"Come on," Poppy said once we stepped outside. "This way."

We walked two blocks with Riccardo following after us.

She leaned closer to me and glanced over her shoulder at him. "Is the creepy, blank-faced guy with cookie crumbs on the corner of his lip with you?"

I peered back at him to confirm that, yes, in fact, Riccardo had cookies crumbs on the corner of his lips.

After stifling a giggle, I nodded and hoped she'd just laugh along too. "Yeah, he's just watching after me because of ... reasons."

"Cool," she said as we walked up to the art vendors. "Your own little bodyguard."

Vendors lined the streets, selling paintings, murals, landscapes, digital art, and pretty much anything. I grinned like a maniac at the sight and spotted an ice cream cart just ahead. I bought an ice cream and decided that Riccardo didn't need any because he couldn't even get all the crumbs off his lips.

Licking the ice cream before it melted all over me, I walked with Poppy down the line of art vendors and smiled.

Laila would love it here. My eyes widened as the urge to text her came and went, my heart racing a bit harder.

Stop it, Sage.

Maybe I'd just get her something.

A gift from a friend ... from a toy.

I gulped and chewed on the inside of my cheek. *A toy.*

After buying a couple of pieces, I tucked them under my arm and continued walking with Poppy through the vendors. I didn't even know if I would give either one of them to Laila. Would that be weird? Would I be overstepping?

Clearly, I didn't mean anything else to her.

The way she had let Bethany toss my food out, then left with her. The conversation she'd had with Constantino last night. The slipping into my room and lying with me, just to touch me this morning …

What if Laila hadn't done anything about Bethany because she *liked* her, even more than a friend? What if Laila was using me until she finally found the courage to ask Bethany out? My hands balled into tight fists, and I gritted my teeth.

"No," I growled.

"What?" Poppy asked.

Eyes widening, I snapped my gaze to hers. "What?"

"You said something," she said.

"Oh," I responded, cheeks flushing. "Sorry."

What the hell was I even thinking anymore? Why was I jealous of Bethany? It wasn't any of my damn business, and I had to stop thinking this shit or else the next twelve months were going to be agonizing hell for me.

Maybe I needed a boyfriend … or a girlfriend to stop myself from having these stupid feelings because, now, I was jealous out of nowhere. Nowhere! I needed help. And a lot of it.

Is having an emotional relationship outside of our thing allowed in the contract?

Hell, maybe I should ask.

When we reached the end of the street, where the vendors stopped, I paused and finished off my ice cream. Poppy bounced on her toes and glanced around for a trash can to dump the rest of her half-drank soda.

"Where do you think—"

"You little bitch," someone said to our right.

I snapped my head toward the voice and spotted Bethany barreling toward us from a tinted black SUV. Heart pounding, I grabbed Poppy's hand and glanced around for Riccardo, who stood near the last vendor, silently watching us.

After giving him *the eyes*—the eyes that begged him to save us—I turned back to Bethany, who had closed the distance. I didn't know what the hell I had done to her, but she looked ready to kill me.

"If you're going to sleep with Constantino, you need to learn your fucking place," Bethany growled, snapping Poppy's soda from her hand, tearing off the top, and hurling it toward us. It sprayed all over my shirt and Poppy's, drenching us in sticky Coca-Cola.

"Stay away from my best friend and her husband," Bethany growled. "Or I will kill you."

32

sage

"I'M SORRY," I apologized to Poppy for the fiftieth time while on our way up to my apartment. When the elevator dinged, I grabbed her hand and hurried down the hallway toward my door. "I'm so sorry."

"It's okay," she said, glancing down at her clothing that Bethany had stained with that soda. Because Bethany had the worst aim in the fucking world, she splashed the soda more on Poppy than on me. "It's just a shirt."

"It should've never happened," I muttered.

But while Bethany might've been a bitch to me, I wasn't the wife of a Mafia don. I had no room to put anyone in their place. I could do nothing but sit back and take the ridicule. After all, I had signed up for it.

Even if I had tried to defend us, Bethany would have cried to Laila. Or worse, hate Laila.

After what Constantino had told me about her being rejected for so many years throughout her childhood, I could feel nothing but pity. I understood why she did it all, and if I caused Bethany to break up with her, then I would loathe myself. Still, that didn't mean I didn't want her out of Laila's life. But maybe that was the jealousy talking again.

Once I quickly typed my pin into the keypad to unlock the door, I shoved it open and ushered Poppy into the apartment. When Riccardo walked into the room after us, I glanced back at him quizzically as I guided her to my bedroom.

"I don't know her," he said blankly, referring to Poppy.

"Well, you knew Bethany," I hissed. "And you didn't stop her from doing what she did."

Riccardo pressed his lips together, and I rolled my eyes. After shutting Riccardo out of my bedroom, I walked to the closet and began digging through my old clothes. I doubted that Constantino would appreciate it if I gave her something expensive.

Maybe he wouldn't if he knew this was Bethany's fault.

"Here you go," I said once I found something suitable that wasn't five years old, way too big, or already stained. "I'll leave so you can get changed."

"Oh, I don't mind." She giggled, tearing off her shirt and taking mine. "Who was that woman anyway? She sure seemed to have it out for you, like you had killed her dog or something." Her red curls bounced as she pulled my shirt over her head. "Like *crazy*, crazy."

"She's"—I scratched the back of my head—"my friend's friend."

"Does your friend know how she treats you?" Poppy asked.

I gulped. *Fuck.*

"That's a yes," Poppy said.

"It's complicated," I whispered, crossing my arms and pacing the room.

So freaking complicated.

Not that I would ever break my contract and tell Poppy that I was the Mafia boss and his wife's sex toy, but if I had to ever explain it ... how?! Sex with benefits with a husband and wife who kill people for a living and sell drugs?

That would go over well, especially with friends and family—NOT.

"I promise that I'll take you out soon to make it up to you," I said.

"Sage, please." She grabbed my shoulders. "It's fine."

But it wasn't, and it would never be.

Bethany wasn't only antagonizing me anymore; she'd now attacked my friend.

Someone knocked on my front door, and my heart leaped. I glanced over my shoulder to my bedroom door and drew my tongue across my teeth. If this was Bethany back to hurt me more, I swore I would tell her off this time.

Maybe.

"I'll be right back," I said.

Leaving Poppy in my bedroom to finish cleaning herself up, I jogged to the front door and pulled it open. Laila and Constantino stood outside, Constantino's arm was wrapped tightly around Laila's small waist.

"We have news," Laila said with a smile. "We're—"

"Sage!" Poppy shouted from the bedroom. "Do you have deodorant?"

Suddenly, Laila's face dropped, and she snapped her mouth closed. Poppy peered out from my bedroom, dressed in my old clothes. She stiffened when she spotted Laila and Constantino in the doorway.

"Oh, sorry," she said. "I didn't know you had company."

"Who's this?" Laila said tensely.

"This is Poppy," I said, shifting uncomfortably on my feet.

Was I supposed to have friends over the place? She wasn't meant to stay that long, but I had needed to give her a change of clothes after what Bethany did to her. Maybe I should've asked before I brought her over.

"Hi!" Poppy said with a smile, her red curls bouncing on her shoulders. "Sorry. I'll be out of your hair. If I had known you were expecting company, I wouldn't have agreed to come over. I don't want to be a bother."

"It's okay." I nervously glanced over at Constantino and Laila to gauge their reaction.

Like usual, when he met new people, Constantino was stoic, like Riccardo, but didn't look particularly angry. He almost looked amused as he gazed at Laila. Laila, on the other hand, scrunched her brows together and pursed her pink-painted lips.

"Do you have a bag for these?" Poppy asked, holding up her wet clothes.

"If you leave them on my bed, I can wash them."

"What happened?" Constantino asked, glancing over at Riccardo, who sat on the couch.

Neither one of us said anything, just glanced at each other. I didn't want to say anything in front of Laila, didn't want her to get angry with me again. Honestly, I didn't think I would be able to hear her tell Constantino I was a toy to them.

At least, I didn't *want* to hear it.

"What happened?" Constantino repeated, looking for a response.

"We went to an art festival and"—Poppy glanced at me—"soda was spilled on my clothes."

My shoulders slumped forward, and I let out a breath. Riccardo hummed on the couch, brow arched hard at me. Later on, I knew he'd tell Constantino the truth—as I wanted him to—but for right now, this was enough.

Laila stared at me, sadness heavy in her eyes. "An art festival?"

Fuck.

"Well," Poppy said, probably sensing the tension between us, "I should be off. I have work soon."

33

laila

"YOU'RE JEALOUS," Constantino hummed, leaning closer to me while Sage showed her *friend* out of her apartment.

Sage had never mentioned her before. Was she the reason that Sage hadn't wanted to spend time with me today? Had she gone to the coffee shop to see her?

And she had brought this *Poppy* to an art festival?

"I'm not jealous," I whispered. "There's nothing to be jealous about. You're mine."

Constantino chuckled, which made me angrier. "I'm not talking about me."

"It was nice meeting you," Poppy said, waving from the front door.

I pursed my lips together and forced myself to smile at her because I wasn't jealous.

Not me. If I were, that'd mean I had feelings for Sage. And I couldn't.

"It was nice meeting you too," I ground out through my teeth.

As soon as Sage closed the door, I let out an unsteady breath. I wasn't jealous. I wasn't jealous. I wasn't fucking jealous.

And to prove it, I straightened my back and regained my composure. "Who was she?"

Fuck, I sound so jealous. So possessive. But Sage is ours.

"Just a friend," Sage hummed.

Just a friend? Constantino had been just a friend until he wasn't.

"Are you okay?" Sage asked me, brows drawn together. "Did I do something wrong?"

Constantino gently squeezed my waist with one hand, stepping in. "No."

"When did you meet her?" I asked, aching to know the details.

"At the coffee shop yesterday."

She was the reason that Sage hadn't wanted to spend time with me today. I balled my hands into tight fists behind my back. Never in my life had I wanted to kill someone, to end someone's life —until now.

Jealousy and possessiveness boiled inside me. My nails cut right through the thin skin on my palm. I hated her. I hated this Poppy so freaking much, and I didn't even know her. Sage was mine. All mine. If anyone even *looked* at her the way I did, I would be forced to kill them.

"Um, I don't know if this is a bad time or not," she said, brows drawn together, "but I wanted to know if the contract specified whether or not I could, um ..." She rocked back and forth on her heels and shook her head. "Never mind."

"What is it?" I asked.

"It's nothing, Laila," she whispered, tearing her eyes away from me.

"If you could what?" I urged, wanting to please her. Desperate for her to choose me.

Not Poppy.

She opened and closed her mouth a couple of times, then gulped. "Can I ask you?" she asked, peering at my husband with flushed cheeks.

My chest tightened. Why didn't she want me to be in the room while she asked? After her night with Constantino alone, she must've sparked an interest in him. Not me. Why would I think she liked *me* like that?

"My wife makes the decisions about this relationship," Constantino said. "Speak."

"Okay," she whispered, glancing nervously at me. "I'm assuming this isn't allowed, but I wanted to know because, well … reasons that aren't important right now … but for the next year, do I have to be solely yours?"

Heat rushed through me. "What?"

"Sorry for asking," she squeaked. "It's so stupid. I—"

I snatched her chin in my hand and forced her to look at me. "Repeat what you said."

Sage widened her eyes. "I-I … I wanted to know if …"

"If you can have another lover?" I finished. My voice was harsh, but I was so scared, so nervous. How could she ask such a thing? Didn't she know that she was *ours*? Was I not fulfilling all of her dirty little fantasies? "Are we not good enough for you?"

"No. No, it's not that," she said, throwing her hands up in defense. "I promise."

"Who else do you want to fuck?" I asked. "Poppy?"

"No!" she exclaimed. "She's just a friend."

"Then, tell me who, so I can take care of them."

When the words tumbled out of my mouth, Sage stiffened. "So you can take care of them?" she whispered, nude-colored lips barely moving. She swallowed again, as if her pretty little throat was dry, and furrowed her brow. "K-kill them?"

"You're ours," I threatened. "And we do whatever it takes to protect what belongs to us."

"There is nobody that I have in mind," she whispered, shoulders curling in to make herself small, as if she wanted to disappear right here in front of me, leave me.

But I'd had too many people leave. She … she couldn't be one of them.

So, I stepped forward, jealousy still pounding through my veins.

"You're ours," I repeated. "Say it."

"I'm yours," she whispered, nearly shaking in front of me.

"Ours."

"Yours."

I slipped my hand around her throat and pinned her to the door that Poppy had just exited a few moments ago, my nails lightly strumming against her neck. I wanted Poppy to know that Sage was mine.

"Nobody touches this pussy, except us," I growled against her lips, dipping my hand between her thighs and teasing her aching little cunt. She was already soaked. "Nobody makes you feel good, except us."

"I-I know," she stuttered. "I didn't want one because of—"

When I tightened my hand around her throat, Constantino moved behind me and pushed some hair over my shoulder, his hands on my waist and his gaze on Sage too. I drew my nose up Sage's fragile little neck.

"I don't want to hear it," I said between my teeth. "You're ours."

"I'm yours," she repeated, breath hitching as she stared at me. "All yours."

"If you want to be treated like a dirty little slut who sleeps around," I murmured against her skin, trying to hold back my jealousy and remembering what Constantino had told me earlier about Sage's enjoyment in degradation, "all you have to do is ask."

"N-no," Sage mumbled, but her pussy got even wetter.

"How wet is that cunt?" Constantino asked her.

She opened and closed her mouth a couple of times, then tried to push her thighs together and whimpered. When she didn't answer, I slipped my knee between her legs to hold them apart and ground it against her pussy.

"R-really wet," she whimpered.

"Slip your fingers into her, doll," Constantino said to me. "And tell me how tight she is."

I shoved two fingers into her pussy and held back a moan, the heat growing between my thighs. Constantino pressed himself against the small of my back, his dick hard and throbbing.

"You're a dirty slut, Sage."

Sage tightened around my fingers and whimpered again. "I really didn't mean—"

"You didn't mean it?" I finished, curling my fingers around her G-spot. "A horny little slut would prove it to us. Get on your knees."

Because once she did, I promised that I'd show her the time of her fucking life. My little slut would know that we were the only ones who could ever make her feel so good.

34

sage

PUSSY THROBBING, I dropped to my knees and pressed my thighs together. Wetness pooled between them, sudden desire ripping through me. When I had asked to be with someone else, Laila had become so possessive.

And, God, it turned me on.

I ran my hands down their stomachs to the waistband of their pants, rubbing Constantino's hardening cock and Laila's clit.

"You want me to prove it to you?" I repeated, breathing heavily. "I'll prove it to you."

Before I could stop, I pulled down Laila's pants, then Constantino's. I needed them, and I needed them badly. I wanted possessive Laila to force me to eat her cunt, then suck her husband off, growl into my ear that I was hers, like a savage animal.

After taking Constantino in my right hand and stroking him, I crawled closer to Laila until my lips were millimeters from her cunt and placed my hot mouth right over it. I had only eaten pussy a handful of times with her and never from this angle, but I wanted to please her.

Badly.

My tongue slipped between her pussy lips and across her swollen clit. She rolled her head back and let out a soft moan, the sound making me tighten even more. I stroked her husband faster, flicking my tongue over and over her clit again.

"F-fuck," she groaned and grabbed a fistful of my hair. "Touch your aching little pussy and don't pull your fingers away, even when you come."

I sank my free hand between my legs and rubbed my clit in torturous circles. Constantino spit on his cock, making it easier for me to stroke him. Raging heat gathered between my thighs.

"Faster," Laila ordered.

Unsure whether she wanted me to eat her pussy or rub mine faster, I buried my face deeper between her legs and did both, her juices decorating my mouth and cheeks. She leaned back against her husband, letting him slide his arm underneath one of her legs and pulling it into the air to give me better access.

"Tell me how I taste," she said. When I pulled back to respond, she pushed my lips back against her clit. "I didn't tell you to stop. I told you to tell me how I taste, Sage. A pretty little slut like you can do both at the same time, can't you?"

Moaning against her pussy, I furrowed my brow, rubbed my clit harder, and nodded.

"Tell. Me. How. I. Taste."

"Good," I said against her pussy, my word muffled.

"What was that?" she asked.

Constantino chuckled darkly and dipped his head to kiss her collarbone. "Doll …"

"Good," I repeated inaudibly.

"Are words hard when your mouth is busy with my pussy?" she asked, pulling away.

"Y-you taste so g-g-good," I said, close to the edge.

"Good girl," she praised, capturing my nipples between her fingers and tugging.

Wave after wave of ecstasy surged through my body. Despite my pussy pulsing, I continued to rub my clit, like Laila had demanded.

She tugged a bit harsher on my tits and moaned against her husband.

"Did our little whore just come for us?" Constantino asked.

I opened my mouth to respond but could only moan.

Laila took my chin in her soft, small hand. "Don't stop rubbing your pussy."

Staring up at her, I rubbed myself harder while I jerked off her husband. She walked to her purse that she had set on the couch after she came into my apartment and pulled out the toy she had told me she had wanted to buy.

A double-sided dildo for us.

"Bring her here, Constantino," she said, spitting on the toy to get it wet. She lay back on the couch, spread her legs, and pushed one side of it into her pussy.

Constantino stepped closer to me, taking my chin in his hand. "Open."

I opened my mouth and hungrily took his hard cock down my throat, sucking as hard as I could while I continued to rub my clit, bringing me closer and closer to another orgasm.

He stepped backward, and I crawled after him, one hand buried between my legs. He moved back again, and I followed. Over and over until we reached Laila. She pumped the toy in and out of her cunt, watching me suck off her husband and furrowing her brow in pleasure for a moment.

"I bet she sucks your cock so well," she said to Constantino, who grunted. "Come here."

When Constantino pulled out of me, I crawled up onto the couch with her, lay down across from her, and lined my pussy up with the other side of the toy, continuing to rub my clit. Pleasure rushed through me.

"Closer," Laila purred.

I scooted even closer until the head of the dildo pressed against my entrance. My heart pounded as Laila pulled the toy out of herself and pushed it into my tight pussy, watching the way my lips spread for it. She scooted a couple of inches closer to me and pulled it out, pushing it back into her. When I moaned, Constantino shoved himself back into my throat.

Clenching around the toy, I stared at the ecstasy on Laila's face as she fucked us with the double-sided dildo. She moved the toy back and forth quickly, my juices beginning to cover her small fingers.

"Tell me you're mine," she ordered.

"I'm yours," I murmured on Constantino's cock, spit rolling down my chin. "All yours."

"My little whore."

"Your little whore," I repeated inaudibly.

"You're so precious," she said almost condescendingly.

And *fuck* …

Fuck. Fuck. Fuck. Fuck. Fuck.

When she shoved the toy deep inside me one last time, my entire body jerked up into the air, Constantino's cock falling out of my mouth and smacking his thigh with a thud. I screamed out in pleasure, eyes rolling back into my head.

"Holy s-s-shit," I stammered. "Holy shit. Holy shit."

Another wave of pleasure crashed through me.

"Oh my God!" I moaned, the ecstasy not stopping.

Laila stared at me with big doe eyes, the sudden dom in her gone and replaced with her usual soft, gentle-hearted self. She pumped her toy into herself a couple of more times, transfixed by my orgasm, and came too, body trembling.

"You're so beautiful," she moaned, staring at me as the pleasure crossed her face. "So fucking beautiful."

35

sage

AN HOUR LATER, I lay on my bed with my eyes shut, trying to sleep. Laila lay on one side of me, Constantino on the other. Neither of them had said anything for the past sixty minutes, and for a while, I thought Laila had passed out.

But then I heard her sniffle.

I swallowed hard, not wanting to disrupt her and make her even sadder. Part of me wanted to comfort her, but after what had happened with Bethany today, I just wanted to find some rest. We could talk tomorrow.

"Please don't leave me," Laila whispered suddenly, clutching on to me tighter and stiffening the way I did when I tried to bite back a sob. "I'm sorry if I did s-something wrong. It won't happen again."

My chest tightened. *Is she talking to me?*

"She's not going to leave you, doll," Constantino said softly, gently stroking her hair.

"She said she wanted someone else."

"And you told me she was just a toy," Constantino responded.

Laila lifted her head off my shoulder, and I wanted to open my eyes to see the facial expression she was giving her husband. Did she really, truly only see me as a toy, or was she hurting right now, almost as badly as I was?

"Stop it," she whispered.

"I'm not the one who said it," Constantino said, shifting next to me on the bed.

"I'm sorry," she said. "But you don't have to repeat it."

"And you didn't have to say it, especially if you are going to be this devastated." After a slight pause, he sighed. "Listen, she's not going to leave us, Laila. I've already paid her. She's indebted to us until she fulfills her duties."

"Wh-what happens then?"

"You tell me."

"I don't want her to go."

"Well then, I hope you know that, one day, you're going to have to choose between the girls and her. If you want her to stay, there is no fucking way that we're going to keep this a secret. The girls will think you're a pushover. And while you might act like it sometimes around Bethany, I know why you really do it."

"You think I'm a pushover?" she whispered.

Constantino paused.

"Okay, I mean ... I might be sometimes, but I hate the thought of people hating me."

"They won't hate you for putting your foot down, for demanding respect."

"Y-yes, they will," Laila whimpered.

My chest tightened as tears pricked at the corners of my eyes. I desperately tried to stay still, to act like I was fast asleep, but I couldn't stop myself from aching to hear every single word they spoke, from eavesdropping on this intimate conversation.

"You put your foot down with Sage tonight," Constantino said. "She doesn't hate you."

"I didn't put my foot down," Laila said, shifting closer to me so her body was snuggled up against mine. "I ... tried to show her why she shouldn't leave." She stiffened even more. "She-she said

she wanted someone else. And I wanted to show her"—sniffle—
"that I'm enough for her."

Fuck. Laila is way more insecure than I thought.

But why? Why the hell was she this way? Constantino didn't put
her down or flirt with other girls in front of her. All I had witnessed
from him was a loving and supportive husband who thought his
wife was incredible.

Damn Bethany.

It had to be that bitch and her other friends.

Still, what if she refused to leave them, to leave *her* because ...
Laila *liked*, liked Bethany? What if she was using me to ease her way
into life with another woman and her husband? Constantino would
never go for that, but ...

It hurt me to think about it.

I stiffened underneath Laila, and she definitely noticed because
she stilled too. Then, she sucked in a sharp breath. "Are you ... are
you awake, Sage?" she whispered, her words soft but guarded.

Deciding that Laila wasn't in the best mindset to know that I had
been listening in this entire time, I shifted in the bed the same way
anyone would do whenever they were fast asleep and wanting to
get more comfortable and turned onto my side.

Laila paused. "Sage?"

I didn't respond.

The room stayed quiet for a few moments until Constantino said,
"She's asleep, doll."

Another short pause.

"Do you think I was good enough for her this time?" Laila
asked, taking an unsteady breath. "We had done stuff this morning
together, but I ... don't think I made her feel good enough since she
met with Poppy and then asked to see other people."

"You did amazing, doll," Constantino said. "And I'm sure you
had done great this morning too."

"I'm so new at this, Constantino," she whispered.

I raised my brows, careful not to draw their attention, but she
had surprised me. *This is new to her? She hasn't been with another*

woman before me? She touched me so skillfully that I could've sworn that she had done it many times over.

"What if I'm not touching her right?" Laila said. "Can you teach me?"

"You made her come twice tonight without my help," Constantino said. "Right?"

"But what if she just acted like that to save my feelings?"

"Laila," Constantino said, the bed shifting as he crawled off it. It sounded like he wanted to stay to convince her that she was good enough, but it was hard, trying to convince someone of something when they were dead set on ignoring it. "You need this vacation. You're way too stressed out around here with Bethany and the FBI always pestering us. Give me a kiss." After I heard them kiss, footsteps padded away from the bed. "Try to get some sleep. I'll wake you when the jet is ready."

36

constantino

AFTER BLOWING OUT A LOW BREATH, I walked out to Sage's living room and gazed out at the New York City skyline. I loved Laila, but she had no confidence in herself ever. We both desperately needed this vacation to relax.

But stress wasn't the only reason I could sense Laila needed to leave. Poppy, Sage's new friend, was the other reason. Sage had been bold as hell, asking if she could have a significant other right after the way Laila reacted.

I glanced over my shoulder at the bedroom door. No way that I'd let Sage be with someone else. My hands tightened into tight fists. No fucking way would another woman or man lay their hands on her. Not while she was ours.

When I walked out of Sage's home to grab our suitcases from the penthouse, I caught Riccardo standing by the front door on his usual duty outside Sage's apartment. I came to a stop, briefly remembering my conversation with Sage before Poppy left.

"What happened today?" I asked him.

Sage had been lying earlier while Poppy was over, and I didn't know why. Maybe those two had already done something together —other than just hang out at an art festival on the NYC streets.

"Did Poppy touch Sage?" I questioned, possessiveness dripping off every word.

"No," Riccardo said.

And usually, I trusted him, but tonight … something seemed off.

"Then, what the fuck happened? The soda on Sage's friend's shirt?"

Riccardo stiffened and peered down at his feet for a moment. "Bethany showed up while they were at the art festival and tossed the friend's soda all over them. I should've stopped it, but I didn't think that—"

As soon as the words left his mouth, I hurled my fist at his face, hitting him square in the nose. He stumbled back, not putting up a fight, and bumped into the wall. Blood spurted from his nose and onto his black button-up shirt.

"You were hired to protect Sage," I growled, wrapping my hand around his throat and slamming him against the wall harder. "I don't care if you know Bethany or not. She is not to *touch* Sage. Do you understand me?"

"She didn't touch her—"

"Don't fucking talk back to me," I snapped. "Or I'll cut your throat."

"I'm sorry," Riccardo said. "I should've been more careful."

"You fucking should've been." I seethed and tightened my grip around his throat. "I told you that if you let anyone harm a hair on her fucking head, you'd be in the fucking shithole, taking punishment for it, didn't I?"

"Yes, sir."

While I wanted to fire him—kill him—right then and there, I stopped myself before I lost even more of my temper. Riccardo had been trying to make a name for himself in the family, trying to rise in the ranks, had stayed with Sage since the beginning.

Not only that, but he also didn't ask questions about our relationship.

He kept his mouth closed, especially around Pietro, who didn't understand us either. If he had been the one to spill to the family, then Pietro would've known about Sage the moment I brought her home that night.

Plus, I needed him to travel with us.

"I'll deal with you once we get back," I growled, shoving myself off him and heading for the elevator. God, I really needed this vacation. "Stay here with the girls until I come back down. Then, we're leaving for a week."

I stormed into the elevator and hit the top button, whipping out my phone to text Pietro.

Me: Going out of town with Laila. Watch Bethany.

Pietro: Trying to shield your wife from your girlfriend?

Grinding my teeth together, I shut off the phone and slammed it into my pocket. Pietro only wanted the best for Laila and me, but, fuck, he was annoying as hell sometimes. Even his playboy ass would never fucking understand.

When the elevator opened, I walked into the house and closed the door behind me. Finding the nearest glass vase, I hurled it across the room.

"Fuck!" I shouted, my breath ragged. "That fucking bitch."

The moment we returned, Bethany would pay for this. I had let it slide for too fucking long because Laila didn't want me hurting her, but I couldn't wait anymore for Laila to put her foot down.

Bethany was threatening my relationship with my wife, putting her down again and again and going to great fucking lengths to torment her. And now, that bitch was assaulting the people close to me. What would she resort to with Laila?

I sure as hell wasn't about to sit around and find out.

37

sage

"CAN we grab coffee before heading to the airport?" Laila asked next to me in the back of the SUV. She gazed out the tinted window while one of Constantino's guards drove us through the surprisingly desolate New York City streets.

This city looked so weird at barely four in the morning.

"The Coffee Club should be open now," I suggested. "They open early."

Laila glanced at me, then dropped her gaze. "We can go there if you'd like," she said quietly, keeping to herself more than usual.

I wondered if this had anything to do with the conversation I had overheard last night.

"We don't have to," I said, not wanting to upset her. Maybe she thought I wanted to meet Poppy there this morning or something. "I just suggested it because it is on the way, but I'm sure that—"

"It's fine," Constantino said as the car came to a stop across the street. "We're here."

I glanced out the window to see a single light on in The Coffee Club and then smiled at Laila. "I can tell you what they have," I said quietly. "Their breakfast sandwiches are really good too, if you're hungry."

While she had seemed upset a moment ago, she smiled softly at me and nodded. After I shuffled out of the car, I glanced over my shoulder at Vincent and Riccardo stepping out of the black SUV behind us.

As we walked toward the entrance, Laila curled her arm around mine. When I glanced down at our arms, she blushed. "Sorry, I was just ..." She peered up at me and pulled her arm away from mine.

But I stopped her and wrapped mine around hers, tugging her to the front.

Perk of getting here early: no line.

"What's your favorite?" she asked, gazing up at the menu.

"I don't drink much coffee," I admitted, "But a lot of people order number five."

"Number five," she hummed to the barista, blindly trusting my judgment. "What would you like, Sage?"

I snapped my gaze to Riccardo, who stood by the door with a swollen black eye. He didn't look over at me, like he usually did, and I hoped that I wasn't the reason for his injury. I hadn't seen him at all today, except when he had been putting out suitcases in the trunk.

And nobody spoke a word about how he had gotten the black eye. Though I assumed Constantino had had something to do with it.

"Two chocolate chip cookies, please," I said.

"And a green tea for her," Constantino finished.

"How'd you know I like jasmine tea?" I asked him while we waited.

"Your kitchen hasn't been restocked since you moved in," he said. "You don't have any left."

My eyes widened slightly, butterflies fluttering in my stomach. I didn't know why it made me feel so giddy inside, but it did. He had actually noticed? Half the guys I had dated before rarely even noticed if I cut my hair.

"Number five!" the barista called.

When Laila released my arm to grab her coffee, I rocked back on my heels and gazed down at the ground, desperately trying to hold back a grin.

I'm not falling for them. I'm not falling for them. I'm not falling for them.

They were a dangerous couple.

At least, that was what I told myself. Because honestly, they seemed like the most genuine, honest, and intimate people sometimes. They truly cared about each other, and I ... I couldn't get in the way of that.

Things were already too messy between us all.

To get it off my mind, I grabbed my cookies off the counter and walked over to Riccardo, who stood by the exit.

"Are you okay?" I whispered while we waited for Constantino's coffee.

"I'm fine," he answered, stoic as usual.

"No, you're not."

"Then, why'd you ask?" he growled.

"Here," I said, handing him the cookie.

He glared at the cookie—yes, *glared* at the inanimate object—and then snatched it from me. I smirked and walked back to Laila and Constantino, hoping that the sweet would make him feel somewhat better.

"Did you just get Riccardo to eat a cookie?!" Laila asked, eyes wide.

Constantino stared at me like I was crazy.

"Yes." I smiled. "Why?"

Laila giggled. "I've only seen him eat steak, rice, and broccoli."

"Your coffee," the barista said to Constantino.

And then we were back on the road to the private jet.

I sipped my green tea and finished off my cookie, gazing out at the pretty sunrise over the city, beams of light bounding out around the skyscrapers. I peered down at my bag on the floor and spotted the painting from the art festival. I had rolled it up and tucked it away in the Birkin bag-purse thing that Constantino had brought down for me way too early this morning.

Is it weird to give it to Laila now?

While I wanted to, I was still so unsure after overhearing her conversation with Constantino. Still, I wanted to ask her if she had really meant everything she said last night. I wanted to tell her that she shouldn't be so insecure about herself, that she was Constantino's wife.

She'd had so much confidence, picking me up at the bar, that I could hardly believe this was the real her. Maybe it had been the alcohol that night. Sometimes, she seemed so confident around me, and other times … she was so distant and unsure.

When I peered over at Laila, she was leaning back in her seat with her coffee cup against her plump pink lips and her gaze on me. She blushed hard and looked away, grinning to herself. "Sorry."

Warmth exploded through my body again.

God, the way they make me feel …

I pulled out the rolled-up art from my bag and handed it to her. "I bought this for you."

"This is for me?" she whispered, eyes widening. "Really?"

"If I had known there was an art festival, I would've asked you to come with me," I said, chewing on the inside of my cheek and wanting her to unravel it. "But I bought this for you there." I shuffled my feet. "It's, um, not worth a million dollars, like some of the paintings in your house, but … I thought you'd like it."

She handed me her coffee and pulled off the rubber band, unrolling it. My heart raced, my mouth drying. I would never be able to afford art the way that Constantino and she could, but I hoped that she sorta liked it.

Or at least pretended that she did.

When she laid it across her lap, she widened her eyes even more. "I love it."

"Do you really?" I asked, smiling softly at her.

"Yes," she said, drawing her fingers across the smudges of paint. "I'm going to hang it up in our bedroom when we return home. We just cleared off a wall so I could hang up artwork I found around the city."

"Girls," Constantino called from the front, jaw clenched slightly while scrolling on his phone. "When we get to Italy, I need you to stay put in the villa. I have some work to do this evening with a friend."

"I thought this was a workless vacation," Laila said.

"A family friend is there and has a matter that he needs help with. I promise it'll be a few hours, and then tomorrow, we'll go sailing on the yacht."

She brushed her fingers against mine while chatting with her husband about his work tonight. I gazed down at them and pushed mine against hers, light enough to make it seem unintentional, but my heart was pounding.

I didn't know why my body reacted this way around her. We had done way dirtier things than brush our fingers against each other. She had literally thrust a dildo into both of us yesterday. But … *gosh*, I felt like I had my first crush all over again.

And I was sure these feelings weren't going to disappear. But I had to remember that my job this year was to be nothing more than their dirty little toy.

38

constantino

HALFWAY TO ITALY, I peered over at Riccardo, Vincent, and a couple of my guards, passed the fuck out, diagonal from us. Laila and Sage were sleeping in front of me, Sage's head leaning on Laila's shoulder, Laila's cheek on Sage's hair. Their skirts riding up their legs.

I drew my tongue across my lower teeth.

No panties either? Had they planned that?

Once I placed my glass down, I stood and walked over to them. I gently pulled Sage's tablet from her arms to put it away and spotted the drawing of Laila she had been working on while my wife slept. I sucked in a sharp breath at how detailed it was.

One day, I'd pay Sage to create a mural of Laila for me to hang in my office.

After depositing the tablet into Sage's Hermès bag, I gently placed Laila's leg over Sage's and parted their pretty little legs. I knelt between Laila's while gently rubbing their cunts, careful not to wake anyone yet.

My tongue traced the slit between her folds, and I placed my mouth on her pussy. I flicked my tongue across her clit, eating her pretty little pussy as my dick hardened inside my suit pants, my balls warm and heavy.

Laila shifted slightly, her hand finding Sage's hand on the armrest, fingers intertwining. I grunted and unzipped my pants, wanting to be inside her now. So, I scooped her into my arms and sat back down in my seat across from Sage, placing my wife on my lap so she faced our toy. She shifted in my arms again, slowly waking up.

"Go back to sleep," I murmured in her ear.

"Wh-what are you doing?" she asked, blinking her eyes open as I slipped inside her.

"Enjoying you."

Her pussy clenched around my cock, tighter and tighter the more she woke up. "Constantino," she whispered, "your … your guards are here. What if they wake up and—"

"And see my wife riding my cock?" I asked. "Then, I'll have to kill them."

She tightened even more, her gaze dropping to Sage, who shifted in her seat and slowly opened her eyes. I wrapped my arm around my wife's waist and leaned her back against me, letting Sage watch me fuck her.

Humming to herself, she blinked a few times and then pressed her legs together. Laila clenched.

"C-come here," she whispered to Sage.

"Eat my wife's pussy," I said to her.

Sage glanced behind her at the guards, then slowly moved over to us, dropping to her knees in front of my wife. I pounded up into her, my balls slapping against her bare pussy. Sleepy-eyed Sage pressed her mouth to Laila's cunt and flicked her clit.

Laila laced her hand into Sage's hair. "His balls too."

Fuck.

I buried myself deeper into my wife and grunted when Sage dipped her head and sucked both my balls into her mouth, gently kneading them with her tongue. They popped out, and she moved back to Laila's clit.

Back and forth and back and forth.

"Baby," she murmured, leaning back further against me and gripping Sage's hair tighter, "d-don't stop. You're going to make me … you're going to make me c-come …" She slapped a hand over her mouth and drew her legs together, body trembling all over me.

When she finished, I sat Sage on my lap next. She curled her fingers into my shoulders and lowered herself onto me, her mouth on Laila's as my wife's tongue slid between her lips.

God, they are so fucking sexy together.

Small whimpers escaped her throat as she bounced up and down on my dick.

"If you don't keep quiet, you'll wake my men," I whispered in her ear.

She tightened around me and clutched my shoulders harder.

"I bet a dirty little slut like her would like that," Laila hummed, finally relaxing into the degradation.

Last night, I hadn't felt as if she was comfortable with it. But this morning, it came out almost naturally.

Sage gazed over at Laila, pussy clenched tightly around me. "L-Laila …"

"Tell her how much you fucking love it," I growled into Sage's ear, taking a fistful of her hair and pulling it back. "Tell my wife how good her husband's cock feels inside you, how much you want my cum."

Whimpering, Sage grabbed on to me tighter. "P-please, Constantino …"

"Keep her *quiet*, Laila," I hummed.

Laila smirked, her eyes hazy, and moved closer to Sage. Sage glanced over at my wife while I plowed into her. Laila dipped her hand between Sage's legs, almost immediately finding her clit and rubbing the sensitive bud back and forth.

"Please," she whined softly.

"Poor baby is begging for it," Laila said, dipping a thumb between Sage's nude lips.

"P-p-please," Sage whimpered. "I-I won't b-be able to stay q-quie—"

Sage dipped her head and bit my shoulder harshly, a drawn-out whine coming from her throat. Laila rubbed Sage's pussy even faster, back and forth and back and forth, making Sage clamp down hard around me.

Laila wrapped her free hand around Sage's chin and pulled her closer, slipping her tongue into her mouth and kissing her. Sage stiffened, her pussy tightening harder and harder and harder until …

Entire body trembling in my hands, Sage threw her head back and came hard. "H-holy s-s-shit," she moaned, lips parted and eyes rolled back far into her head.

Her pussy convulsed around me, and I could do nothing but fill it.

With every last goddamn drop of my cum.

39

laila

CONSTANTINO: **Be ready in ten.**

I readjusted black bikini in the mirror, eyeing the gold chains that snapped together behind my neck, and frowned. Today, we were supposed to be relaxing on a yacht somewhere off the Amalfi Coast.

But I had changed into ten swimsuits and couldn't find one that I liked.

My gaze dropped to my tits, and I frowned. They looked too small in this bikini.

Sighing, I crossed my arms and leaned against the bathroom counter. I scrolled through Bethany's Instagram and tapped on a couple of her bikini selfies with her tits hanging out of them and stared at all the comments and likes she had because of her body.

After I peered back up into the mirror, my chest tightened. It wasn't fair.

"Do you have—" Sage started from behind me.

"Sage!" I said, jumping up in surprise and scrambling to put my phone away.

As far as I knew, she didn't particularly like Bethany, but if she saw the way that Bethany showed off her body online, she might change her mind. She might … might fawn over her the way that everyone else in this family did.

Sage's gaze lingered on my phone, even after I stuffed it away, and she looked away. "S-sorry, I didn't mean to disturb you. Constantino said I should ask you if you have any sunscreen. I'm definitely going to burn."

I crouched down beside one of the bags that Constantino had packed for me. He had thrown everything in there like any man would, without a care in the world, just happy that we were going on vacation. No sense of organization at all.

"I don't know if Constantino packed sunscreen," I said, scrounging through my bag and hoping that I had something for her. If he had let me pack myself, I would've grabbed a bunch of sunscreen. Sage was so fair-skinned. "Do you want tanning lotion?"

"I don't tan like you." She smiled softly. "No worries. I can go pick some up—"

"Found it," I said, popping back up with a small bottle. "We can pick up more later."

"Can you put some on my back?" she asked.

Anything to touch her like yesterday on the plane.

My lips curled into a smile, heart pounding. Nearly five years ago, when I had started dating Constantino, he had asked me to rub tanning lotion on his back while on vacation, giving me every opportunity to touch his body. I remembered all those butterflies fluttering in my stomach.

Now, all those little feelings returned.

She sat on a small stool in front of the mirror and hummed. I squeezed some pasty sunscreen into my hand and lathered it on her shoulders before my fingers ran over all her curves that I so desperately wanted again, especially after that flight.

"Were you talking to Bethany?" she asked quietly a couple of moments later.

I stiffened. "No. Just scrolling through her Instagram."

"You must really like her, huh?"

"She's my friend," I said. Though Constantino had kept telling me otherwise. "Why?"

Sage set her lips into a tight line and shrugged. "No reason."

"Do you think she's attractive?" I asked before I could stop myself.

Sage shifted uncomfortably and nervously gazed into my eyes. "Do you?"

I opened and closed my mouth, not knowing what to say. *Why didn't she answer? Did she see that picture of Bethany on my phone?* Of course, Bethany was fucking beautiful, but ... but I didn't want Sage to think so.

Sage was mine.

"She's attractive," I whispered, watching to gauge her interest.

"Oh," Sage said, voice falling as she looked away.

"Do you think she is?" I asked again.

"No."

"What about your friend?"

"My friend?" she asked, brows scrunching for a moment. "You mean, Poppy?"

"Yeah, her," I said, loathing the sound of her name.

"She's pretty, but not my type."

"Who's your type?"

"I hope it doesn't offend you, but I would usually go for someone like Constantino, except without the whole *gangster, mob boss* thing." She giggled, eyes flickering up to me again and cheeks flushing. "But I make exceptions sometimes."

Exceptions ...

I stared at her for a few moments, wondering if I should ask her if one of those exceptions was me. By the way she stared back, I sorta felt like it was, but ... but ... she had done this for the money. Not because of me.

Sometimes, I still couldn't get my head around why Constantino liked me.

My body wasn't as naturally sexy as most of the women who hung around the family. Hell, I couldn't even give him a child. I didn't know what the hell he saw in an average woman who couldn't produce a family.

I turned back to the mirror and swallowed hard, my chest tight.

"Do you think I should get a boob job?" I asked casually, adjusting my top again.

Sage froze. "Wh-what?"

"Breast enhancement," I said, nerves bubbling in my stomach.

I wasn't sure what I hoped she'd say, but I didn't want surgery. Getting my lips done, botox, and lipo … that had been enough. My breasts were already sensitive enough, to the point where I could come from stimulation alone, and I didn't want to lose that if the doctor hit the wrong nerve.

"Of course not!" Sage said, eyes wild. "What made you think that?"

"I just …" I swallowed hard. "I think I'd look better for Constantino."

And you.

"You think you'd look better?" Sage whispered. She blinked a couple of times, shook her head, and grabbed my hands, tugging me away from the mirror. "Constantino fucking loves you for you, Laila. He doesn't care what your body looks like. You don't have to do anything for him."

"So, no?" I asked.

"I'm not going to tell you what to do," she said, pushing some hair off my forehead and tucking it away behind my ear. "You should do what makes you happy and the most confident, but you don't need it at all."

"You promise?" I whispered smally.

Sage held out her pinkie and smiled softly. "I promise."

40

laila

I LAY on my stomach next to Sage on the back of the yacht, staring out at the rippling blue waves behind us with the sun beating down on my back. Constantino sat back on a chair, his dark Italian skin glistening with tanning oil.

"I feel like I'm in a toaster," Sage mumbled, glancing over at me through her glasses.

When I peered over at her, her pasty skin had turned a shade of pink. I grabbed the sunscreen and squirted it all over her back, rubbing it into every inch of her that was exposed to the sun, slipping my fingers underneath her bikini strings.

Once I collapsed back down next to her, I pushed a couple of her curls off her forehead and tucked them behind her ear. I squirted some lotion on my fingers again and dabbed some on her nose, which was burning. She watched me closely and stayed quiet, her pretty eyes following my movements.

God, she was the most beautiful woman I had ever seen. I didn't know how the hell I had gathered up enough courage to walk up to her that first night and bring her back into my husband's office. Probably the alcohol.

Still … this didn't even feel real.

But every time I looked at her, I never wanted her to leave. *What will happen a year from now, when Sage has a million dollars in her pocket and the agreement is up? Will she leave us?*

"What do you want to do in the future?" I asked.

"Hmm?"

"What do you want to do in the future? As in … a job or for your life," I clarified, nerves bubbling up in my stomach. "Where do you want to go? What do you want to see? Where do you imagine yourself in five years?"

Sage paused for a moment and sucked on her inner cheek. "I don't know, honestly," she said. "I really loved working in animation, but that studio environment was so toxic. Maybe starting my own business." She hummed softly, raspberry-painted lips tugging downward. "I wanted to have a family by my late twenties, but that's a stretch."

"It's not that much of a stretch," I whispered.

"I'd have to meet and marry someone within the next few years."

I pressed my lips together to stop myself from saying something stupid and closed my eyes. If Sage thought I was falling in fucking love with her, all this would be ruined. She might like sleeping with another woman, but loving them was something different entirely.

And I was scared. Scared of getting my heartbroken. Terrified of scaring her off.

I didn't want to lose her. Not now.

"Constantino mentioned that you've been trying for a baby," she whispered.

Dropping my head between my arms, I stared down at the padding underneath my body. Constantino had told Sage we'd been trying to get pregnant. Had he mentioned how much, how long, how many different fucking things we'd tried, and still … I had been useless in that too?

When Constantino's brother, Pietro, asked about it, Constantino always told him we weren't ready. But the family kept pushing it, which only stressed me out more. Constantino had even gone to an fertility doctor to see if he could do anything, but everything was okay on his end.

It was me.

"Yeah," I whispered, the tears building in my eyes, "we have."

"I can't wait," she said.

"You can't wait?" I asked, lifting my head.

She rolled onto her back and grinned. "Your kids are going to be so cute! I can just imagine a whole bunch of little Lailas and Constantinos running around your house in the city, driving you crazy."

Warmth spread through my chest, the tears in my eyes getting hotter. But unlike every other time I thought about the stress of *not* being able to have kids, I found myself smiling, feeling hopeful.

What would life be like with a handful of young kids running around the house? Constantino would offer to hire a nanny, but I would want to raise them myself. Sage could help me. We could create art all day. And—

I swallowed hard. All this was *if* Sage was still with us.

"Do you want a boy or a girl?" she asked.

"It doesn't matter to me," I whispered honestly. "I just want to have a family that I can care for." Because I never had one myself. I wanted kids who would come running to me when they fell off their bikes, who would hug my thighs to feel safe.

It was something I never had, and I vowed to devote my life to my family.

"I want a girl," she said.

We fell into a relaxing silence until Sage glanced back over at me.

"You should put on some sunscreen too," she said. "The sun is strong."

While I didn't use sunscreen often, I handed her the bottle. She sat up, squirted some into her hands, and rubbed it across my shoulders. I closed my eyes once more, relaxing further under her touch and smiling.

Sage wanted a girl.

She'd be a good mother to her too. I held back my tears. And I'd bet she would find an amazing husband to raise her daughter with, someone who would support her through anything, someone who would inspire her to follow her dreams, bring her out on dates and not ditch her for his friends.

God, what was wrong with me?

She leaned down closer to me. "Do you think Constantino would put any on?" she whispered in my ear, wiggling the sunscreen bottle at me, peeking up at my husband, and stifling a giggle.

We both knew he wouldn't; he had been reapplying his tanning oil every thirty minutes.

"Only if we squirt it at him," I hummed.

She laughed into my shoulder. "You do it."

While I hadn't been serious about squirting my husband with sunscreen, I sorta wanted to do it now. He would freak the hell out, probably think that a bird had shit on him because I had never done something so silly before, but—I grabbed the lotion—why not?

From this angle, I could see his eyes closed underneath his sunglasses.

I slowly stood up and pulled Sage up with me, moving closer to her to whisper in her ear. "When he gets up, run. Fast."

She grinned and nodded, stepping closer to Constantino with me.

When we approached, Constantino arched a brow at us. "Why do I get the feeling you girls are about to get yourselves into trouble?"

"Now!" I shouted, whipping out the sunscreen and squirting it all over his chest. Then, I dropped it, grabbed Sage's hand, and ran with her to the other side of the yacht. I peered over my shoulder at Constantino, who ran after us. "Faster!"

Sage burst out into a fist of giggles, nearly stumbling over with her shorter legs. "Get sun-screampied!"

Giggles erupting through my body, I clutched my stomach and pressed my back against the edge of the yacht. "Wh-where did that come f-from?" I said between my laughs, barely able to hold myself up.

Constantino's arms came around her stomach, and he flung her over his shoulder. She stared at me from behind him, upside down and in a giggling fit. Her face was red, cheeks flushed. But, God, was she beautiful.

"You're not getting out of this either, doll," Constantino said, his hand wrapping around the back of my neck as he pulled me to him. "Come here."

41

sage

AFTER CONSTANTINO TOSSED me onto the couch, he tugged his wife closer and pushed her down on top of me. She straddled my waist, her tits swaying in her tiny black bikini, the gold chain glimmering in the sunlight.

Her pussy was flush against mine and wet. So damn wet.

She placed her hands on my tits to steady herself and glanced back at her husband, who unclasped the straps of her bikini and tore it off her body. She gasped and curled her fingers into my breasts almost instinctively.

Warm spread throughout my core, and I ground my hips up against hers in an attempt to rub myself off. Constantino walked between our legs, placed a hand on Laila's lower back, and arched it so her tits hung in my face.

I latched my teeth around one of her nipples, sucking and tugging on it until she moaned. Constantino spit on his cock and then slid it between us, pushing our pussy lips apart. Instead of slipping into either of us, he thrust himself back and forth between us, his head rubbing against each of our clits.

Laila moaned again and stared down at me, her pink lips parted in pleasure and her brow furrowed. She took my nipples between her fingers and pulled. "Oh, just like that, baby," she whimpered, beginning to buck her hips back and forth against us.

A moan escaped my lips as I sucked harder on her breast, kneading the soft flesh in my hands. Constantino wrapped his arms around my thighs and pulled my ass toward the edge of the couch, spreading my legs as far as they could go.

"Keep your back arched, doll," Constantino said. "It's time for your punishment."

Laila arched her back harder so her stomach and tits pressed against mine and our pussies were stacked instead of pressed against one another. She dipped her head down and sucked on the flesh just above my collarbone.

Constantino thrust hard into her, then pulled out and slammed into me. I tilted my head back against the couch as much as I could and moaned, the sound getting lost in the waves around us.

"More," Laila murmured against my skin. "Please, Constantino."

Constantino slid into her once again. Then me.

One thrust. One thrust.

One thrust. One thrust.

One thrust. One thrust.

Until I felt Laila's juices dripping down onto my pussy.

He grunted and pulled away from both of us, crouching down between our legs. He placed his mouth against our pussies and flicked his tongue between both our clits, his fingers sliding in and out of each of us.

After he rested my thigh on his shoulder to hold my legs apart, he grunted and devoured our pussies with even more hunger. My legs began to tremble, the pressure building higher and higher in my core. I threw my head back and grasped the edge of the couch.

"Oh my God!" I moaned. "D-don't s-stop!"

He moved his tongue in circles around our clits, his fingers curling into us at just the right angles, massaging our G-spots. I curled my toes, on the brink of an orgasm, when Laila threw her head back and screamed out in pleasure.

I came undone, my entire body trembling as an orgasm ripped through me too.

Constantino continued to pound his fingers into us, his mouth on our bodies until we both came down from our orgasm. Then, he stood back up, his dick raging hard, and moved between our legs.

He smacked his hand against our clits. "Arch your back, Laila. We're not done."

Laila whimpered against me but arched her back hard again, her lips millimeters from mine. He seized her hips from behind and began pounding into her tight cunt, slamming his cock into her pussy over and over. Every time he thrust, she brushed her lips against mine, moaning into and kissing on me.

Again, he brought her to another orgasm and tipped her over the edge. And when he was done using her, he shoved his cum-covered cock into my dripping pussy. She sat back up and bucked her hips back and forth against my clit.

"Take my husband's big cock," she murmured, seizing my nipples and tugging.

Pleasure shooting through my body again, I arched my back and came hard for a second time tonight. He continued to pound into me, and for a moment, I thought he was going to fill me up again.

But then he pulled out and tugged Laila and me to our knees at his feet.

"Open your mouths," Constantino ordered, grunting and stroking himself.

While we both had our mouths wide open, he came all over our faces instead, completely missing our lips and decorating our forehead, eyes, and cheeks with his thick load of cum. I blinked my eyes a couple of times, a salty strand lying across my lid.

Over the sound of waves crashing against the boat, I heard shuffling from a room on the upper deck. My cheeks flushed. God, I could only imagine what kind of show Vincent, Riccardo, and the other guards had just witnessed.

Laila licked her lips and grabbed Constantino's hand to stand up on the yacht. She tugged me up after her and headed toward the bathroom, but Constantino captured her waist.

"No cleaning off. I'm taking you girls out like this." He pulled him to her and dipped his head into the crook of her neck. "Your punishment isn't over. You get to walk around town with your faces drenched in my thick load tonight."

42

constantino

WE WALKED UP to Luca's, the dirtiest bar I could find in the area for my filthy little sluts. Laila and Sage walked together beside me, Laila's arm looped around Sage's, both their eyes wide with excitement and my cum decorating their pretty faces.

When I opened the door, a cloud of smoke drifted out from the inside. After I gestured for them to enter, I followed them into the smoky room. Stripper poles stood in the center of the bar with cheap dancers dressed in raggedy clothes.

While we never attended places so run-down, neither Laila nor Sage seemed to mind. If Laila were with Bethany the Bitch, she wouldn't dare step into a bar this disgusting, but she was here with me and Sage tonight, being my good little whore.

Older men looked over at my girls, who had my cum all over their faces, checking them out, like all the guys in the city did. I should've been a jealous bastard, like the rest of the family men were over their women, but I knew these girls were going home with me.

And only me.

My cum was on them, like a savage territorial mark.

I slipped onto a barstool between Laila and Sage, my hands on their thighs, and motioned for the waiter. He walked over to us, placing three glasses on the bar in front of us and nodding at me like I had won the fucking lottery.

"Get us three of whatever your specials are tonight," I said. "You girls are filthy," I murmured in their ears, drawing them closer to me once he walked away.

A drop of my cum ran down Sage's cheek to her mouth, and she licked her lips clean and swallowed. My cock hardened inside my suit pants again, and before the waiter could even come back with our drinks, I pushed out my seat, took them both, and found the restroom.

I knew that I wouldn't last an hour tonight with them like this.

After I shoved them into the small, dirty bathroom, I locked the door and unbuckled my belt. Laila pressed Sage against the sink, her hands traveling across our toy's body and her mouth on Sage's neck.

Sage tugged on the straps of my wife's dress, yanking them down her shoulders and letting her tits bounce out of it. Sage slipped onto the sink and spread her legs, letting my wife finger her tight hole. I arched Laila's back and stepped behind her while she ate Sage's pussy, slamming myself into her, their moans getting lost together.

Laila pulled up and stared at me through the mirror, thumb brushing against Sage's swollen clit and fingers buried deep inside her. "Fuck her," she whispered, brows drawn together. "Please, come inside her."

Groaning, I pounded into my wife for a couple more thrusts. I'd fuck Sage now, but Laila was getting my cum tonight. Sage had had it yesterday. But my wife … she seemed desperate—her pussy had tightened on me when she said it.

After I pulled out of her, I moved between Sage's legs and slipped into her.

"Take your lipstick out of your purse," I growled.

Laila shakily unzipped her purse and rummaged around for her raspberry-colored lipstick. After she pulled it out of her bag, I tossed the purse onto the ground.

"Write *Property of the Burattis* across your dirty little toy's pussy."

While I pounded into Sage, Laila drew the bright pink lipstick across Sage's pussy, following my orders. I gripped Sage's thighs harder, spreading them further so I could pound myself deeper into her.

When Laila finished, she set the lipstick on the counter and slipped her hand over Sage's leg and rubbed her clit in small circles. "You're ours," Laila said, moving closer to Sage to kiss her on the mouth, their tongues tangling together. "We own you. Say it."

Sage tightened around me. "Y-you own me."

"Again," I growled.

"You own me."

"Louder," Laila said.

"You own me!" Sage cried, her pussy exploding around me. She jerked her legs up, her entire body trembling on the porcelain sink countertop. She gripped the edges of it. "You own me. You own me. You own me!"

Once she came down from her orgasm, I pulled out of her and stepped back, taking my wife by the hair and pushing her to her knees.

"We might own her, doll, but I own you," I growled, slipping my dick into her mouth when she opened like a good girl for me. "I'm your fucking god."

Laila wrapped her full lips around my dick, bobbing her head back and forth wildly. "Give me your cum," she murmured once she pulled away for air, wrapping her hand around the base of my cock. She sucked my balls into her mouth, stroking me and staring up into my eyes. "Please."

I grunted each time her small hand traveled up my shaft, tightening around it. Then, I snatched the lipstick from the counter and grabbed her chin, tilting it upward and writing *Dump cum here* on her throat.

"Open your mouth, doll," I ordered.

As she opened her mouth, I drew an arrow from the pink lipstick on her throat to her pouty mouth and shoved myself deep into her throat, watching the way the lipstick and words on her neck bulged from my cock.

While my dick was deep inside her, I handed the lipstick to Sage.

"What do you want me to do with this?" she asked, eyes wide.

"Make my wife pretty."

After she pressed her thighs together, Sage hopped off the sink and crouched in front of Laila. She gently took Laila's chin from me and twisted the bottom of the stick so she'd have some lipstick to work with. Then, she placed it on Laila's forehead.

Slut.

I grunted, my cock throbbing inside of Laila's mouth. "Tell my wife what you wrote."

"*Slut,*" Sage whispered, brow furrowing as she watched me thrust my dick in and out of Laila's mouth.

Spit and drool rolled down her chin, decorating her full tits. Her warm mouth squeezed my cock.

"Repeat it, doll."

"Slut," Laila gargled on me. "I'm a slut. I'm a slut. I'm a—"

I exploded inside her mouth. She widened her eyes and gently pushed on my thighs, but I didn't pull away. I kept my dick in her mouth until every last drop of cum dripped out of my balls and into my wife.

When I finally pulled back, I leaned against the chipped tiled wall. Laila leaned over on her hands and stared up at me, her pretty face ruined, flushed and dripping with spit, my cum in her mouth and pooling around her tongue.

Sage moved closer to her, cupped her chin, and tilted Laila's face toward her, kissing my wife right on the mouth. I grunted again, my balls growing warm and heavy. I wrapped my hand around my wet dick and stroked it a couple more times.

Sex with Laila before Sage had been amazing, but this was fucking phenomenal.

"God," I growled, "I fucking love how dirty you girls are."

43

laila

"WHY DID you ask me to come inside Sage the other day?" Constantino asked me.

We sat in a luxury restaurant that overlooked the water while Sage used the restroom. I shifted in my seat and took a sip of my Afterglow wine, heart pounding. I didn't want to say it out loud, so I opted for the first thing that came to mind.

"Because I thought it'd be sexy."

"Mmhmm," Constantino hummed.

"What?" I asked, placing my glass down and avoiding eye contact.

"You didn't have a reason other than that?" he asked me, nudging at it.

I peered over my shoulder to make sure that Sage wasn't on her way back. "I'd really like to not talk about it now. We are at dinner with her, and she could be back any second, Constantino. Why don't we wait until we get home?"

"We're going to talk about it," Constantino said. "We've put it off all week."

"She'll be back any moment," I repeated.

"Then, you'd better start talking."

Mouth drying, I stared at him and pressed my lips together. How could I tell him that I wanted a kid so badly that I would be okay with him getting Sage pregnant? It was so fucking wrong, but I didn't want to lose her.

"Because," I whispered, "it will make her stay."

Constantino was about to respond, but he paused and furrowed his brow, as if he hadn't expected that answer. "I thought it was because you wanted me to get her pregnant for us to have a family."

"That too," I said, guilt washing over me.

This past week, I had thought endlessly about both scenarios, but I had realized that Sage couldn't leave me because I ... I loved her. Which was ridiculous because it had only been a couple of weeks, but ...

"Fuck." I ran my hands through my hair. "I don't know, Constantino. I—"

"The restroom is so nice," Sage said, sliding onto her seat beside me.

I froze and straightened out, hoping she hadn't heard a word I said to my husband. She took a sip of her water, her silky royal-blue dress clinging to the curves of her breasts, and looked between us.

"I didn't interrupt, did I?"

"No," Constantino said. "We were just talking about how Laila wants a big family."

Cutting my gaze to him, I kicked his leg underneath the table.

"She was telling me about it the other day," Sage said, rolling spaghetti around her fork.

Constantino arched a brow at me. "Is that so?"

So that he wouldn't say anything else, I shifted the conversation.

"I've been thinking a lot about starting that foundation we were talking about at the museum the other day," I said to Sage, lightness flowing through my body and a smile creeping onto my lips. "I want to help kids in foster care and in adoption agencies through an art auction."

"I can help you," Sage said.

"You-you would? I mean, you don't have to do it to please me, but I was going to ask you if you would donate some of your art to the auction," I said, nerves biting my insides. "I think it'd go for so much."

"On one condition," she said, "You have a piece of art in the auction too."

My eyes widened. "Sage, I'm being serious."

"Me too."

"My art in the auction?" I said, shaking my head. "Nobody would buy it."

"I would," Sage and Constantino said at the same time.

Butterflies bubbled up in my stomach, my cheeks flushing red. Sage bit back a giggle and glanced at my husband, blushing. He looked over and smiled at her, and my heart fucking jumped in my chest.

I didn't understand why my body reacted this way when they were together, but it made me so happy to see Constantino relaxed. When we were in New York, everything was always so tense. He barely smiled.

"So, why foster care?" Sage asked.

"What?"

"Why do you want to support children in foster care?"

I had never told anyone, except Constantino, the real reason I wanted a family and to support that kind of charity, not even Bethany. It wasn't that I didn't trust her with the information, but I didn't want the entire family to know that I had been in foster care, being handed off from one family to the next.

Never having a stable place to live or people who loved me.

But if she was going to be with us forever, if she was going to have our child, then … she would have to find out sooner or later. She would have to know why I acted the way I did sometimes around her and my friends. She would have to know the way I had grown up.

"I, um …" I glanced over at Constantino. "I was in foster care for a long time, growing up, and never had a family." I paused and stared down at my food, not wanting to tell her everything, but all my problems fed into each other. "I hate the thought of anyone leaving me."

We stared at each other for a long time, and then she placed down her fork and set her hand over mine.

"I'm not going to leave you," she whispered.

But that was what everyone said before they left. That was what everyone said before they broke your heart. Every foster parent had crouched down in front of me as they picked me up and told me that they wouldn't leave me. They put on a big show.

And then they had hurt me.

"Don't say that," I murmured.

Sage furrowed her brow and glanced at Constantino. I hadn't meant the words literally, just the meaning behind them. But I felt like the biggest bitch after the words tumbled out of my mouth. I was sure Sage probably thought I was crazy, too, for asking her to stay with us and then telling her not to.

"I don't mean it like that," I said. "But everyone has said that to me before they walked away."

She leaned forward. "As long as you want me around, I will stay."

But did that mean forever? Would she stay forever, even after she asked if she could have a boyfriend the other day? I feared she was already getting tired of my craziness, of my indecisiveness.

"I never had a chance to apologize," I said. "For the way I acted with Bethany that night."

"Please leave her out of our dinner," Constantino said, clenching his jaw.

I stared at Sage, feeling so utterly heartbroken and angry with myself for what I had done that night. I still thought about it nightly, how I had almost screwed something amazing up with Sage because of her.

"That's why I left with Bethany that night," I whispered, my chest tightening as I relived the moment. My stomach had been so tight that I felt like I would puke, my heart racing. "I didn't want her to hate me, but I … I'm working on being better. So, please be patient with me."

While I would try hard to be better, I couldn't change myself overnight. Nobody could.

It had taken decades for me to find someone who loved me for me, searching and hoping that I would be loved, only to have my heart broken every single time. I couldn't unlearn all that trauma within a day, not even a couple of weeks.

But I feared that if I didn't tell her now, I would make a horrible mistake in the future while I tried to please everyone. I feared that I would do something stupid that Sage would never forgive me for, something so much worse than ditching her for dinner.

44

sage

AFTER DINNER, Constantino brought us to an exclusive BDSM club that cost a hundred grand per ticket to enter. Laila wrapped her hand around mine, intertwining our fingers. Half-naked women danced in glass boxes inside, others around poles.

I swallowed hard and pressed my thighs together. I couldn't believe that we were here. We had done worse together at that dirty bar the other night, but this felt different. Everyone here was drinking or fucking, or drinking and fucking. Grinding up all on each other. Kissing and touching.

"Are you girls going to be good for me tonight?" Constantino purred, wrapping his arms around each of our waists and pulling us closer to him. He planted a kiss on Laila's neck, then one on mine, his nose traveling up the column of my neck. "We have a surprise for you tonight."

My eyes widened. *A surprise?*

"Maybe," Laila teased.

She had convinced me to pull off our underwear in the restroom after we had dinner earlier, and now, I knew why. She wanted to be bratty with Constantino tonight, the way we had been the night he locked us in his sex room, chained us to the walls, and forced us to come.

After buying us each drinks, Constantino led us to one of the many back rooms with glass windows. He thrust the key into the lock, opened it, and gestured for us to enter. Laila pulled me along inside and leaped onto the bed with her wineglass.

"Come here," she murmured, one hand on the back of my neck.

Pussy tightening, I crawled onto the bed with her and placed our glasses on the side table. Constantino approached us from behind, footsteps low and daunting. I closed my eyes and climbed between Laila's legs, the anticipation building between mine.

When the bed dipped behind me, I sucked in a sharp breath. We weren't even naked yet, but people were looking inside the glass windows at us kissing and touching on each other already, handsome men and women getting themselves off.

Constantino snaked his large hand around my throat and strummed his fingers, crawling behind me. "Do you know what this throat needs?" He pulled his hand away for a moment, then fastened a collar around my neck. "My collar."

Laila gazed up at it and drew her fingers across it. "Slut."

A wave of pleasure rushed through me, my nipples hardening.

Constantino handed me another collar. "Put it around my wife's pretty throat."

After I locked the collar around Laila, Constantino moved closer behind me and pulled my dress up my ass, giving everyone watching a whole view of my pussy. Laila sank her hand between my thighs, rubbing my clit.

I took her breasts in my hands and rolled her nipples around my palms while I ground my pussy up and down against Constantino's suit pants, completely coating them in my juices. He took a fistful of my hair and pulled back.

"Look at my two little sluts, getting each other off in front of everyone." He sprawled a hand across my ass. "So fucking desperate for my cock that you can't even wait for me to pull myself out of my pants."

"P-please, fuck me," I begged as Laila pulled the straps of my dress down and let my tits bounce out of it. She took my face in her hands and pulled me down closer to her, tilting my head so I stared out at all the people watching.

"Tell them that you're a whore for sleeping with my husband."

"I'm a whore," I said to the onlookers.

"Louder."

"I'm a whore."

"Louder."

"I'm a whore!" I screamed loud enough for the men and women to hear me. "I'm a whore. A dirty little whore for sleeping with your husband and loving every single second of it." I arched my back hard, sticking my ass into the air. "Please, fuck me!"

"Please what?" Constantino asked.

"Please, sir."

"Good girl," Constantino praised, lining the head of his cock up with my entrance.

A rush of heat warmed my core.

Laila released my face and seized my nipples between her fingers, tugging harshly on them. "Tell them how much you love being filled with my husband's huge cock."

"I-I love it!" I cried out in pleasure.

Constantino slammed into me. I fell forward against her, my breasts pressed against hers so that I could feel her hard nipples sliding against mine. Another wave of pleasure rushed through my body.

"Come inside her," Laila said to her husband as she stared up at me, her eye contact unparalleled, which only made me tighten around Constantino.

A wife telling her husband to come inside me?

Fuck, it was so fucking sexy.

"Beg for it," Constantino growled, slamming into me. He seized my hips tighter, and I could only imagine his hair flopping against his forehead with every thrust. "Both of you beg me to come inside Sage's pussy."

I slipped my hand between our bodies to massage Laila's clit, wanting her to feel pleasure from this too. "Please!" I cried out, rubbing her pussy in small, torturous circles. I slipped my fingers inside her, the heel of my palm against her clit.

"Please come inside her! God, please."

Hearing her beg for him to fill me—"Fuck!"—it tipped me over the edge. Pleasure soared through my body as my legs trembled.

Constantino slammed deep into me and filled my tight pussy to the brim with his warm cum. He rolled over onto the bed, keeping me on top of him and grasping my hips.

"When I pull out of her, I want you to thrust my cum deeper inside her, doll."

Laila shoved her hand between her legs and continued rubbing herself off, then nodded eagerly as she knelt beside us. I captured one of her nipples between my fingers.

And when Constantino pulled out of me, Laila immediately stuffed her fingers deep inside me. She wiggled them around, making sure to get his cum as deep as it could go, and then I felt a slight pinch.

Constantino wrapped his arm around my waist, playing with my clit and making the pain disappear completely. "Relax, princess. She's filling you up with my cum. Isn't that what you wanted?"

I bit my lip as Laila pulled her fingers out of me, looking as if she was on the brink of an orgasm, and when she stuffed her cum-covered fingers into her mouth, she screamed out in pleasure.

45

sage

OUR LAST NIGHT IN ITALY, I lay between Laila and Constantino in the bed, staring out at the stormy ocean. Rain pattered against the balcony outside, the thin drapes whooshing into the room from the wind.

I tucked myself into Constantino's arm as Laila held my waist, her head on my shoulder. She rubbed small circles around my naked hip in a soothing manner, humming lightly to herself.

"Thank you for coming with us," she whispered.

"She didn't have much of a choice, doll." Constantino chuckled.

Laila glanced up at me through wide eyes as a giggle escaped my mouth.

Well, he had a point.

But still, I wanted her to feel appreciated because nobody had ever done this for me before—especially between all the shopping and dining.

I brushed some hair out of her face. "Thank you for bringing me," I said, peering outside at the ocean again. "I've never been to Europe before. It's really beautiful here."

After sending me a soft, sleepy smile, Laila slipped further down in the bed and rested her head on my breast. Her body became heavier, her breathing evening out for the night. Once she fell asleep, I cuddled closer to Constantino and closed my eyes.

Part of me wished we could stay in Europe forever. I didn't want to go back home, where Bethany ripped Laila away from me every chance she got, where Laila's supposed best friend made her feel bad about herself.

Furrowing my brow in annoyance, I squeezed my eyes closed tighter and wished I could just forget about it all and enjoy the last few hours we had in Italy before we left tomorrow morning. It had gone by too quickly.

A couple moments later, light flickered in front of me. I blinked my eyes open to see where it was coming from and spotted Constantino scrolling through his pictures on his phone. Once my eyes readjusted to the bright light, I shifted in the bed.

"Can I see?" I asked.

Constantino tensed and looked down at me. "I thought you were sleeping."

"I'm too anxious right now," I whispered honestly.

"Is Laila rubbing off on you?"

"No, I just don't want to go home. It's so peaceful here."

"No foul-mouthed best friends," Constantino agreed.

My lips curled into a small smile. "Nope."

He stared at me for a long moment, his playful gaze traveling across my face, and then he handed me his phone. I sat up against him, laying Laila on my lap and resting my head on his shoulder. I scrolled from left to right, glancing at all the pictures he had taken on our trip to Italy. All of Laila in her most candid moments.

Butterflies fluttered through my stomach, a smile creeping onto my face. She looked so happy, like she wasn't an insecure mess, the way she was back home, like she absolutely loved her life with Constantino. And, God, I wanted that so badly.

I wanted the love that they had for each other. I wanted to feel so happy with somebody.

When I scrolled to the left once more, I stared at a candid shot of me with a dab of sunscreen on my nose.

My eyes widened, and I sucked in a breath.

Constantino grabbed the phone from me and looked away, his cheeks tinting bed.

"What was that?" I whispered, still in shock.

"Nothing," he said a bit too quickly. "It's nothing."

"Did you take pictures of me?"

I wasn't angry. I just couldn't believe it.

He had all these pictures of Laila and some of me too? Maybe Laila had asked him to take some pictures of us together. But ... she wasn't in that picture. It was of me alone, lying in the middle of his yacht.

"I just ..." he stammered, cheeks flushing even redder.

I never thought I would see it in my entire life, but Constantino —the big, macho Mafia boss who didn't give a shit about anything —was blushing because I had called him out on taking a picture of me.

"Can I see it again?" I asked, nervously.

After a couple of quiet moments, he handed me back the phone. I stared at the image and smiled softly, butterflies fluttering in my tummy. He must've taken it after Laila dabbed sunscreen on my body. I thought he had been sleeping that whole time, but he had been watching us.

"Do you have any more photos of our trip?" I asked.

He paused for a moment, an uncomfortable expression crossing his face, but then he wiped it away quickly. "Yes," he said, his voice sounding the same way it had the first night I met him—hard and almost cold. Or maybe he was just guarding himself.

Hesitantly, I scrolled to the left again and saw another picture of me. And then I scrolled again and again and again. The rest were of me, sometimes with Laila scattered in with me, ordering breakfast or smoothies by the beach.

I handed him back the phone and gazed up at him, my heart racing. I didn't know what to say. What were you supposed to say when the guy you had a crush on had pictures of you on his phone? I wasn't sure, but my heart was racing.

"Why?" I asked. "Why do you have pictures of me?"

He stared at me for a long time, not saying anything, but his eyes searched mine. I expected a cold, callous answer from him because he was the big, bad boss of the city, but he moved closer to me and took my chin gently in his hand.

"Because I wanted to."

"Because you … because you wanted to?" I repeated.

What did that mean? Why would he just randomly take pictures of me if it didn't mean anything? Would he even admit it if he felt something for me? His wife was lying on my lap, but I couldn't shut off the feelings I had for *him*.

"Is that a problem?" he asked, moving closer.

I stared into his eyes for a long time and moved closer to him. My heart was racing, pounding against my chest so loudly that I could almost hear it in my ears. His lips were millimeters from mine.

"Are you going to answer me, princess?" he murmured.

"No," I whispered. "It's … it's not a problem."

"Good," he said, brushing a thumb down the center of my lips. "Because I wouldn't stop even if it was a problem for you." He paused for a moment, gaze searching my eyes and then dropping to my lips. "You belong to me."

And then he crashed his lips onto mine.

46

sage

ON OUR FLIGHT back to the States, Laila and Constantino sat together, both working on their laptops. I brushed my drawing pen across my tablet and hummed softly to myself, desperately wanting to draw Constantino, but not in front of him.

I had never been kissed the way he had kissed me in bed last night in such a long time. Even my ex-boyfriend—who, honestly, I was surprised hadn't reached back out to me since I'd broken it off with him—hadn't kissed me like that. Ever.

Instead of drawing Constantino or Laila, I drew Riccardo with a funny nose and a cookie in his mouth. He would get a kick out of it … or maybe not, but I didn't care. He was too easy to piss off that it was sorta, kinda funny.

"What are you up to?" Laila asked, tilting her laptop down to look over it at me.

Turning the tablet in her direction, I showed her the drawing. She stifled a giggle and glanced over at the guards, who all sat together. I didn't know what their problem was, but they were serious all the time, never smiling once.

"I'm working on an outline for the auction," Laila said with a genuine smile.

Warmth spread through my chest at her smile. She was actually going to go through with it, making plans and writing out all her ideas. It made me so freaking excited for her. She had told me she had wanted to do this since she had met Constantino.

But Bethany was the reason she hadn't planned anything.

And now, after we had talked, that had changed. I hoped that I had given her the confidence to do what she loved from now on, but I still feared that as soon as Bethany found out, she would put Laila down and force her to stop.

Laila would tell us that Bethany didn't have anything to do with her decision, but Constantino and I would know better.

I needed to figure out a way to get rid of Bethany for good because if Laila wanted me to stay with them far past the contract length of a year … I didn't know if I would be able to deal with Bethany for the rest of my life.

Though … I really did want to stay with them.

Sure, I hadn't spent more than a month with them, but I …

I think I love them.

After swallowing hard, I shook my head and returned to my drawing. *Stupid, Sage. Stop it.*

They couldn't feel the same way about me. They were married to each other and had a happy life together. But that kiss last night with Constantino and spending this week with Laila without her best friend …

It had been the happiest week of my life.

The only way I could think of possibly getting Laila to finally dump Bethany was to—

No.

I pressed my lips together and scolded myself for even beginning to think *that.*

That I needed to use Laila's desires against her. That was dark as hell and such a betrayal. I couldn't allow myself to betray her trust like that. I couldn't allow myself to … to think about helping her have a family with Constantino just so she would have to choose between us and Bethany.

Her fingers whizzed across her keyboard, a gentle smile painted on her pink lips.

At the same time, I couldn't let Bethany destroy her happiness. I needed to do something. After slamming my tablet into my purse, I stood up before I could stop myself.

"I'll be right back," I said, then hurried to the bathroom at the rear of the private jet. My stomach twisted into knots, and I ... I wanted to stop myself.

But I couldn't.

Bethany wouldn't take away more of Laila's happiness. I would give Laila what she wanted.

I hope she wants this.

Once I shut and locked the door behind me, I pushed my pants to the ground and squatted over the toilet. Thoughts whirled through my mind.

What the fuck am I doing?! Why am I doing this at all? Removing my own IUD to get pregnant?

Does Constantino want this? Does Laila want this?

By the way she had been acting this week, she did. She had been giving me *all* the signs.

And last night ... last night had made me so happy. I hadn't felt that way with another guy in so long, and to know that he had taken candid pictures of me the same way that he had snapped pictures of Laila on vacation ... the way he had kissed me ...

God, I can still feel his lips on mine.

There was nothing in the contract about what would happen if I got pregnant or that I had to be on birth control, and my crazy, possessive brain rationalized that to mean that they didn't care if I was on birth control or not.

Swallowing hard, I plunged two fingers into my pussy.

Why am I ...

How can I be doing this?

It was dark. Disturbing. Maybe illegal.

But Constantino and Laila did far more illegal shit. They were in the mob, for fuck's sake. I was the Mafia boss's and his wife's toy.

Their toy. Their toy. Their fucking toy, who is now fishing around in her vagina for her IUD string.

Fuck it.

I closed my eyes and reached inside my pussy with my fingers. I pushed deeper and deeper into my cunt, trying to reach the IUD because it must've been buried deep, deep inside me. So far that it … almost wasn't there at all.

47

sage

AFTER TEN MINUTES or more of trying to find the string in different positions, I collapsed onto the toilet with my legs spread and tried one last time to find it. I fished around for it, my fingers moving in all different directions.

And nothing.

Nothing!

It wasn't inside me. *When did it fall out? How long has it been?*

"Sage!" Laila called from right outside the bathroom door. "Are you okay?"

Heart pounding, I snapped my head up from between my thighs and stared at the closed door. My pants were on the ground, my fingers covered in my pussy juices. I opened my mouth to respond, but I didn't know what to say.

Yes? No? That I don't have my IUD anymore?

Should I ask her to help me find it? Maybe I just couldn't get it from this angle.

I didn't know why the fuck I was freaking out. I had literally come into the bathroom to remove it, to snap it out of my pussy and get pregnant with Laila's husband's child.

Now, fear rushed through me. *What if she … what if she doesn't want me to get pregnant with their child?* But she had made it seem like that was what she wanted all week, constantly asking me about children, how I would raise them, and then telling her husband to come inside me.

Multiple times.

It wasn't a one-off thing. She had ordered him to come inside me twice at least.

I swore that she wanted it.

Now, I was second-guessing everything. Maybe she had said that because she knew I had an IUD, that I was safely on birth control.

"Sage?" Laila said again, twisting the knob. "What's going on?"

I sucked in a deep breath and yanked my pants up. "I-I'm fine."

"You've been in there for twenty minutes. Do you need medicine? Are you nauseous?"

Nauseous? A pregnancy symptom. That was a weird question to ask … or maybe I was blowing this out of proportion, connecting things that weren't even related. Why the hell would Laila mean that? She probably thought I had gotten sick off that food we had eaten last night.

"Sometimes, when I fly, my stomach doesn't feel good," she called. "I have medicine."

"It's okay," I answered. "I'll be out soon."

"Are you sure?" she asked.

"Yes!"

Please don't come in. Please, don't come in. Please don't come in.

When I finally heard her walk away, I buckled my belt and readjusted my clothes. Then, I placed both hands on the sink and stared at my reflection in the mirror, my stomach twisting into tight knots.

What the actual hell am I going to do?

Does she want this? What if I get pregnant? Should I get Plan B once we get home? Go to the doctor for another IUD insertion?

If I did, Constantino would know. He wouldn't let me go to my old doctor, but would want me to go to a better physician, one he knew personally. Maybe Laila's.

After I calmed myself down, I unlocked the door and walked back to my seat. I stared at the ground throughout my entire walk back to my seat, thoughts racing through my mind. As soon as I sat, I knew Laila would have questions.

But I didn't want to ruin this vacation.

We'd had an amazing time this week, and we had problems back home we needed to deal with first. Like *Bethany.* We only had a few more hours of complete peace before we landed in New York. *What am I going to do?*

Once I sat across from them, they both looked up at me, Constantino arching a brow and Laila staring worriedly in my direction. I snapped my seat belt back on and peered up at them, forcing myself to smile.

"I'm fine," I said before they could say anything.

No, I'm not! I am freaking out because I went into the bathroom to take an IUD out of my pussy to get pregnant by the couple who I am contracted to be their toy, and I couldn't even find the birth control device.

"Just feeling a little light-headed," I said. "That's all."

"Nauseous?" Constantino asked.

"No," I whispered, then paused. "Would-would it be bad if I was?"

They shared a long look, and then Laila shook her head. "No."

We all stared at each other for a few long moments without saying a single word. My heart pounded against my chest, threatening to jump out of it. I swallowed hard, my throat beyond dry.

"Laila has medicine if you need it," Constantino said, breaking the silence. "For nausea." He glanced at his wife. "She'll make you feel better if you ever … get sick in the morning."

My eyes widened, and I snapped my head to the window.

Is he talking about what I think he's talking about?

"Isn't that right, doll?" Constantino said.

I could feel Laila's worried gaze on me. "If she needs it," she whispered.

I ran a hand through my hair and looked out the window. *Fuck, this is dark.*

Never in my life had I done something so … so shady.

While part of me wanted to tell her, I couldn't get myself to open my mouth. She wanted me to stay with them longer than a year, and if I got pregnant, this would bind me to them forever. And … not only that, but she would also have to choose between her friend and her family.

She would have to choose us.

48

constantino

AS SOON AS WE LANDED, I led Laila and Sage to a car and ordered Riccardo and the guards to bring them home and to keep them there for the rest of the night. Laila lingered by my side before slipping into the car.

"Where are you going?" she asked, staring up at me through wide eyes.

"I have someone I need to take care of," I said, opening the door and ushering them inside the car.

"We just got home," she said.

After sighing softly, I nodded and shut the car door. I didn't want to disappoint her, but I needed to take care of that bitch, Bethany. She had hurt Sage before we left—which was one of the reasons I had wanted to leave as soon as possible.

Laila rolled down her window. "Please, be quick."

But I couldn't make her promises. I was going to kick the shit out of that bitch and take my time. She would know not to fuck with any of us any longer. All she did was feed into my wife's insecurities and try to get into her head about me cheating.

We had been so great this week, and I didn't want that to change.

Especially with the way she treated Sage.

My gaze drifted to Sage, and I grimaced. I should've never kissed her last night because, now, I couldn't get her out of my fucking head. All this morning, she had become my obsession, something I had to protect.

She gave me a small smile, and I forced myself to look away.

Once their car disappeared from view, I slid into another black car with a couple of other men and placed my phone to my ear, calling Pietro. He picked up on the third ring.

"Have fun on your vacation?" he hummed. "Sleep with both of them?"

"Cut the shit," I growled, not about to be bullied by my own brother. "Bring Bethany underground."

He paused. "Underground? Why?"

"Do it," I growled and shut off the phone.

I wasn't going to answer any of his questions over the phone. I didn't have time for his shit and really didn't need to explain anything in my personal life to him either. He might've been my brother, but he didn't know shit about my relationships.

"Drive Underground," I said to the guard.

After removing my wedding ring—so I wouldn't get blood on it —I placed it into my pocket and cracked my knuckles. I had been waiting so fucking long for this night, and I would finally be able to let loose on Bethany because she had crossed the line.

Thirty minutes later, we arrived at our home outside the city. I stepped out of the car and walked into the house, down the closest set of stairs to the basement, where we conducted *discreet business.* Surrounded by guards, Pietro stood next to Bethany, who he hadn't restrained yet.

The fuck does he think I want her here for?

"What am I doing here, Constantino?" Bethany asked, arms crossed. She snapped her gaze down to my hands. "Not wearing your wedding ring. Did something happen on the vacation that you failed to tell me about, where you took my best friend and your little plaything—"

Lunging forward in front of all the guards, I grabbed the bitch by her hair and hurled her onto the ground. I never laid my hands on a woman, but she had not only threatened the family, but also my relationship with my wife.

"What the fuck are you doing?" Pietro said, grabbing me by the shoulder.

"Get the fuck off me." I shoved him away and dragged Bethany by the hair across the concrete basement floor to the thick chains we used to restrain people.

She tried to scramble to her feet, but I knocked her back down every single fucking time.

"Someone is finally going to teach you a fucking lesson."

"Constantino!" she screamed. "Let go of me!"

I snapped cuffs around her wrists, then her ankles.

"Wait until Laila hears about this!" she shouted. "I'll tell her that you restrained me to a fucking pole Underground, ripped off all my clothes, and raped me. And she'll fucking believe me because of the shit you're pulling with your maid—"

I punched her square in the face. *This fucking bitch.*

"My wife won't do shit about it," I growled. "Not when she finds out what you did to Sage."

"Sage? Is that her name?" Bethany exclaimed, spitting out blood. "You think she'll give a fuck when she knows that you've been sleeping with that bitch so much that you took off your wedding ring?"

"I didn't remove my wedding band because of Sage," I said, stepping closer to her and meeting her glare, aching to kick the living shit out of her. "I removed my wedding band so I wouldn't ruin it with your blood."

49

constantino

"LET ME OUT!" Bethany screamed, blood rolling down her face from the gash in her forehead. Her cries echoed throughout the basement as all my men watched me beat the shit out of her. "I'm sorry! I won't do it again! I'm so sorry!"

But it was a fake apology. It had been fake since the moment I'd ripped off one of her manicured nails with pliers. That bitch had been declawed like the stray sewer cat she was.

Her screams filled me with immense pleasure in ways that it shouldn't have. Part of me wanted to call Sage to watch so she could enjoy this too. It was sick, twisted, and fucked to be torturing my wife's best friend. But Bethany deserved it all.

"That's enough, Constantino," Pietro said, stepping forward. "You're going to kill her."

"Good."

Pietro snatched my shoulder and flung me back a few feet. Then, he stepped between me and Bethany and slammed his hands into my chest again. "You're going to punish the bitch when *you're* in the wrong?" Pietro spit. "Because *you* can't admit to yourself that you have a problem. Because your wife has been begging you for a kid, but you decided to sleep with your maid—"

I hurled my fist at my brother's face in front of all my men. Blood spurted from his nose.

"Everyone, out!" I growled.

If Pietro wasn't going to keep his head out of my shit, then I would have to settle this right here and now. No way would he continue to disrespect me in this family. We had the FBI on our ass; he should be on my side for everything.

No matter what.

One of the guards undid Bethany's chains, and she stumbled out of the basement, leaving a trail of blood. I gritted my teeth, wishing that I had just killed her, but I had run out of time. When I had told Pietro to watch Bethany this week, I hadn't meant for him to get so fucking close to her that he would stick up for that bitch.

Once everyone, except my brother, had scurried out of the room, I balled my hands into tight fists. Deep down, I feared that I'd have to gut this family from the inside out. When my father—that fucker —had passed the family business down to me, he had left it in shambles. And I had to be the one to fix it.

And the only way to do that was to kill those who betrayed us.

I slammed my fist into my brother's face. "Back the fuck up, Pietro."

Maybe that started with Pietro.

When he lunged back at me, I stepped out of the way. "I've taught you to fight better than that. Stop being a dick and fight me if that's what you really want because my family is none of your fucking business."

He ran toward me again and caught me in the jaw with a hook. "If you're not going to respect Laila, then I will."

What did this fucker just say?!

Rage blinded me. *How the hell is he going to threaten to take my wife away from me and still be fucking standing?!*

Leaping forward, I hurled fist after fist at Pietro. Even when I knocked him onto the ground, I continued to beat the shit out of him.

I didn't care anymore.

Nobody took my family away.

"If you're going to cheat on your wife, then—"

"I'm not fucking cheating on her!" I snarled. "I've never fucking cheated on her." *Slam.* "Out of all people, you should know that I wouldn't do that shit." *Kick.* "If it wasn't for her, this family would be six feet under already."

When my knuckles began aching, I stumbled back and glared down at him. He slowly sat up and spit out blood. His white teeth were coated in red, his eye already swollen. He was the only family I had left, and I didn't have the fucking heart to kill him.

"Then, what about your maid?" Pietro said. "Does Laila know?"

"Yes, she knows," I growled before I could stop myself. "And she's not our fucking maid. We *both* have an agreement with Sage, so stop fucking accusing me of shit. Stop listening to Bethany. Stop threatening my authority in front of the family."

"You have an agreement that you can fuck her?" Pietro asked. "*Pfft.*"

"That we can both fuck her."

"Does Laila know that it goes both ways?" Pietro spit.

This fucker isn't listening to me.

"Why don't you fucking ask her, Pietro? Why don't you ask Laila how many more times she has slept with Sage compared to me? I'm at work all day and night long because nobody in this family can do shit right, and they stay home together, sleeping with each other!"

I loathed that I had betrayed my wife's request to stay quiet about this all, but I hated being accused by my own family now. My own men had been smirking and giving nods of approval at me for apparently cheating on my own wife, and that shit wasn't okay with me either.

If I didn't put my foot down and demand respect with my own brother, nobody else would respect me in this family. And I had been working day and night to keep everyone out of prison. I had uprooted this family and breathed life into them after my father died.

"What is this all for, Pietro?" I asked. "Are you doing this because you want to lead the family? Turn them all against me? Make it seem like I betrayed them? If you want to run the fucking family, have fun taking the fall and rotting in fucking prison for the rest of your life."

The reason the FBI hadn't put me away yet? They didn't have the evidence.

Everything I'd orchestrated couldn't be pinned directly on me. My men were good at covering shit up, but I was better at diverting the blame from me to the family members who worked for me. And if they didn't think I would stoop so low to protect Laila, Sage, and myself, they were wrong.

I couldn't kill my brother, but I could put him in prison.

I wouldn't betray my family—unless they forced my hand.

On the last night of the trip, when I had kissed Sage, I'd promised myself that I'd do anything for the both of them. And anything meant anything. They were my fucking world. And in this life, they were all I truly had.

"I thought you had my fucking back," I said.

"I do have your back," he said, standing up and reaching for my shoulder. "I didn't know—"

"Fuck off, Pietro," I growled, ripping myself away from him. "Don't bother me again with this shit."

50

sage

TWO HOURS after we returned from the airport, Laila and I cooked pasta in their kitchen for Constantino. He hadn't said much about what he had to do, but he had looked stressed when he left. So, I'd thought it'd be nice for him to come home to a warm meal.

"Can you grab the strainer?"

"The strainer?" Laila asked, glancing into the pantry.

"The strainer is a metal bowl with holes in it," I said. "It should be in a cabinet."

Laila didn't know the first thing about cooking. Honestly, I wasn't sure she had cooked a day in her life. And I mean, I wasn't the *best* at making pasta, especially the Italian way, but we were trying our hardest to make something ... *edible.*

"Laila!" someone screamed from outside the door, banging harshly. "Let me in!"

Stirring the pot of spaghetti, I froze and glanced over my shoulder. That was Bethany.

How had she known that we were back already? Had Laila really texted her in the two hours we'd been here? Asked her to come over?

"I'll be right back, Sage," Laila said, handing me the strainer.

I tightened my grip on the wooden spoon until my knuckles turned white and glared at the boiling water. My vacation was officially over, and now, I had to return to acting like the maid, like the last week had meant nothing to me.

"Oh my God!" Laila cried, opening the door. "What happened to you?"

I bit back the urge to glance at Bethany to see what had happened. Before I could turn around to see what was going on—not that I cared about that bitch—Laila pulled her past me and toward the bathroom.

I continued stirring the pasta like it wasn't my business and added some more salt.

"Sage!" Laila called from the bathroom. "Grab me the first aid kit!"

"No!" Bethany shouted. "I don't want to see that bitch. This is her fault."

Biting back my annoyance with her—because I hadn't done shit—I hurried to the bathroom and pulled the vanity chair to the closet, standing on it to grab the first aid kit from the top shelf. When I hopped off, I placed it on the counter and unzipped it.

"What do you mean?" Laila asked Bethany.

Briefly, I glanced over at Bethany, who looked beaten to hell. All her nails had been ripped off and were bleeding profusely. Blood dripped from a huge gash in her forehead. Bruises covered her arms and legs. If she hadn't been a bitch to me, I would've maybe felt bad for her.

"Why don't you ask her?" Bethany snapped.

Brow furrowed, Laila glanced over at me. "What did you do?"

All I could feel was hurt. *Why does she blindly believe Bethany?* I had spent the entire day with Laila. I didn't have time to ask Constantino to do anything like *this* for me. Not only was I not going to stoop down to Bethany's level, but I couldn't. I hated the thought of hurting anyone, especially this badly.

Death would've been an easier punishment than this torture.

"Sage?!" Laila exclaimed, eyes blazing with anger. "What did you do?"

"Nothing!"

"She's lying," Bethany snapped. "The bitch is lying."

A plethora of emotions crossed Laila's face—anger, confusion, sadness, then betrayal. She shook her head and blinked back tears. "Sage, what did you do? What did you say to Constantino? Why did he do this?"

"I didn't do anything," I explained.

Why doesn't she believe me? Does she really think that I would ask Constantino to hurt her best friend like this? I wanted her to choose between us, but ripping off all her fingernails and giving her bruises and bumps everywhere? That wasn't me.

Laila sighed softly. "Please, go get me an ice pack, Sage."

I hurried to the kitchen and grabbed an ice pack for stupid little Bethany, who had gotten herself in trouble and was now trying to pin this all on me. Once I returned, Laila was crouched in front of Bethany and handed her the ice pack.

The front door opened.

"Laila!" Constantino shouted, his footsteps pounding against the floor. "Are you okay—"

When he reached the bathroom and spotted Bethany on the toilet seat with an ice pack on her forehead, he growled. "You have some fucking audacity, coming here."

He lunged toward her, but Laila stepped in front of her.

"Stop it, Constantino!" she shouted. "What did you do to her?!"

"Move, Laila."

"You nearly killed her!" Laila screamed. "I'm not moving away from her!"

"Move!"

"No!" Laila seethed. "Are you fucking insane, Constantino?! Why did you do this?"

"That bitch is not allowed in my house anymore," Constantino growled, his nostrils flared and his knuckles bleeding too. It looked as if he had hurt more than just Bethany tonight. "If she's not out in one fucking minute, I will kill her." Constantino's voice was as sharp as glass.

"You won't," Laila said, glaring at her husband with her arms crossed.

"Try me, Laila. Fucking try me right now." He looked at Bethany. "I will fucking kill you."

With tears heavy in her eyes, Bethany stood up and rushed out of the house, crying.

Part of me wanted to reach out my foot and trip her while she ran by, but I thought against it. Laila already thought that I had caused her husband to beat up her best friend. And I needed Laila to trust me.

When the door slammed closed, Constantino growled in my direction, "Leave now, Sage."

I sucked in a sharp breath and hurried out of the bathroom. After taking the boiling pot of water off the stovetop, I grabbed my phone and rushed out of the penthouse. Constantino was fuming, and I didn't want to be in the way of his wrath right now.

Some shit had gone down with him and Bethany. For him to come home to find her in his bathroom, crying to his wife ... I could only imagine how he felt right now. If I were him, I'd be more than angry.

He wouldn't hurt Laila, but I feared what was about to happen between them.

51

laila

"I'M GOING AFTER BETHANY," I said, rushing past him.

"No," my husband growled, grabbing my wrist. "We need to talk."

"Get your bloody hands off me," I snapped and pushed him back.

Blood dripped off his hands, the skin on his knuckles broken open. *What is he thinking? Is beating Bethany up what he had to do for work today?! How can he do this?* We had been on vacation all week long. She couldn't have done anything!

Blinded by rage and upset that my husband—who I trusted—would nearly kill my best friend without telling me anything, I shook my head and glared at the man. From the moment that I'd met him, I had known he was a monster, but I ... I couldn't believe what he had done.

What he was capable of doing.

He had completely mutilated her. He had made Bethany so ugly that even surgery wouldn't fix it. He had embarrassed her to no end, and, God, I hated him right now for it. He had threatened my relationship with her.

"Can you get it through your head how much you just hurt her?!" I screamed.

"Of course I can," he shouted. "She has been threatening Sage!"

My eyes widened. "What?"

"She has been threatening Sage," he repeated, voice sharp.

"You're lying," I said.

Of course Bethany didn't like Sage—she thought Sage was sleeping with my husband behind my back—but that didn't mean that Bethany had been threatening her. They had barely even seen each other. And never alone.

"We have been on vacation for the past week," I said, unable to believe that this had happened.

Sage would've mentioned it at some point, wouldn't she? It never even seemed like anything was wrong.

"When she went to that art festival, Bethany showed up and threw soda at her and her friend. That's why they were at her place." Constantino stepped forward, nostrils flared. "And then I came home to find her in my house. *Again.*"

I crossed my arms. "It's not fair. You can't be angry with me when nobody even told me that this happened! How am I supposed to believe anything you say after my best friend comes crying to me, completely mutilated?"

"Because I'm your husband!" he shouted, his voice almost … trembling.

He sounded so vulnerable, so defeated.

"I'm your husband, Laila," he said. "That's why you're supposed to believe me." He turned away from me, ran a hand through his hair, and shook his head, his entire body tensing again. "But you want to know why nobody tells you?" he growled. "It's because you never believe them! I have been telling you all this shit about Bethany for years now, and you haven't believed a word I said about her."

Guilt rushed through me, and I stared at the ground. "Sage didn't say anything."

"Why would Sage think you'd believe her if she did say something?" Constantino asked. "You acted like a bitch to her after Bethany tossed her food into the trash. Of course she's not going to say shit about Bethany in front of you."

Tears welled up in my eyes. If this was true … if Bethany had threatened her, then I would need to talk to Bethany. But that didn't give Constantino the right to rip out all of Bethany's fingernails and beat the shit out of her.

"I know you pulled out her IUD. If you're going to make me put a baby inside her and also let Bethany threaten her," Constantino growled, "then I can't fucking do this. I'm not bringing a baby into the world when she's still your fucking friend. So, choose."

"I'm not going to choose after what you just did to Bethany! You hurt her."

"You think everyone has a good heart and good intentions because you do," he said. "But they don't, Laila. Some people, like that bitch and my brother, are out to fucking get you. Get us. So, choose."

52

laila

"PLEASE DON'T MAKE me do this," I pleaded with my husband.

I didn't want to choose between Bethany and Sage. Bethany had been my friend for years, and Sage had just come into my life, but I didn't want to get rid of either of them. Though after what Constantino had told me about what Bethany had done to Sage …

I didn't want to believe it, but I did.

Bethany was a bitch to the woman I wanted to spend the rest of my life with. And I had been a bitch to Sage in so many ways. Pulling out her IUD so my husband could get her pregnant? Ditching her for Bethany? Blaming her when Constantino had hurt my best friend?

"Please don't make me choose between them," I whispered.

"I'm not making you choose between them," Constantino said, but there was more than that. There had to be more than that. "I'm making you choose between Bethany and us. Between Bethany or Sage and me. Between your lousy friend or your family."

Tears welled up in my eyes at the guilt and hurt that I felt for

Constantino even having to *ask* me that question. We had been together for years. He had done anything and everything I had asked of him, even let another woman into our marriage.

Of course I would choose him.

"Laila," Constantino growled, "now."

"You should know the answer, Constantino," I cried. "Why are you even asking me—"

"I want to hear it out of your fucking mouth," he said, the vein in his neck pulsing violently against his skin. He clenched his fists and shook his head, tearing his gaze away from me. "Because as soon as you say her name, I am taking Sage and leaving."

"You-you're gonna leave me?" I asked, my voice barely a whisper.

Pain rushed through my body as tears raced down my cheeks. This wasn't really happening, was it? Maybe I was just hallucinating from seeing all that blood. My husband really, truly thought that I wouldn't choose him?

And this was all my fault. I had made him—made *them*—feel this way.

"Choose," he snapped, this time much harsher.

I stared at him and shook my head. No matter what name I said, I would hurt someone. And part of me believed that if I said his name, he wouldn't believe me anyway. He wouldn't care. He was fuming right now.

But I swallowed my pride, my pity, my cries.

"Constantino ..." I whispered.

After impatiently waiting for a few moments, he twirled around and stalked toward the door, smashing my little broken heart into tiny little pieces. Constantino had never walked out on me in all the years we had been together. We always talked through our problems, never went to bed angry with each other.

"Wait!" I exclaimed. "Please don't go."

But he continued forward until he reached the door. When he grasped the handle, my heart sank even further in my chest. I ran forward so he wouldn't leave me here alone, so he would know that no matter what happened in this world, I would always choose him.

"I choose you, Constantino," I whispered, wrapping my arms around his torso and resting my forehead against his hard chest. "I don't know why you would even ask that. I will always choose you."

Unlike usual, he didn't wrap his arms around my body to comfort me. Instead, he stood like a statue in front of me and stared down coldly at me.

I stared up and furrowed my brow, chest tightening even more. "Please, don't leave me."

"Get your hands off me."

"Constantino …"

"Your choice should've been instant," he growled, shaking me off him and stepping back. "You should always choose your husband. We promised ourselves to each other the day we married. Do you remember your fucking vows, Laila?"

"Of course I do," I whispered, stepping forward. "But—"

"No fucking buts," he snapped.

"You're not giving me a chance to explain myself," I whispered.

"You don't get any more chances."

"You know what happened to me."

Constantino gritted his teeth. "Stop using that as a fucking excuse to be weak, Laila. We've all had shit happen to us. We all go through shit. You're supposed to learn from it and know when to be better."

"It's not an excuse," I cried. "I-I'm trying. But how am I supposed to react when someone walks into my house, nearly dead?! This is how I would react if you had tortured anyone the way that you tortured her!"

"Bullshit," he growled. "You know the monster you married."

"Please," I whispered, not even sure why I was pleading with him. What was I asking for? For him not to leave? He wouldn't do that to me. He wouldn't ditch me. Deep down underneath the monster he chose to be, he was a good man.

A really good man.

"If you really choose me—choose *us*—prove it," he said.

"Prove it?" I asked. "How? How do you want me to prove it to you?"

He ran his tongue across his lower lip. "Kill Bethany."

53

sage

RAIN POURED OUTSIDE MY WINDOW, deep gray clouds capturing the city skyline. I curled up in my bed and pulled the blankets to my chest as a tear slipped down my cheek. It was so stupid to cry because I had done nothing wrong.

But Laila had made me feel terrible.

After everything that Bethany had done to her, all the insecurities that she had caused, Laila had still blindly believed her. She hadn't even given me a chance to explain myself, to tell her that I'd had nothing to do with Constantino hurting her.

In fact—while I wasn't complaining that he had done it—I would never have asked him to do such a thing. Bethany was a bitch, but that didn't mean I wanted Constantino to hurt anyone because of me. I was just his ... toy.

Another tear fell down my cheek, but I pushed it away.

I knew that it wasn't true, but I had an awful way of hurting myself more with words. Constantino and Laila both meant more to me than a stupid contract. And this past vacation, I'd realized that I meant more to them too. I wasn't just a toy. They had taken me out to dinner and cuddled with me, smothered sunscreen on me while I burned on their yacht.

But honestly, tonight, I felt like I was just their toy. Laila had been so hurtful.

And it wasn't her fault. She had trauma. We all did. Still, her words had had meaning.

Someone banged on my door. I curled up into a ball on my bed and pulled the blankets over my head. Tears were streaming down my face now, and I couldn't even stop them. I didn't want to face whoever was outside my door.

Especially if it was Laila.

The bang came again, this time harder.

"Please," I whispered. "Go away."

"Open the door," Constantino said from outside the apartment.

He was still angry, furious. I didn't know if I wanted to deal with him right now. *What will he say to me? Will this be my fault too? Will he tell me that me being with them is causing too many problems for him?*

"Sage!" he called. "Open up."

If I didn't open the door, I knew he would come in anyway. I stood up and swaddled myself in my blankets, and then I walked to the front door. I took a deep breath. I didn't want to do this right now. We had spent all day traveling.

After his second knock, I opened the door. He stood in the hallway, his expression much softer than I'd expected. We stared at each other for a couple of moments before I lunged forward and wrapped my arms around his waist, burying my face into his chest.

More tears sprang from my eyes and rolled down my cheeks. I wanted to stop crying because I had no place to feel anything in this relationship, but, damn … this fucking hurt so much. I hadn't realized it before tonight.

"Sorry," I whimpered, sniffling.

I didn't know why I was so weak around him, but he made me feel safe. Especially after what he had done to Bethany for me. It made me feel like he would do anything for me, just as he would do anything for his wife.

"You have nothing to be sorry for."

"Yes, I do," I whispered. "For causing so much drama between you and Laila."

"You're not causing drama."

"You're fighting with her."

Constantino wrapped his arms around me, walked with me into the apartment, and shut the door behind us. "We are fighting because she keeps making terrible decisions, because she ..." He paused, his entire body tensing. "Because nobody—"

He stopped completely, as if he wanted to tell me what was on his mind but he didn't want to say a word aloud. Instead, he grasped me even tighter as the rain pounded against my windows and buried his face into the crook of my neck.

I held him tightly and cried. I didn't want to opt out of the contract early. I didn't want to opt out at all. But Laila was making this so hard. I didn't know why she just kept choosing Bethany over and over, even after everything she had done to her. I'd thought I was making her feel good about herself.

But I guessed I wasn't. I guessed what I'd said had no effect on her whatsoever. She didn't love me the way I had thought she did. Maybe all those nights in Italy, those dinners, our laughs and memories meant nothing to her.

After five minutes, Constantino pulled away and turned toward the door before I could even look at his face. "I'm going to handle it for you," he said, shoulders tense and body rigid. "I promise."

54

constantino

"PLEASE, COME WITH ME," I pleaded with Sage.

My back was still turned toward her because I was a fucking mess of a man. Hot tears burned my eyes, and I didn't let anyone see me cry. Not even Laila. My mind was jumbled with how hard it had been for Laila to choose, to say my fucking name over Bethany's.

I never begged anyone for anything, but I really couldn't be here right now. I might not have loved a lot of people, but I loved Laila. If I stayed here any longer, I might go back upstairs to the penthouse and comfort her. She had always been my weakness.

"But ..." Sage started. "What about Laila? What happened?"

"Nothing," I whispered, voice trembling. "All I did was give her a choice. And she hesitated. So, I gave her an ultimatum. There's nothing more you need to know besides that. Until she does what I asked her to do, you're not going to see her."

Sage stayed quiet for a few moments, then stepped toward me and placed her hand on my flexed back. "I don't wanna get in between you and her," she said. "Please. You had an amazing relationship with your wife before I stepped in. Don't let me ruin that."

"Since you signed the contract, you've been under my protection," I said. "Even from people in this family. Even if that's my wife. You're not getting in the way of anything. This is for your protection."

"Fuck the contract, Constantino," she said. "You need your wife."

"My wife doesn't need me," I shouted, louder than I meant.

But the pain ... the fucking pain of Laila hesitating had hurt me.

"But ... I ..."

When she didn't finish her sentence, I wiped the tears from my eyes and turned in her direction, capturing her chin in my hand and forcing her to stare into the eyes of a fucking monster. "Don't try to get out of our agreement because I'm not letting you leave me too."

She stared up at me with her brow furrowed and opened her mouth to respond. But I didn't want to argue anymore about this. I wouldn't. I had known what I was getting into the moment I signed the contract, the moment she brought it to me. I just never thought I would feel this way about her.

"Come," I ordered, holding out my hand.

To my surprise, she placed her small hand in mine. "Where are you taking me?"

I led her out of the apartment and into the elevator. When we made it to the ground floor, we walked to my car with the guards. I'd never walked out on my wife like this, but I couldn't handle it anymore. She had always chosen Bethany. Always.

It was never me.

Every time I brought up how Bethany made me feel—how Bethany made *her* feel—she didn't give a fuck. She brushed it to the side, like my opinion didn't mean shit to her. And I was so tired of it.

After ushering Sage into the car, I slammed the door harsher than I'd meant to and then slipped into the driver's side. Riccardo and a couple of my men followed us in the car behind us. I drove out of the lot and onto the New York City streets.

I hadn't wanted to go, but I had no choice.

Rain pounded down on the windshield. Laila would never learn if I didn't do anything. She would always choose Bethany. It was harsh to make her kill her, but I had to do it. If I killed her, Laila would hate me forever. But if Laila did it herself, after realizing how shitty of a person she was, maybe it wouldn't be as bad.

I gripped the steering wheel hard and continued driving, pressing my foot on the gas. I spent two hours driving through New York City until I finally pulled into the gated neighborhood that we lived in outside of the city.

Sage stared at the statues out front, eyes wide with excitement. We had never taken her here before, but Laila had mentioned it to her a couple of times while in Italy. She would love the artwork here. At least, I hoped.

Because she was my fucking prisoner until Laila stopped being a fucking baby.

After pulling into the garage, I shut the door and turned off the car. Instead of getting out of the car, I stared at the rain droplets sliding down the windshield and gritted my teeth.

Why the fuck did Laila react that way?

I slammed my hand on the steering wheel and growled, "Fuck!"

Sage gripped her seat belt in fear and glanced over at me. "Are you okay?"

We both knew I wasn't.

"I'm fine," I said, blowing out a deep breath and reaching for the door.

Before I could open it, Sage gripped my wrist. "You can talk to me."

But if I talked to her, if I opened up to her for the first time, she would realize how weak of a man I was. I'd never wanted to be this broken, this vulnerable to anyone but Laila. But Laila was slowly breaking my trust and breaking my fucking heart.

I clenched my teeth and gripped the steering wheel even tighter, not wanting to show her how broken this had made me. I couldn't trust anyone anymore. My own brother—my own fucking brother— had betrayed me. Now Laila? It wasn't fair. It wasn't fucking fair.

"I do everything for this family," I said, my voice coming out shakier than I'd meant to, "fucking everything, and nobody cares. Nobody gives a fuck. All that everyone cares about is themselves. Even my wife."

"Constantino …" Sage whispered. "That's not true. Laila loves you."

"Then, why?" I cried, pain etched into every fiber of my being. "Why does she keep choosing her over me? I am her fucking … husband, and she would choose Bethany over me any fucking day."

"That's not true," Sage said. "She's just hurting. I know it's so fucking hard. And I haven't even been married to her. I haven't even been with her for more than a couple of weeks. But she …"

Sage couldn't even finish her thought because we both knew it was bullshit.

Utter bullshit.

Hot tears built in my eyes. Sage undid her seat belt and took me into her arms, letting me rest my head on her shoulder. She gently ran a hand through my hair.

"Come here," she cooed. "You can cry. You can let it all out. It's just us."

55

constantino

I'D NEVER CRIED over anyone, especially not in front of somebody who I ... loved.

But as soon as Sage told me that I could let it all out, I couldn't stop the tears from springing from my eyes and running down my cheeks. I couldn't push back the pain any longer. My wife had hesitated to choose between me and her bitchy best friend.

How fucking terrible was that? I had never felt more like garbage.

Sage unbuckled my seat belt and laid my upper body on her lap, her fragile fingers running down my arm. My shoulders bucked back and forth, the heartache almost too unbearable. She trailed her fingers to my hair and gently stroked it.

"Why ..." I cried, voice cracking.

I didn't even know how to finish the sentence. I had so many questions that couldn't be answered by Sage. So many rhetorical thoughts that I didn't even know I would be able to answer myself.

Why had Laila hesitated? Why hadn't she chosen me after everything we had been through, after I spent all my money on her and took her places, after I made sure that she was the happiest fucking woman on this planet? Why could nobody ever choose me?

"I don't know," Sage whispered, as if she understood. "I'm sorry."

Wrapping my arm underneath hers, I grabbed her shoulder and pulled her closer. Thank fucking God that it was just us here and the windows were tinted because I would never *ever* let my guards—my men who trusted me—see me like this.

For this family, I always had to be the protector. But nobody ever protected me.

Sage wrapped her arms around my body and rested her head against mine. While I wanted to say that I had let Laila see me like this, I hadn't. I hadn't given Laila the option of seeing me this fucked up because I knew she wouldn't know how to protect me.

She was even more broken than I was. I needed to shield her from more heartache.

As far as I knew, Sage was the only one of us who had her head on straight, who didn't have trauma to unpack—at least not as badly as Laila and me. And breaking down in front of her didn't feel like a burden.

It felt so good to let Sage hold me. Nobody had held me since my mother had died.

"Maybe we should give you a bath," Sage suggested. "To help you relax."

But I didn't want to relax right now. I wouldn't be able to relax in a bath with her without clearing my mind first. I had brought Sage here for a reason—and not to a luxury hotel to hide us away. I wanted to spend time with her, to show her the home that she'd live in for the rest of her life—with or without Laila.

My chest tightened. Hopefully *with*.

So, I moved off Sage, turned away to wipe the tears from my cheeks, and shook my head. "I wanna show you around first. We can take a bath later." I opened my car door and walked around the car to grab hers too. "Follow me."

When she exited the car, she took my hand and squeezed it. "Are you sure?"

"Yes."

Without questioning it, she followed me into the house and passed the guards. Sage gawked at the foyer, mouth slightly ajar. She moved closer to me and scanned the room, a grin painted on her full nude-colored lips.

"This is your house?" she whispered. "It's grander than the penthouse."

A weak chuckle escaped my lips. I wanted to be happy and wished that Laila and I could've shown her the house together because Laila would've completely gushed about every single piece of artwork hanging on the walls.

Sage released my hand and sauntered through the halls, to each and every room. She'd walk up to a painting, stare at it for a few moments, then get distracted by another, and hurry over to it with a smile.

As she explored the home, I ran a hand through my hair and paced on the hardwood floor. Laila plagued my thoughts.

I shouldn't have walked out, but I had no choice. I kept telling myself that.

I had nothing else I could've done.

But I was wrong. This was my fault. All my fault.

Still, I should be home with Laila because if she made a mistake while trying to kill Bethany … the FBI would be on her ass in a heartbeat. If anyone from the family found out we had gotten into a fight, they might try to … hurt her.

"These are beautiful," Sage gushed, walking back up to me and taking my hand.

I gave her another weak smile. "Aren't they?"

Art really wasn't my thing, so I had nothing else to offer in this conversation. I chewed on the inside of my cheek—something I never did—but my stomach was in tight knots. Maybe I should go home to make sure Laila killed Bethany cleanly.

"What are you thinking about?" Sage said, the happiness suddenly gone from her voice.

Which wasn't what I wanted.

"Nothing," I said quickly, trying to lead her to the door.

"Talk to me," she said, refusing to follow. "What's wrong?"

But I didn't want to tell Sage that I had forced Laila to kill Bethany to prove herself to us. It felt so fucking wrong—I had known that it was wrong when I said it—because Laila had never killed *anything* before.

I doubted she'd be able to kill a mouse.

"What good husband would give his wife that choice?" I said, stiffening when I realized I had said the last bit aloud.

"A husband who wants what is best for his wife," Sage said, pushing some hair off my forehead. "Laila isn't going to learn without you putting her in her place. You shouldn't have to because you're her husband, but you deserve to be put first too. You don't deserve to come second to anyone, especially Bethany."

I pressed my lips together. She was right.

If Laila wanted to save our marriage, she would have to get rid of Bethany in some way, shape, or form. I didn't care how she did it. She could hire someone in the family to permanently remove her.

But would she?

After all these years of marriage, I still didn't know what my wife would do.

I rubbed my sweaty palms together and took Sage's hand. "Let's go take that bath."

56

sage

FIFTEEN MINUTES LATER, we sat in a hot bath together. I relaxed in his lap while he gently grasped my hips. We stared at each other in silence for a few moments until he moved forward and kissed me.

Contractually, I should kiss him back. And while I wanted to comfort him, this didn't feel right. I didn't want to sleep with him while he was angry with his wife. I was annoyed with her, too, but this just felt so wrong. So disgusting. Like something Bethany would do.

"I don't think we should," I whispered, hands on his chest. "I want to, but it feels wrong."

Constantino stopped, lifting his gaze to me and tightening his jaw slightly. After a moment, he slumped his shoulders forward and blew out a deep breath. "I know; it does." He shifted in the tub, the water sloshing over the edge. "I just want to get my mind off her."

"Let me actually give you a bath then," I suggested, taking the loofah.

I smothered the loofah with soap, then deposited it back onto the shelf. When I rubbed the loofah against his shoulders, he blew out another breath.

Head lolling forward, he closed his eyes. I shifted in the tub so I sat behind him and continued to wash his body. We were doing things backward, but I didn't care. I would wash his hair later. He needed to relax.

"You know you didn't have to do that to Bethany for me," I whispered.

"Yes, I did. And I'd do it again. She deserved it." He paused. "I should've done it sooner."

I swallowed hard because I wasn't going to disagree with that. Bethany had deserved it. Still, I felt so wrong. So dirty. He didn't have to do anything for me. It wasn't in the contract to kick the shit out of Laila's best friend.

None of *this* was in the contract, especially not the part about me washing him in the tub.

After I finished washing his body, I hung the loofah on the faucet and grabbed the bottle of shampoo. Suds fell down his body and into the warm water, creating small bubbles. I squeezed a dollop of shampoo into my hand and gently rubbed it into his thick brown hair.

"What happened anyway?" I asked, staring at the bruises he had all over his body.

I highly doubted that Bethany could do that much damage to him. These bruises were dark enough to have been done by a grown man.

"My brother is a dick," he growled. "If it wasn't for him, I would've killed her."

"Killed her?"

"Pietro stopped me, so I kicked his ass too." He suddenly tensed and snapped his head to the side. "Nobody is on my side. I do so fucking much for this family. I keep us out of prison, would kill every member of the FBI if I had to. And nobody appreciates a damn thing."

"I'm sure they do," I whispered, trying to comfort him.

"No, they don't. I told my brother to watch Bethany this week, and instead, she sank her claws into him too, just like she had with my wife. She needs to go. Now. I can't do shit around here with her."

I wrapped my arms around him, my breasts pressed against his back, and lay back in the tub. I gently washed the suds and shampoo from his body and hair. I hadn't been in this family long—barely a month—so I didn't really have space to talk.

"Part of me just wants to let the FBI have them. They have no shit on me, but I have shit on them. I can send them all to jail, start this family over. Get my wife back …" He gulped. "And our fucking family back."

Chewing on the inside of my lip, I continued to splash the water over his chest to get off the soap. Guilt washed over me when he continued on about their family. I should really tell him about my IUD. He wanted a family with Laila so badly, and here I was, knowing I'd attempted to pull out my IUD, only to find that I didn't have one anymore.

"I have something to tell you," I whispered, sitting back up and shifting in the tub so I sat in his lap. I draped my arms over his shoulders. "I, um … I know you and Laila wanna have a family together. I have no intention of getting in the middle of it …" My voice barely came out as a squeak. "But on our flight back to the US, I realized that … my IUD must have fallen out."

Constantino tensed, but didn't say anything.

"I'm sorry. I should've told you the moment I found out." I dropped my head. "I was actually looking to pull it out myself because I selfishly wanted Laila to choose us and not Bethany, but when I tried to pull it out, I couldn't find it." I winced. "Please don't hate me."

"Hate you?"

He drew his tongue across his teeth, then suddenly seized my neck in his large hand. I sucked in a sharp breath, hoping that he wouldn't do to me what he had done to Bethany.

"Why would I hate you? I was the one who helped Laila pull it out of you."

My mouth dropped open. "You ... you guys pulled my IUD out?"

To be honest, I honestly didn't care about when. My body grew warmer by the second. *They talked about this? Did they want me to get pregnant? Did they want to put a baby inside my stomach?*

With any other couple, I would've been freaking the fuck out. This was wrong. Dark. Fucked the hell up! But this was Constantino and Laila—mob boss and his wife, who did far worse than reproductive coercion.

If I had gotten pregnant without wanting it, I knew that Constantino would pay for an abortion. *Maybe.* But I had been trying to get pregnant without their knowledge too. We were both in the fucking wrong. That didn't make it any better or any more legal, but still ...

They want me pregnant.

"You were trying to get yourself pregnant with my baby?" He shifted in the bath and tugged me closer, his hand slipping between my legs. "God, you're a bad fucking girl, Sage." He brushed his lips against mine. "A bad, bad girl who's going to take every last drop of my cum until Laila comes to her senses."

57

laila

I PACED AROUND the penthouse with my mind all over the place. I hadn't slept at all last night, turning and twisting in the bed, waiting for Constantino to come back to me so I could apologize for hesitating.

Sure, I'd spent my nights without him while he was at work, but this had been different. When he left me last night, he looked so heartbroken and hurt that I had paused for even a moment. I would always choose him, but he hadn't believed me.

My stomach twisted, and I glanced at the front door. Waiting.

Not for him, but for Bethany. I had asked her to come over to talk, but really …

My gaze drifted to my gun that sat on the counter, the early morning sunlight glimmering against the metal handle. I wasn't sure that I would be able to do it. I'd never killed anyone in my entire life. I had never ever *thought* about it.

What can I do? Shoot her? Torture her?

I wanted to hurl at the thought.

If Constantino wanted her dead, he could've killed her yesterday. What had stopped him? Why make his wife—who didn't like to kill *anything*—do it? He hadn't liked that I'd hesitated, but I didn't like it when he forced me to make decisions like this.

And while the FBI is on our asses?!

Blowing out a breath, I forced myself to stop pacing and walked to the kitchen island. I slid onto one of the stools and opened up my laptop. I needed to keep my mind off of this. There was nothing to think about, nothing to decide.

If it would get Constantino to stay with me, I would do it. I would have to. But I didn't know if I could do it now or *when* I would actually be able to muster up enough courage to pull a trigger and end someone's life.

I pulled up a couple of tabs and sent emails, finalizing the venue and the plans for our charity event. That had to be at the forefront of my mind because it gave me a goal. Sage and Constantino would be back in my life before the event.

Once I finished that, I glanced at the digital clock in our kitchen and strummed my fingers against the marble countertop. I opened a new tab and stared at the blinking line, my stomach in knots. Bethany should be here by now.

I didn't know what I wanted to do, how I could pass the time. My mind was reeling, racing. All I could think about was Bethany's dead body sitting in the middle of the living room. I didn't know how I would get rid of it. *If* I could get rid of it.

What would our friends think? Would they hate me? Think I betrayed them? If I were them, I sure as hell would think that I was next. I wouldn't want to be my friend. I ran my hand through my hair until it became greasy.

Fuck. Where was she?

My gaze drifted to the gun on the table again, my stomach twisting.

A knock echoed through the penthouse. I leaped up from my seat, hand resting over my heart. She was here. Bethany was here, like I had asked her to come. And now … I would have to kill her.

Tears welled up in my eyes. I closed my laptop and reached for the gun on the counter. My hands lingered on the handle for a moment, feeling the smooth metal underneath it. I held it in the air, my hand trembling.

I didn't want to do this.

I really did not want to do this.

I tucked it away in my waistband, like I had seen Constantino do so many times. *How am I going to do this?* I didn't wanna take a life. I couldn't. She was my best friend. This was so harsh, so cold. And this wasn't me.

But I was about to lose my husband and Sage.

I was about to lose the opportunity to have a family.

So, I swallowed hard, closed my eyes, and prayed I could do this. I walked to the door and opened it up, expecting to see Bethany, but instead Poppy—Sage's coffee-shop *bestie*—stood at my door.

58

laila

WHAT IS POPPY DOING HERE?

I opened the door a little wider and furrowed my brow, extremely confused. *What do I even say to her?* I didn't like her. Bethany was about to come over. And I had a fucking gun in my waistband.

"Hi. Is Sage here?" she asked.

"How did you find my home?" I asked, chewing on the inside of my cheek.

My guard stood watch at the end of the hallway near the elevator. I didn't know why he had let her in. Had she said something to him? Had she bribed him in some way? If Constantino were here, he wouldn't have let anyone up here besides Sage.

"Oh." She giggled. "I just followed the big guys." She laughed again, her cheeks tinting red. "I went to Sage's apartment, but she wasn't there. She hasn't been home all week, and she hasn't been answering my messages."

I didn't know where Sage and Constantino were. We had been gone on vacation all week, but I had spent all night alone. If I had to guess, they were probably at the house. But I sure as hell wasn't gonna tell her that.

"I don't know," I said, grasping the doorknob tightly. "I haven't seen her."

"You haven't seen her?" she repeated. "I thought for sure you would have. When we went out to the art festival the other day, you were all that she could talk about. I guess ... I was wrong. Sorry for bothering you!"

My eyes widened. *I am all that Sage can think about, all that she can talk about?* Warmth exploded through my chest, a small smile tugging at the corners of my lips. *Is that true? Or is she lying to me?*

"If I talk to Sage," I said, "I'll tell her that you were asking about her."

"That would be great! Thank you." She turned around to head back down the hallway, her red hair flying in every direction. "Oh." She twirled around to face me with a big grin on her face and stuck out her hand. "I know that we kind of got off on the wrong foot the other day, but I'm Poppy again."

I stared at her extended hand for a moment, then shook it. I really just wanted her to get out of here as soon as possible, especially before Bethany came. I sure as hell didn't want her seeing what I was about to do to Bethany.

"Laila," I said, shaking her hand. "And I heard about what happened the other day. That somebody threw soda on you. I just wanna apologize. That's not how ..." Guilt washed over me. "That's not how anybody should act."

"Oh, it's fine. I'm over it."

"By the way, was there a reason why you wanted to see Sage?"

Poppy twirled her finger around the lock of her red hair. "Oh, I just had some tickets to an art gallery for tonight, and I wanted to see if she wanted to go with me. She seems really into art. Are you too?"

"Sorta," I lied, glancing down the hallway when the elevator chimed.

The elevator doors opened, and my heart raced inside my chest. I impatiently waited for Bethany to walk through the doors, to march down the hall toward me, so I could … attempt to murder her.

But instead, another guard walked from the elevator to change shifts.

"You don't think that she'd be back later, do you?" Poppy asked. "The tickets are for tonight. They were sold out, but I scored these from some scalper on the street. She was telling me she wanted to go the last time we spoke."

"Really?" I asked.

I didn't want them hanging out. I wanted Sage all to myself. But Sage wasn't gonna be back by tonight. Well, I highly doubted it. My stomach twisted. I honestly didn't know if she'd be back by next week or next month. I didn't know when Constantino would let me see her again.

"Where is the art gallery?" I asked.

"Near the coffee shop."

"What time?"

"Nine." She paused, then sucked in her bottom lip. "If you want them, you can take them. I don't really wanna go by myself. I don't really have any friends around the city yet, so …" She shrugged and awkwardly peered down at her feet. "I don't mind."

While I really wanted to go—because *art*—I needed to take care of Bethany. I really fucking needed to do it. Somehow, someway. I didn't know what was gonna happen. I didn't know how long it was going to take. But it needed to be done.

I couldn't be distracted.

But maybe … if I went with Poppy, I could attempt to figure her out a bit more. Figure out what her intentions were with Sage. See if she really liked Sage the way I did, if she wanted to take Sage from me.

I chewed on the inside of my cheek, pulled out my phone from my pocket, and spotted one message from Bethany. Because I could be a rude bitch sometimes—I saw that now and was working on it—I glanced at the phone before responding to Poppy.

Bethany: I can't make it tonight, sorry. I'm at the doctor.

I sighed.

"You could come *with* me if you don't want to go alone either," she suggested.

The offer was tempting, and I was almost going to accept. But I had already broken Sage's trust more than once. If she found me going out with one of her friends, just so I could try to figure out her intentions, I didn't know if she would ever be able to trust me again.

So, I shook my head. "No, thank you. I'll let Sage know you were looking for her."

59

laila

ONCE POPPY LEFT, I paced around the penthouse. I debated on what to do. I could go after Bethany and just get it done now. Or I could wait. But waiting meant that I would be longer without my husband and Sage, longer without a family.

My mind was racing a million miles a minute. If I went out and found Bethany at the doctor's office, I would have to do it in public or spend the day with her and bring her back here. Or maybe I could have somebody else do it for me. *Will that even count? Will Constantino accept that?*

So, I texted Bethany.

Me: Where are you? Which doctor?

Bethany: Plastic surgeon. I need to fix my nose, thanks to your husband.

My stomach twisted and turned. I cursed to myself and slipped my phone into my back pocket. I didn't fucking want to do this. I really wish that I didn't have to. I loathed myself more and more with every moment that passed.

But I had to do something. I couldn't just sit here and wait. Who knew when she'd be able to come over? I just … I knew I wouldn't be able to do it in public. Hell, I wouldn't be able to do it in any place other than this house.

What if somebody caught me? What if the FBI watched me kill her? They would send me straight to jail. Straight to fucking prison. And then all my hopes and dreams of having a family would be erased for good. I wouldn't get a chance at having a baby.

Me: Wanna meet me at the club later on?

I chewed on my nail and paced around the apartment, waiting for her response. I didn't know what she would say. But if I were her, I wouldn't want to go anywhere near the club now. Hell, I wouldn't even wanna be my friend.

Bethany: I don't know. We'll have to see how long this takes.

Stomach twisting into knots, I took a big, deep breath and grabbed my purse. I didn't know where I was going, but I couldn't stay cooped up in here any longer. This house reminded me of him. Everything reminded me of him. Of what I was about to lose.

I closed up and walked to the elevator, barely looking at any of the guards. I felt so ashamed that I wasn't with Constantino, that Constantino hadn't shown back up. I felt like my husband was leaving me for good. His guards probably thought that he was cheating on me anyway.

They didn't know the real story, and that was because of me. Because I couldn't admit to wanting to be with another girl. Because I was nervous, afraid. *What will they think of me? What will anyone think of me?*

This was all my fault. I stepped into the elevator and balled my hands. This was all my fucking fault. Bethany was going to die because of me, because I couldn't tell her that I liked Sage. That Sage was in our relationship because *I* wanted her to be in our relationship.

Tears streamed down my face. All just because I wanted people to like me.

God, it felt so stupid. *I* felt so stupid. *How can I let this happen? Let my husband believe that I don't choose him before anyone else? That I would gladly support my best friend over him? What the fuck is wrong with me?*

"Are you going to push the button?" my guard for the afternoon asked.

I let out another deep breath and hit the lower-level button. Once we made it to the bottom floor, I walked to my car and decided just to drive. I didn't have a destination in mind. Sage and Constantino were probably back at the house, but they didn't want me there, so I wasn't going to go.

I needed to fix this first.

So, I drove, and I drove, and I drove, and somehow, I made it back to The Syndicate myself a couple of hours later. I parked in the back and spotted Pietro's car in the alleyway. Constantino wasn't here yet, but he had work soon.

They were supposed to be working on an important shipment this week.

After frowning, I walked in through the back door. Pietro sat at the bar, one hand grasping a glass and the other scrolling through his phone. I glanced around at the few people here for an afternoon and walked toward him.

He had always been so sweet to me. Maybe he knew where his brother was.

"Hey," I said, sliding onto the chair next to him. "Do you happen to know where your brother is?"

"Constantino? No."

I glanced over at him and saw that his nose had also been broken, just like Bethany's. My eyes widened.

"What the hell happened to you?" I asked nervously, my stomach twisting. "Please don't tell me that my husband did that to you too."

"What's gotten into him?" he asked, peering at me. "I don't understand what's happening." He ran his hand through his hair. "Why is he with that girl? And why the fuck are you letting him run around with her?"

I swallowed hard and rubbed my sweaty palms together. I really didn't wanna tell anyone, but holding it back and keeping this a secret was hurting everyone, especially my husband and Sage.

"Please don't tell anyone," I whispered, clutching on to his forearm. "I … asked Constantino if she could spend some time with us. In the bedroom." My voice was barely a whisper. It was so hard to say that out loud to people who didn't understand how I felt. I had felt this way about women for so long in secret that …I could barely articulate it. "I wanted to explore."

"Shit," he said. "I didn't think he was telling the truth."

"Why? Did my husband say something?"

He had promised me that he'd keep it a secret, but things had been getting out of hand so much lately. If he had said something to his brother, I wouldn't blame him. I knew that Pietro wouldn't look at me any differently. It was Bethany and my friends that I worried about.

"We got into a little fight yesterday," he said. "And he might've mentioned something."

"Did you tell anyone else?" I asked.

"No," he said. "But everyone in the family thinks he's cheating on you. Why didn't you just say something?"

"Say something?" I repeated. *How can I say anything in this family?* I swallowed hard. "Because I'm nervous about what my friends are going to think. Because I … I don't just like her. I love her," I whispered. "I love her, and I want to have a family with them."

This was the first time I had said it out loud to anyone other than Constantino. I hadn't even told Sage yet that I wanted her in my life forever. Maybe she didn't feel the same way, especially after what had happened yesterday.

Maybe she didn't, but I wasn't going to let either of them go.

Not now.

60

constantino

"I HAVE TO GO TO WORK," I said to Sage, grabbing my wallet and walking to the garage. "No talking to Laila while I'm gone. She needs to fix something before she's allowed back. And I don't want her to find out that you're here."

We had been cooped up in here all day, and I needed to get back to work. I couldn't have my brother continue to run things around here or else he'd get us all locked up. I loved him, but he was getting on my fucking nerves.

Especially with that comment yesterday about my wife.

Did he want her? Was he planning to try to overthrow me? Maybe he wanted to turn me into the FBI. I didn't know what the fuck he was up to, but he would never take what was mine from me. Ever.

"What should I do?" she asked. "All my stuff is back in the city."

"I'll have somebody bring you your tablet, so you can do some art."

She widened her eyes, painting a smile on her face. "Okay," she whispered. "And if you see Laila, can you please tell her to make the right decision? I don't want to see either of you hurt because of me."

"None of this is because of you," I said.

I doubted that she would ever believe it, but it was true. This little problem that we had with Bethany had been going on for far longer than just a few weeks. Having Sage with us had really set Bethany over the edge and turned her into a monster.

"Do you understand that?"

After she nodded, I walked to my car and left for work, driving down the back roads until I merged onto the main highway to head back to New York City. I navigated the busy streets in nearly stand-still traffic, then drove into the garage underneath the club.

Not wanting to chat with anyone, I walked straight to my office and sat at my desk. I had peace and quiet for ten minutes. Ten fucking minutes before my door swung open without a knock and Laila walked into the room.

"Where is she?" she asked, hurrying into my office.

I stared at her for a few moments, my chest tightening. It had been a whole night that I had spent without her. Just one fucking night, and it'd felt like a fucking eternity. I didn't want to go home without her again.

But I hadn't heard anything about Bethany yet. From anyone.

"Have you done it?" I asked calmly.

I didn't want her to know how badly this was affecting me. I didn't want anyone to know. I was out in public, around my guys, my men, my family. If they thought I was weak, Pietro might try to start shit again.

"Please, Constantino, tell me," Laila pleaded. "Is she okay?"

"Laila, you're not getting off that easily. Did you do it?" I asked again, more sternly this time so she knew I was serious. I stood up, hands on the table and my dark eyes on her. "No excuses."

"It's not that simple," she said.

"I do it fucking daily," I said. "All you do is stick a gun to her head and pull the trigger."

"It's easy for you because you do it every single day!" she

repeated, balling her hands into fists by her sides and glaring at me. "I've never killed someone in my entire life. And I don't wanna start now."

"So, you haven't done it yet," I said.

I had known she hadn't done it the moment she walked into my office. If she had, her hands would have been covered in blood; she would've been shaking and scared and fucking terrified, like I had been my first time.

"You chose her," I said blankly.

"I didn't choose her," she said back, tears in her eyes. "I already told you, I choose you. I choose you and Sage. A family."

We stared at each other for a long time, and I didn't know what the fuck to say. I had always been able to find the right words around her, but today, I was lost for them. I didn't want to hurt her, but she was killing me on the inside.

"You haven't done it yet."

"Why didn't you do it?" she asked, crossing her arms. "You had every opportunity to when you were beating the fuck out of her. Why didn't you just kill her then? I can't get my head around it. Do you wanna torture me? Is that what this is for?"

"I want you to understand that your actions have consequences, consequences that I've been enduring since we've been married. I've been trying to keep this family away from the police, away from the FBI. But people keep on fucking with me. I can't protect anyone if we have rats in our family."

"Bethany isn't a rat," Laila said, standing up for her *again*. "She's just a bitch."

I paused for a moment because that had never come out of her mouth. She had always thought that Bethany was some sort of saint, some sort of goddess that she could look up to, that she could imitate.

Now, she thought her best friend was a coldhearted bitch.

We were making progress.

"A bitch who is poisoning you," I snapped. "You might not have killed Bethany yet, but you're going to." I cleared my throat as I walked to the door, pulled it open, and gestured to one of the guards. "Find Bethany and bring her to me. Now."

What Laila didn't know was that Sage would be down here tonight, too, and I would force Laila to pull the trigger on one of them. Just as she had chosen to rip the IUD out of Sage and not give Sage a choice, Laila wouldn't have a choice tonight.

By the morning, Laila would be a cold-blooded killer.

61

sage

SWIPING my pen across my tablet, I finished up the drawing that I had been doing of Laila while traveling to Italy. Especially after the fight last night, I hadn't dared to ask for my tablet because I didn't want to set Constantino off. But thankfully, he had kept his promise, and one of his men had brought it to me a couple of hours ago.

My lips curled into an easy smile as I colored in her dark brown hair.

I hadn't ever drawn anyone from my real life before her, and while I usually didn't love my first drafts, this was ... pretty fucking amazing. I really wanted to show Laila how beautiful it was—she was—because when she was with Bethany, I knew she didn't feel that way.

Once I finished up her hair, I placed my tablet down and munched on some homemade chocolate chip cookies that I had made for Riccardo. He had told me that he didn't want anything and disappeared into the large mansion, but as soon as the scent drifted down the hallway, he came strolling into the room, as if he suddenly wanted to check on me.

"Boss wants you down at the club," he said, shoving his phone into his pocket and stealing a cookie from the tray on the counter. He grabbed another in case he got hungry and nodded to the door. "It's urgent."

"How urgent?" I asked, arching a brow. "Like ... *someone died* urgent?"

"Like *if you don't get your ass in the car now, Constantino will kick* my *ass* urgent."

After nodding, I saved my work, turned off my tablet, and grabbed my purse from the foyer, then followed Riccardo to the car. He opened the back door for me, and I slipped into it, pulling out my phone to see if Laila had texted me.

Constantino had technically told me not to talk to her, but I could at least see if she had messaged me, right?

I had a few missed texts and calls from Laila, but most were from Poppy earlier in the day, the last being at two thirty-eight p.m.

Poppy: Hey, are you busy?

My eyes widened as I glanced down at all her messages that I had missed while in Italy. I sighed to myself and threw my head back against the seat. And this was why I didn't have any friends ... because I was hella bad at keeping up with them.

Me: SORRY!!!

Me: I totally missed all your messages. I've been traveling.

Me: I'm so sorry! Don't hate me!

Poppy: Ha-ha, no worries! I was worried something had happened to you. I even stopped by your place and chatted with Laila a bit. I was just wondering if you wanted to go to this art thing with me tonight, but it's probably too late!

Me: Oh no! I can get us tickets for next time!

Poppy: Don't worry about it. <3 Whenever you're free!

Poppy: Will you be at the coffee shop soon? You can tell me all about your trip to Italy!

Me: Hopefully tomorrow, but I'm not sure.

"We're here," Riccardo said from the front seat.

I chewed on the inside of my cheek, remembering the first time I'd stepped foot in this club, how Laila and Constantino had flirted with me from across the bar. I pressed my thighs together and hoped that they were finally on better terms.

While I wasn't sure what kind of ultimatum Constantino had given Laila, I really hoped that she chose us. And if he wanted me to swing by The Syndicate, then she had to have chosen us, right? Or maybe he wanted me to come by for him. Maybe all his men would see him with another woman, and more drama would ensue. The thought gave me a freaking headache.

Me: I'll talk to you tomorrow, hopefully!

With that, I slipped my phone into my purse and shuffled out of the car. Riccardo walked beside me, guiding me to a side entrance. I spotted a tinted-out SUV in the alleyway across the street and gulped, my stomach twisting at the thought of the FBI watching our every move.

"This way," Riccardo said, leading me into the entrance that he had led me *out* of that first night.

After taking one last look at the SUV, I followed him into the hallway and to Constantino's office. Two large men stood in front of it, dressed in dark suits with their hands crossed over their torsos.

Riccardo knocked on the door. "Boss, Sage is here."

A moment later, Constantino opened the door, a devilish smirk on his face. "Sage, so glad you could join us."

He took my hand and led me into the room with Laila, who jumped up from her seat and hurried over to us. But Constantino stopped her from touching me.

"You don't get to touch Sage until you choose."

Laila's face dropped. "Why is she here then?"

"You'll see." Constantino's smirk widened as he looked over his shoulder at his guards. "Any word on Bethany?"

Eyes widening, I tensed. *Bethany will be here? But why?*

I tugged on Constantino's wrist and swallowed hard. "I don't know if my being here with Bethany is a good idea," I whispered, brow furrowed. I peeked over at Laila, not wanting to upset her, but also scared that they'd blame me again for what had happened to Bethany.

"Bethany won't be a problem for you," he said, glancing at Laila. "Right?"

Laila looked between us and nervously chewed on the inside of her cheek.

Before she could answer, Riccardo cleared his throat. "Bethany is here now."

62

constantino

RICCARDO GRABBED BETHANY, who was zip-tied and gagged, and shoved her to the floor at my feet. He nodded and exited the room, closing the door behind us and leaving the four of us.

Sage pressed her lips together and stared at Bethany, nervously chewing on her inner cheek. Laila opened her mouth to say something, but one look from me, and she snapped it shut.

I pulled a spare gun out of my desk drawer, took off the safety, and handed it to Laila. "Choose."

Bethany began shaking her head back and forth, scooting across the floor to Laila, while Sage snapped her head toward me, her eyes wide in shock.

"Constantino, I …"

While I wished that I could've told Sage about this, I needed her reaction to be as believable as possible. I needed tears, sobbing, begging, and pleading. I needed Laila to hold a gun to Sage's head and choose not to pull the trigger.

"Your life is in my wife's hands," I said to Sage.

As if Sage didn't think my wife would choose her, she collapsed onto her knees, threw her head into her hands, and began sobbing uncontrollably. Her shoulders shook back and forth, and all I wanted to do was pick her up and reassure her that I would never let *anything* bad happen to her.

That even if my wife chose Bethany, I would choose her.

Laila grasped the gun in her trembling hands. "Constantino …"

"Choose."

"I don't want to hurt anyone."

"Well, if you don't"—I pulled my gun out of my waistband and pointed it at Sage's head—"then I will." I clenched my jaw and glared at my wife. "Stand up, Sage."

Weeping, Sage stood to her feet and wrapped her arms around herself. "I … I'm sorry. I'm sorry. I'm sorry," she murmured. "I should've never accepted your invitation. I should've never"—she sobbed—"never c-come to this club."

Laila's eyes widened, a frown tugging at her raspberry-colored lips. "Don't cry," she cooed. "Please don't say that. Take it back, Sage. I fucking love you." She squeezed her eyes closed and looked back at me. "I fucking love her."

"Prove it."

"You're not going to pull the trigger, Constantino," Laila whispered, tears streaming down her cheeks. She still pointed the gun at Bethany, but she stared at me. "You're not that heartless. You're not a monster. You fucking love Sage just as much as I do."

"I *am* a monster." I curled my lips into a smirk at her. "And you know it too."

"Stop crying, Sage," Laila said through her sniffles. "He's not going to kill you."

A low chuckle escaped my lips. "You're right, sweetheart. I'm not going to kill Sage. My plan was never to kill her. The only one of us who is going to kill someone tonight is you. It's your choice who dies. Bethany … Sage …" I lowered the gun to Sage's belly. "Or the baby in Sage's belly."

Tears rippled in Laila's widened eyes. "The what?"

"The baby."

Laila dropped her gun, her hands beginning to tremble uncontrollably. "S-stop. Y-you're lying to me. Sage isn't pregnant." She doubled over onto the floor and stared up at me, shaking her head. "She's not pregnant." She looked over at Sage. "Y-you're not pregnant, right?"

I pressed the gun against Sage's belly, wanting her to comply. Sage sniffled and nodded down at Laila, following my lie. A lie that Laila could never know about. I would fuck Sage every waking moment of my life to get her pregnant before Laila had a chance to schedule a doctor's appointment, if that was what it took.

"No!" Laila cried, doubling over once more, but this time, she was clutching her belly, as if the pain inside her was unbearable. And I hated her for it because it shouldn't have been this hard to choose.

"Choose, Laila," I growled.

"I-I want the baby!" she cried. "I want the baby."

"Prove it." I kicked her gun toward her. "Prove it to us."

With shaky hands, Laila grabbed the gun and slowly stood up, using my desk for support. She pointed the gun at Bethany's head once more and stared into her eyes.

"I don't want to kill anyone," she cried. "Please, Constantino. I'll do … I'll do anything else you want me to do to Bethany. I'll torture her if you ask me to. Just don't make me into a monster."

"You've already been a monster to Sage. To me." I grabbed her by the back of the neck and growled into her ear, "This is what happens when you get yourself into trouble. Do it."

"I don't want to kill anyone!" she cried.

"Enough with the fucking hysterics," I snapped, taking her left hand and wrapping it around the handle of my gun. I forced her to curl her finger right over the trigger, so when I pulled it, *she* would really be the one to pull it.

She would be the one to end any chances of Sage getting pregnant again. She would choose her best friend over a family for good, and I would have to leave her.

"Three," I warned.

She stared at her best friend, the gun in her right hand trembling against her forehead.

"Two."

Tears streaked with black mascara rolled down Bethany's cheeks as she begged Laila not to shoot through her cloth gag.

"One."

I yanked back the trigger of the unloaded gun.

"No!" Laila screamed as she shot Bethany through the skull and unloaded all the bullets into that bitch's brain.

63

laila

I DROPPED THE GUN, collapsed onto my knees, and cried out for Bethany. Blood poured out of the holes in the center of her forehead. Yet she stared up at me through wide eyes. Dead. Completely and utterly dead.

"No!" I cried, tears streaming down my cheeks. Pain ripped through me, my insides twisting and turning. I laid my fingers on her cheeks and pulled her head off the ground, holding it in my hands. "I-I'm a killer. A killer."

When I had married Constantino, he had promised that I would never dirty my hands in the family business ... but tonight, I had murdered my best friend. I cried out. I'd killed her! She was dead. Cold. Gone. Lying in my arms lifelessly.

I sat with her on the floor for hours, curling up by her side and wetting my hair with her blood. How could this happen? How could I betray her trust? Kill her dead? She was a bitch, but ... but why couldn't Constantino have done it?

And while I wanted to continue to blame Constantino for this, I had been the one to pull the trigger. I had been the one to make that choice. I had been the one who … said I loved Sage but hurt her by staying with Bethany.

Sage had broken down into tears when Constantino said I would be the one to choose if she lived because … she didn't think I would choose her. She didn't trust me. She had expressed her dislike for Bethany, and I hadn't listened so much that she decided to not even tell me about how my best friend had tossed soda all over her and Poppy.

More tears fell from my eyes, but I finally released Bethany from my grasp and sat up. I stared down at her and wiped my cheeks, my gaze narrowing by the second. It wasn't my fault that she was dead. She had … continued to snoop into my business after I told her not to worry about it.

She had betrayed me.

She had …

I dropped my gaze to the floor and pressed my lips together, remembering the first day in Italy with Sage, how I had told her about wanting plastic surgery just because Bethany had made me an insecure mess, how I had gotten lip injections, chin lipo, and Botox to stay in the family's *in* club.

I liked looking pretty, but …

I glanced up at my husband and Sage, who hadn't left the room yet.

Being pretty wasn't everything in life. I would take having a family over being attractive any fucking day.

"I'm sorry," I sobbed, forcing myself to stand. "I'm sorry I took so long to choose you both."

Sage looked away from me, her head down and her cheeks stained with dried tears. I wanted to reach out for her, to comfort her, to tell her that it would never happen again, but I … I had fucked up so much. She didn't trust me.

And I didn't blame her.

"I'm sorry," I whispered, staring at my husband.

He grimaced and peered down at Bethany. "Are you done with her?"

"Yes," I whispered.

"Riccardo!" Constantino called.

Riccardo opened the door.

"Get the men to remove the body from my office and clean this place up. And call Pietro to come here too." Constantino looked at me. "We need to talk about his place in the family."

"Why Pietro?" I whispered, eyes widening. "You're not going to force me to kill him too?"

"No."

"Pietro is"—Riccardo glanced into the hallway—"busy right now."

Constantino rolled his eyes and followed Riccardo, who carried Bethany out of the room. They shut the door, leaving me alone with Sage. Sage sat on the edge of the couch, pressing her body against the arm and staring at the wall to her right.

I slowly approached her and sat on the other side, knowing that she probably didn't want me anywhere near her. But I wanted to make it up to her for being such a bitch, for letting Bethany treat her that way, and for believing Bethany blindly.

"How can I make it up to you?" I whispered, staring at the bloodied ground.

Sage didn't respond, so we sat in another long silence.

"I know you probably hate me," I whispered. "But—"

"I don't hate you," she said, gaze locked on her legs now. "I'm not allowed to have feelings in this relationship. You've told everyone, including me, that I am just your toy … so whatever happens between us means … nothing."

"Sage," I whispered, voice cracking, "I didn't mean it. I fucking love you."

Tears trembled in Sage's eyes, but she looked over at me. I wanted her to tell me that she loved me too, that she would never leave me, that she would be here with us forever. But I … didn't want to rely on her, like I had relied on Bethany.

She wouldn't lead me astray, but I … was scared.

"So what if you love me?" she asked. "The only place you show it is in private. To everyone in the family, I'm Constantino's mistress, the woman who is sleeping with your husband, the measly help who is having an affair." She tore her gaze away. "I don't know if I want that for the rest of my life."

I scooted closer to her and grabbed her hand. She tensed, but didn't pull away.

"You won't be anymore. Please, give me another chance." I grasped her hand tighter. "I can't lose you, Sage, especially not now. I will do anything you want me to do. I'll tell the family what you really mean to me, who you are, why you're here. And that … I love you."

She stayed quiet for a long time. "Did you only choose me because of the baby?"

"What?"

"Did you only choose me over Bethany because Constantino told you that I was pregnant?"

"No," I said immediately. Because it was true.

I had chosen Sage over Bethany last night, but I hadn't wanted to kill.

She peered over at me again, tears threatening to fall. "Will you always choose me?"

I drew my thumb across her cheek. "I promise."

And before I knew it, Sage threw her arms around my torso, tucked her head into my shoulder, and cried into me. "I love you too."

64

constantino

"WE NEED TO HAVE A LITTLE TALK," I growled at Pietro, snatching him by the back of the neck and yanking him away from some pretty girl who probably only wanted him for his money. I shoved him through the crowd and back toward my office. "Now."

"The fuck do you want?" he said, trying to tear himself away from me.

But I clutched him tighter and pushed him into the back hallway.

When I walked into my office with Pietro in tow, Sage was holding on to my wife with her face buried into Laila's neck as she sobbed. I clenched my jaw and shoved Pietro farther into the room, shutting the door behind me.

I had completely fucked up.

I should've told Sage what was happening. At least that I would put a gun to her stomach, force her to lie, and then push Laila to the edge in order to get her to kill her best friend. Sage's brain must've been scrambled because she looked more than terrified.

And for longer than a moment, she had looked afraid that Laila wouldn't choose her.

That was what had really broken me.

"Riccardo," I called from the office, shoving Pietro down in a seat.

Riccardo peered into the room. "Boss?"

"Bring Sage back to her apartment," I said.

"Sage is staying here," Laila said, holding her tightly. "You promised that if I did everything you asked, you would let me see her again. I ..." She stared at me with heavy tears in her eyes. "I just killed my best friend, as you'd asked."

I pressed my lips together. She had killed her best friend, but not quickly enough. She had chosen the baby, not Sage and not her own husband. Part of me didn't give a fuck that those words had come out of her mouth because I'd do anything to keep her as mine. I was a monster who didn't give a fuck about what she thought.

But Sage ...

How would this affect her?

I wasn't supposed to love her. I wasn't supposed to fall for her. I wasn't supposed to feel anything for her. But here I was, in love with two women, as my father had once claimed to be when he continued to sneak out and cheat on my mother.

"You'll see Sage later," I said, my tone final. "We're not done."

Laila burst out into tears. "We're done! I'm not killing anyone else!"

Pietro lifted his head, about to stand. "Kill anyone else? Laila, what'd he make you do?"

I grabbed him by the shoulder and shoved him back into the chair, so he didn't even have a chance to comfort my wife. This little conniving bastard wanted to take my place as boss and as Laila's husband. He had always been a little too close to her.

"Sage," I growled, glaring at my brother, "out. Now."

Sage quickly stood from the couch and scurried past me.

I snatched her arm before she could escape and leaned down to whisper in her ear, hoping it was enough for now, though I knew it wouldn't be. Nothing could turn back time, not after she had just watched someone die at her feet. "I'm sorry. I should've told you my plans."

While Sage stared down at the floor and nodded, I could tell that she only did so because she was afraid. Maybe of me. My chest tightened, and I peered over at Riccardo, telling him with my eyes to keep her safe because this was breaking my heart.

All of it.

I did so much. So fucking much for this family. And nobody appreciated it.

Once Sage scurried out of the room with Riccardo, I shut the door and turned toward my brother. I snatched a fistful of his hair, ready to finally unleash on him, and hurled him to the ground by it. The chair clattered onto the floor, and he scrambled back to his feet.

"The fuck are you doing?" he growled. "I thought you wanted to talk."

"Next time you fucking flirt with my wife, put Sage down, or threaten my position in this family, I will put a bullet straight through your empty fucking head, Pietro. No more chances. I have too much drama to deal with, and I don't need you stirring up any other shit. Do you understand me?"

"I don't flirt with your wife," he said through gritted teeth.

I pulled my gun out of my waistband and held it to his head. "Bullshit."

He stared up at it, then at me. "Fine."

"Say it," I growled, pressing it to his forehead.

"I won't flirt with your wife or threaten your position."

"And what about Sage?"

"I won't put her down," he snapped, grimacing. "But I don't like that bitch."

"She's not a bitch," Laila said, sitting down with her arms crossed. "Don't call her that."

"Fine," Pietro said, slamming his hands into my chest. "You happy?"

I shoved my gun back into my waistband and glared at him. "Get out."

After he scurried out the door, I turned to Laila. "I said, get out."

"I don't get it," Laila cried, Pietro now gone. "Why are you still angry with me?"

"I'm not angry with you," I said, avoiding eye contact with her so I didn't fucking explode.

I wanted to go home. I wanted not to constantly worry about the FBI. I wanted to have a family again. But Laila … choosing the fucking baby over me, over Sage? I would never have done that to her. If she could get pregnant and had a problem with childbirth, where I had to choose between her and the baby, I would *always* fucking choose her.

If roles were reversed, would she choose me?

"Go back home," I said, sitting at my desk and busying myself with work.

She slammed her hands down onto it. "Constantino, you're angry. Why?"

"Because," I growled, finally losing it, "you chose the baby."

Laila stared at me like I was insane. "Over Bethany, yes, I did. What's the problem?"

"The problem was that you had a choice between Sage and Bethany, not a baby and Bethany." I balled my hands into tight fists by my sides and stood. "And you fucking chose the baby over Sage, over me, over *us*. The baby was what pushed you over the edge, not the two people you claimed to love." Hot tears burned my eyes, but I wouldn't let my wife see me cry.

I had been the strongest man alive for her. I couldn't be weak now.

While I expected her to roll her eyes or deny that it had ever happened, she dropped her gaze. "I'm sorry."

"Is that how you really feel?"

"What?" she whispered, peering back up at me. "Of course not."

But that was a lie.

I had killed too many people to know that when they were in a desperate position, they spoke the truth. Maybe Bethany could lie in that kind of position, but it was hard to do when there was a gun pointed at someone you loved.

And Laila had never been a good liar.

"I'm sorry," she whispered, moving closer to me. She gently grasped my face. "Don't cry." Tears streamed down her face, her shoulders caving in. "Please, don't cry, Constantino. I will always choose you. No matter what."

I ripped myself away and turned my back toward her, wiping the tears from my eyes. "Leave."

"Constantino, please."

"Leave, Laila," I growled. "I need a break."

"A break?" she whispered. "A break from us?"

I stayed quiet. I loved my wife, but I ... couldn't do this right now. I couldn't.

"Leave," I said harsher, not turning around.

She shuffled toward the door, whispered, "I love you," and then walked out of my life.

65

laila

TEARS STREAMED DOWN MY CHEEKS. I hurried through the grinding bodies in the club and headed straight toward the exit. My husband was … tired of me. After all these years, he had finally decided that he didn't want to put up with my shit any longer.

A sob escaped my mouth, but the music drowned it out.

I didn't blame him. I had been a hormonal wreck lately.

This was what I deserved.

Drunk men and women pushed back against me, and I stumbled through the crowd.

While I had killed Bethany unwillingly, I didn't feel stuck anymore, didn't feel the need for her approval. I was free for the first time in the past few years. I was dying on the inside because my husband didn't want me around, but this was the first time in a long time that I felt so good without her.

So, so good.

"Laila!" someone said from my right.

I ignored them—because it wasn't Constantino or Sage—and hurried through the front door. Tears blurred my vision. I glared across the street at the blacked-out SUV and headed straight for my car. I needed to get out of here now.

After shutting myself away in my car, I screamed at the top of my lungs. My heart broke, shattering into a million little pieces. I had just killed my best friend, watched my husband threaten to kill his brother, and hurt the one man who I loved the most.

At least Sage … at least she had forgiven me.

I hoped …

Once I turned on the car, I gripped the steering wheel and sped off into the New York City night. Constantino should've never brought Sage into the room—or into the damn club—while all that shit went down. And to hold a gun to her head, then her stomach?!

He had frightened her to no end. She had collapsed into my arms and cried so hard. I wanted to go find her, to comfort her. But I was too broken up over my husband asking me to leave him alone. Because for how long?

How long would he refuse to be with me? Forever?

I slammed my foot harder on the accelerator and gritted my teeth, crying out. I had screwed up so badly. Too badly! I should've dumped Bethany a long time ago. I shouldn't have accepted the way she treated Sage. If I had loved her the way I'd said I did, I wouldn't have let that happen.

The light turned red in front of me, and I slammed on the brakes.

"I love her," I whispered, body lurching forward from the sudden stop.

I wasn't trying to convince myself. There wasn't a doubt in my mind that I loved her. But I … had also loved Bethany in a different way. I'd loved her because I wanted to be like her. I wanted people to love me the way they loved her. To admire me the way they admired her.

Why had those words come out of my mouth? *I choose the baby?!* I had meant to say that I chose a family, but I wanted a baby so badly. Yet I didn't want to lose Sage for more than just that. I didn't want to lose her because I loved her.

More than a friend. More than I loved Bethany.

When the light turned green, I gently tapped on the accelerator once more. I wanted to go home and paint my heartache away. I wanted to sculpt. To draw. To throw myself back into my art and finally be happy again. I had spent the past few years depressed without it.

Red and blue lights flashed behind me.

Fuck.

I swallowed hard and pulled over to the side of the road, hoping to God that they just needed to go around me. And when the police car passed me, speeding up ahead through traffic, I blew out a low breath and slumped my shoulders forward.

Thank God.

After glancing back into my rearview mirror, I merged back into traffic. I gripped the steering wheel hard and drove toward the skyrise. My gaze flickered back up into the rearview mirror, spotting a blacked-out SUV three cars back.

Immediately, I turned down a street that led away from my home. And so did the SUV.

Fuck.

Fuck. Fuck. Fuck. Fuck. Fuck. Fuck.

When I turned right again, they followed. I drove slowly as I desperately tried to figure out what to do, who to call, where to go. I didn't have that much gas left in the car. I would run out sooner or later, and they'd … stop me.

Arrest me.

Take me away.

And maybe even put me in prison.

66

sage

"I CHOOSE THE BABY," *Laila says, smiling at me as she points the gun at my head. "Not you."*

"L-Laila," I sob, holding my hands up. "Please, don't do this."

She presses the gun against my temple. "It's never been you, Sage."

"Laila," I whimper. "P-please."

"Do it," Bethany says from behind her. "Kill her. She's trying to steal your husband."

"Please, Laila, I love you," I beg. "Don't kill me."

Laila pulls the safety off the gun. "You're trying to steal my husband. I've never loved you. I only loved you for what you could do for me, for the baby you could give me. I choose the baby, Sage. I would never choose you."

And then she pulls the trigger.

Screaming at the top of my lungs, I sat up in the bed and clutched my blankets to my chest. Tears streamed down my cheeks. The dawn streamed into the room from the open curtains. I sniffled and clutched my tight chest.

Maybe I was misremembering.

My mind was scrambled, my emotions all over the place. I had never been in that situation before, never had a gun pointed at me like that, never seen someone die right before my eyes. I had to be remembering wrong.

Right?

Suddenly, my bedroom door swung open, and Riccardo barreled into the room, one hand on his gun.

"What's wrong?" he asked, scanning the room. "Is someone in here with you?" he asked, rushing to my closet and tearing open the door.

"No," I whispered, tears trembling in my eyes. "Nobody is here."

"Why were you screaming?" he asked, cutting his gaze to me.

I pulled the blankets closer to my chest. "I had a bad dream."

Facial expression softening, he slid his gun back into his waistband and dropped his tense shoulders. After giving me a curt nod, he walked back to the bedroom door and slipped into the hallway, leaving me alone with all these horrible thoughts.

Did she … really choose the baby over me? I stared at the blank wall across from my bed and pressed a hand to my mouth, muffling a sob. I couldn't remember. Things had happened so quickly that I couldn't process it all.

After sitting there for a while, I forced myself to lie back down and close my eyes. But every time I did, I saw Laila. I saw Bethany's corpse. Heard their lies, their bullying. All of it. Their words were so loud that I couldn't even think.

I snapped my eyes back open and scrambled out of the bed and went to my closet. If I stayed here any longer, I would go insane. I needed fresh air. I needed to breathe. I needed to get my mind off Laila and Constantino for a couple of hours, a day, maybe even longer. I had been doing nothing but spending time with them for the past few weeks straight.

Once I threw on some clothes, I hurried out into the foyer of my apartment and grabbed my belongings. Riccardo sat on the living room couch, watching something on his phone.

He glanced up at me. "Where are you going?"

"Out."

He stood up.

"You don't have to come with me," I said, wanting to be alone.

"If I don't come with you, he'll kill me," Riccardo said.

Grimacing, I marched out into the hallway with Riccardo behind me. We walked down the hall in silence and stepped onto the elevator. I crossed my arms over my chest to keep myself as small as possible. I didn't want anyone talking to me, and I sure as hell hoped I didn't see Laila and Constantino this morning.

Why would she choose the baby? Did she only choose me because I could give her a family? Is that the only reason she loves me?

I had stupidly told her that I loved her back, but I'd actually truly meant it.

When we stepped into the underground parking lot, a light wind chilled my skin. I slipped into the backseat of Riccardo's SUV and rested my head against the window as he drove through the city at sunbreak. Part of me wished there were traffic, so I could stay in the car and ignore the world forever.

At a red light, Riccardo peered in the rearview mirror. "Do you want to talk about it?"

Riccardo wants to talk? He rarely even spoke two words to me.

I stayed quiet. When the light turned green, he gently hit the accelerator.

"When I took my first life, I was shaken up too," he said.

I arched a brow and peeked into the mirror at him. "I … I didn't kill anyone."

"Oh."

God, this is awkward.

"Not even Bethany?" he asked.

"No, Laila did."

"Damn," he said, a deep chuckle escaping his mouth. "About time."

My lips curled into a small smile. I almost couldn't believe that Riccardo—the man who seemed to *hate* me—had decided now was a time to be chatty. And while I didn't want to laugh at someone dying a horrid death, we were talking about Bethany of all people.

Riccardo glanced into the rearview mirror, lips set in a soft smile when he saw me. "Bethany was a bitch, so don't worry about it. She got what she deserved. This had been a long time coming. I'd thought Constantino would do it sooner."

Warmth exploded through my chest. I sat back in my seat and looked out the window as we pulled up to the curb. Riccardo parked his car across the street from the coffee shop and then opened my door. I hopped out of the car and headed inside.

"Tea, please," I said to the barista, sliding my card across the counter.

After paying for my drink, I stepped to the side.

Riccardo leaned against the counter with one forearm and peered over at me. "Two chocolate chip cookies," he said to the young woman. "Warm them up for us."

My lips curled into another soft smile. All this time, I'd thought that he hated me.

When the barista gave him the cookies, he handed me one. "Don't tell anyone about this."

67

sage

"YOU'RE HERE EARLY," Poppy said, bobbing up the steps to the second floor of the coffee shop.

Riccardo grabbed his phone and his third cookie of the day, then walked to a table across the floor. He had been surprisingly nice to me so far today. I mean, I would hope that he would because I had literally witnessed someone get murdered right in front of my eyes. But still ...

He was never nice.

"You know you don't have to sit alone," I called to him.

But he didn't even look up at me. Back to being the cold, hard-headed asshole.

"You have to tell me all about your trip!" Poppy cheered, sipping on tea. "How was it?"

"Good," I gushed, attempting to forget about last night. *Think about all the good times I have had with them, not the cold-blooded murder that I witnessed.* "We went to the coast of Italy for a week, and it was the most beautiful place that I have ever seen!"

"Oh my gosh, stop!" she said, eyes wide. "I've always wanted to go. Was the food good?"

"Amazing!"

"And the eye candy?"

My cheeks flushed. "They were cute, but …"

I hadn't really checked them out. I had been with Laila and Constantino the entire time, who were both jealous, possessive monsters that sorta, kinda turned me on more than they should've.

"Oh, come on," she hummed. "No sexy Italian men? Or … women?"

My cheeks flushed even harder. "Women?"

She shrugged. "If that's your thing. Laila seemed very protective of you when I talked to her. I figured that you and she might have a thing going on?" She leaned across the table and placed her hand on mine. "And if you do, don't worry about it. I don't judge on little things like that."

I laughed nervously. "Poppy, Laila has a husband."

Her eyes widened, her lips forming an O. "Who?"

"That guy you met a couple of weeks ago in my apartment."

"Oh, I thought he was another one of those big, scary guys who follows you around all the time." She glanced over at Riccardo and giggled. "Like him." Her gaze lingered for a long moment, her pupils growing wide.

Does she have a crush on him?

I shook my head and pushed the thought away. If I wasn't still trying to get over this whole *murder Bethany and Laila only saved me for the baby* type of thing, I would hook them up together. But I couldn't get my mind right.

"Why does he follow you around anyway?" Poppy asked, still gazing at him.

"Oh, um …" *Think quick!* "My family has … money."

Fuck, that is the worst thing to say. But it was much better than *I'm connected to the mob.*

"Makes sense," she said, finally pulling her gaze away.

Thankfully, she didn't push it any further. Instead, she dug into her chocolate-filled croissant, cutting it in half with a knife, and entertained me with the latest gossip in her life, which was apparently a lot because she talked for nearly half the day.

At four p.m., she yawned. "Gosh, we've been here for hours. Sorry for keeping you."

My lips curled into a smile. "Don't worry about it. This was … nice. Very nice."

So much less drama than Constantino and Laila. It felt good to have a friend outside of the family. Even if Riccardo was becoming a friend too, all he thought about was the family, climbing the ranks, and doing business.

I appreciated it, but it got boring after a while.

Once I packed up my belongings, I stood with Poppy and walked with her and Riccardo to the exit. When we walked out of the coffee shop, three guys were pushing and shoving each other on the sidewalk. One slammed his hands into a female bystander's chest, sending her flying into the window. Glass shattered everywhere, onto the sidewalk and into the building.

Riccardo scowled and pushed us to the side so we were out of the way. "Wait here."

Poppy looped her arm around mine and stared in horror at the scene. "Do you think we should help her?" she whispered, chewing on the inside of her cheek. Her gaze dropped to the woman's back when she stood up, and then Poppy leaped forward. "Gosh, you're covered in blood!"

I swallowed hard, unsure about what to do. Riccardo had told me to stay put—and after the past few days I'd had, I didn't want to disobey any orders—but the woman's entire back was covered in a sheet of blood and glass.

"Sage, come help me pull this glass out of her back," Poppy said, ushering the woman to a small bench at the end of the block.

Poppy knelt by her side, brow furrowed, and examined the glass lodged into this woman's flesh.

Once I took one look at Riccardo, who had his hands full, shoving the men back from each other, I hurried over to Poppy and the woman. After dropping my purse, I crouched down behind the woman and pulled my sleeve over my hand so her blood wouldn't come into contact with my skin. While I felt sorry for her, I didn't know this woman at all. And in NYC, you didn't know who was clean. It was dirty as hell out here sometimes.

I gently grasped a jagged piece of glass from the woman's back and pulled it from her flesh, wincing from the mere sound of it. But before I could pull another piece from her flesh, someone grabbed my arms from behind and slapped a hand over my mouth. They pressed something circular and cold to the back of my spine.

"Don't fucking scream, or I'll blow your brains out."

68

constantino

AFTER I'D SLEPT at my damn desk last night because I didn't want to come home to face Laila and then working nonstop at the club with Pietro, who wanted to be helpful for once, I stepped into the elevator in my building and hit the button to the top floor.

I leaned against the metal wall and pressed on my temple, my head pounding since I had woken up. Usually, Laila would grab me some aspirin whenever I had a headache, but today, I had gone without them completely. But, fuck, I needed one now.

When the elevator doors opened, I stepped onto my floor and tapped my code into the lock. The door clicked open, and I walked into the quiet house. I expected Laila to be home, curled up in the bed, sobbing that she had just killed her best friend.

But there was nothing.

Not even a muffled cry.

Once I grabbed some medicine, I walked to our bedroom and tried to figure out what I would say to her. If she gave me the silent treatment, she was pissed. But still, I wanted to see her, to kiss her, to tell her that we would work this out.

We always did.

"Laila," I called, knocking on the door before I opened it.

The bedroom was empty, the bed untouched. I pressed my lips together and stepped into the room, peeking into her walk-in closet.

"Laila, are you in here?"

Silence.

My stomach twisted, and I pulled out my phone. No messages from her. No calls.

I tapped on her contact and put the phone on speaker as I walked back to the kitchen to grab a snack from the fridge. The phone rang three times, and then her voice drifted through the speaker.

"Hi. This is Laila. Sorry I missed your call. Please leave me a message."

Fuck.

Ignoring me was even worse than the silent treatment.

After calling her five more times and texting her about twenty, I sighed and placed my phone down. Where did she go? It didn't even look like she had come home at all last night, no crumbs on the kitchen counter, like she usually left during breakfast.

Once I pulled off my suit jacket and tossed it onto the couch, I picked up my phone again and dialed her number. I waited and waited and waited until she finally picked the goddamn thing up.

"Hello?" Pietro said through the phone.

"Pietro," I growled, "where the fuck is she?"

"Who?"

"Don't play stupid," I snapped, tugging off my tie. "Laila."

"Don't know," he said. "Someone found her phone on the ground of the club after you left. Must've dropped it here when she ran out last night. Surprised she hasn't come to get it yet. Before you fucking … *you know* … to Bethany, she was glued to the thing."

My stomach dropped. *Fuck no.*

"She's gone?" I whispered, remembering how I hadn't seen the tinted-out SUV outside the club when I left.

I thought that they had given up, but … they must've fucking taken her. They had taken my wife!

"Pietro, search the cameras outside the club for Laila. Get back to me as soon as fucking possible. I'll be down there in twenty minutes."

While my thoughts were racing, I tried to stay calm. Tried to think clearly. I wouldn't let those fuckers win. I wouldn't let them trick me into making a mistake. But I also needed to save Laila. I didn't want them harming a fucking hair on her head.

After snatching my keys, I ran to the elevator and hit the bottom button, slamming on the Close Door button. What felt like an eternity later, I reached the lowest floor and sprinted straight for my car. Those assholes would pay for kidnapping my wife. I would cut their fucking—

My phone buzzed. I slid into the driver's seat of my car and answered the call.

"Laila?" I asked.

"This is Riccardo," he said. "We have a problem."

"What is it?" I growled. "Did you find Laila?"

"Laila is missing?" he muttered. "Shit. Shit. Shit. Shit. Shit."

My stomach twisted even more. "Tell me you're with Sage."

He paused for a moment. "There was an incident at the coffee shop today. I can't find her."

"God," I shouted. "I'm going to fucking kill you too! Meet me at the club. Now!"

I slammed my finger down on the End Call button and sped like a maniac to the club, hoping that by the time I showed up, both my girls would be there. But when I parked my car and sprinted into my office, the girls were nowhere to be found.

They were gone.

And for all I knew, they could be dead too.

69

laila

I CHOKED on water by the mouthful.

After they finished pouring water over the wet rag that covered my mouth, my shoulders jerked up, and I coughed until my throat burned. Tears streamed down my cheeks. My mind was heavy, broken. I wanted Constantino.

"What'd he make you do?" one of the men asked, pulling the rag off me.

"Nothing."

"It didn't look like nothing," he growled, smacking me hard across the cheek. "What was it?"

"Nothing!" I screamed.

"Come on," the other *good cop* cooed. "Give us something, Laila."

"Fuck you!" I said, spitting at him.

If they thought they'd break me, they were wrong. I was already broken. I had killed my best friend. I had surrendered everything for a family. And these dickheads thought waterboarding me would force me to give up vital information that would put Constantino in prison?

Fuck that!

After seizing the rag from the *bad cop*, he frowned down at me. "Don't make me do this."

"Do it," I growled through gritted teeth. "I have nothing to hide and nothing to say to you fuckers."

He draped the rag back over my mouth and nose. I struggled against my restraints, my wrists nearly bleeding with how much I tugged and pulled in an attempt to break free, to escape. They had been interrogating me for … hours, days maybe.

They poured another gallon of water through the rag. Tears burned my eyes. I opened my mouth in an attempt to breathe because it felt like I was drowning. But I wasn't going to break. I wasn't going to break. I wasn't going to fucking break for them.

When the water stopped, they ripped the rag off me once more. My eyes stung, and my nose burned. I coughed until I tasted blood. I wanted this torture to finally be over, but I refused to give up any information about my family that could send anyone to jail.

I wouldn't betray them.

Someone banged on a metal door to my right. I finally opened my eyes and blinked back the tears, watching a man shove in another two sobbing women. My vision was so blurry that I couldn't make out who was who or if I knew them.

Chances were, I did.

"Laila," Sage sobbed from the corner of the room.

"No," I cried. "No!"

This couldn't be happening. This couldn't fucking be happening.

When my vision finally cleared enough, Sage and Poppy came into my sight. I cried harder, chest heaving up and down, shoulders bucking back and forth. They were going to torture her the way they had with me all night.

They couldn't!

"Tie them down," the dickhead growled at the new man. "Then, get the fuck out of here."

"Let me out!" I screamed, wanting their attention on me and not on Sage. "Now!"

But the man tied Sage and Poppy up anyway.

The good cop crouched by my side. "We don't have to hurt them. Just give us information, Laila."

I spit right in his face again. "Let me out. Now! Or I will kill you myself."

The second cop grabbed my wet rag, yanked Sage's head back by her hair, and draped it over her face.

"Laila," she whimpered, voice trembling. "What's going on?" She sniffled. "P-please, don't hurt me. I-I'm s-scar—"

Before she could finish her sentence, they poured a gallon of water over her face. Her body convulsed as she desperately tried to breathe, but she must've been swallowing water by the mouthful.

"Stop!" I screamed at the top of my lungs, snapping my shoulders back and forth. Tears streamed down my cheeks.

They couldn't hurt her. Not her. She was so vulnerable, especially after what had happened with Bethany. She hadn't been in this family for more than a few weeks, and she wouldn't be able to handle it.

"Please, torture me!"

"Tell us, Laila," the good cop hummed, "and we won't hurt her."

My eyes burned. I didn't want to tell them shit. I wouldn't get my husband thrown in prison. But, fuck, I didn't want them to hurt her. I couldn't watch or listen to her scream out in agony, sobbing and begging for them to stop.

"She's pregnant. Please," I whispered, hoping that they'd have some sympathy.

If begging for her life wasn't going to do it, then maybe a baby would. But when those words left my mouth, I knew that Sage would have a hard time believing that I cared about her. Constantino had brought it up last night, so Sage must've at least been thinking about it.

I stared at Sage as tears flowed down my cheeks, hoping she'd understand that everything I had said was to protect her. I loved her, no matter what. I wanted her forever—and not just because she could give us a family. If I had wanted that from the beginning, we would've gone the surrogate or adoption route instead of picking up a random woman at our bar.

"Please, don't hurt her or the baby," I begged.

"If only we could do that," the shithead cop said, walking over to me.

He hurled his fist right at my face and knocked me out cold.

70

constantino

MY BULLET WHIZZED through a guard's head, and the corpse smacked hard onto the ground with a thud. I stepped over him and ripped open the door to an abandoned building, rage pumping through my veins.

They weren't fucking cops. They were monsters for taking women.

I slammed my fist into another fucker's jaw, sending him to the ground. Hurling my foot into his head over and over and over, I didn't stop until he wasn't moving. Pietro, Riccardo, and a couple of other guards took care of the other men around me.

"Please, stop!" a woman cried from down the hall. "Stop! Please, don't hurt her!"

Feet moving faster than my mind, I sprinted down the hallway toward the plea for help. It had taken us two hours to track down the SUV that had been hanging out near The Syndicate, using street cameras around the city with the aid of a dirty cop.

Two hours where my girls had had to endure torture.

A single guard stood at the door to what looked like a basement. Adrenaline kicked in when Laila screamed at the top of her lungs for them to stop torturing Sage. I shot three bullets into the man's skull, then sprinted down the stairs.

One man grabbed Laila, the other Sage, who had a wet cloth covering her face. She coughed, her neck red, which looked to be from a lack of oxygen. With Pietro behind me, I lunged forward, shooting the man who held Laila straight in the head.

Then, I tossed my gun because I didn't have any bullets left and finished the other guy off with my fists until he was knocked out cold on the floor. My hands were covered in blood. My girls were still restrained.

"They're not cops," I growled. "Men from another family." I snagged him by the hair and hurled him across the room to my brother's feet. "Take him to the house and interrogate him. I want to know everything the girls told him and everything he has spoken to the FBI about."

Pietro yanked him up by the throat and dragged him out of the room and through the back to our cars. Other guards walked into the room, picking up the mess that we had been forced to make by killing those fucking bastards.

"What about her, boss?" Riccardo asked, looking over at Sage's friend.

"Pay her to keep her mouth shut," I said through gritted teeth. "And get her out of here."

"Come on," Riccardo said, picking her up off the concrete. "You're coming with me."

Once they disappeared, I walked over to Laila, who was a snotting and bleeding mess. After I pulled her restraints off her, she grabbed her stomach and sat up, wincing from the pain that I could only imagine she was in right now.

"We're bringing you to Dr. Lin."

"No." She pushed me away. "Make sure Sage is okay first."

"Laila, you have multiple open wounds."

"Constantino," she snapped, "take care of Sage. I'll be fine."

While I didn't want my wife to be in any more pain than she already was in, I hurried over to Sage and helped her out of her restraints. She cried hysterically, grasping on to me tightly and sobbing into my shoulder.

I took her in my arms and brought her out into the car. Then, I walked back into the basement to find Laila stumbling to the door. I whisked her off her feet.

"No walking for you," I murmured against her lips. "You're mine to take care of now."

71

laila

"I WANT them both tested for drugs in their system," Constantino
ordered Dr. Lin.

I walked with Sage into the doctor's office that I had been to
about a million times while Constantino and I were attempting to
get pregnant. Dr. Lin had been paid off many times over to keep her
mouth shut about all the business we did.

She was in the business of money, and we had more than enough
of it.

Holding my stomach, I sat in one of the rooms and lay back in
the bed. Bruises and wounds covered my body. Constantino helped
me out of my shirt so a couple of her assistants could stitch up my
wounds.

It hurt. Badly.

But I wanted to be strong for Sage. I wanted to prove myself to
her. These past few days had been a complete mess for her, and I
didn't want her to leave because of it. We would get through this,
like Constantino had told me.

Once my wounds were closed, the assistant gave me a small

plastic bottle with a label that had my name written across it in black Sharpie.

"We need a sample of your urine. Do you need help getting to the restroom?"

I slid off the bed and stumbled toward the restroom. "No."

After peeing in the cup, I returned to my room, where Sage sat on the bed alone, crying. When she saw me, she threw her arms around me and pulled me into a tight hug.

"I'm sorry," she whispered over and over. "I'm sorry. I'm so sorry."

"What're you sorry for?" I asked, tucking some hair behind her ear. "You did so amazing tonight. We should be the ones apologizing for putting you in that situation. You should've never been in harm's way."

"I-i-it's not that," she said, snotting.

Handing her a tissue, I took her face in my hands. "Then, what is it?"

"I don't know how to say this," Sage whispered, tears trembling in her eyes. "But I need to tell you because I can't ..." She bit back a sob. "I don't know if I can handle this anymore, Laila. I'm not ... I'm not really pregnant."

My eyes widened slowly. "Wh-what?"

They had ... both been lying to me? Constantino had lied so I'd kill Bethany?

Sage dropped to her knees. "Please don't be angry with Constantino. He has only ever looked out for you and wants the best for your relationship. I'm so sorry that I went along with his lie, but I need you to know before our test results come back, i-in case they can tell. Forgive me."

"I-it's okay, Sage," I stuttered.

But they had lied to me. How would that ever be okay? How could I trust them?

"No," Sage sobbed, shaking her head. "It's not. I'm so sorry."

After a couple of moments, Constantino walked back into the room. "Laila—"

"You lied," I said blankly.

"What?"

"About Sage being pregnant."

Constantino frowned, but didn't look at Sage in an attempt to blame her for telling me, which was one of the reasons why I loved that man. But still … he had lied to me about this. He had … given me false information in order for me to kill Bethany.

And, *fuck*, I needed to get over it already.

If I didn't want this to seem like it had all been for the baby—because it hadn't been—then I would leave it as it was. I didn't care that Sage wasn't pregnant. Sure, I wished that she could officially become part of the family, but if we had to wait for that, then we would wait.

Lying though?

"If I had told you the truth, you would've let me kill Sage," he said, his words a slap in the fucking face. He pressed his lips together and cut his gaze away. "It doesn't matter at this moment. Let's not get into it now. We'll talk later."

And while I wanted to hash it out now, he was right. I had been tortured for the past twenty-four hours straight. I would say something stupid that I didn't mean at all. I would hurt him more than I already had.

Dr. Lin returned and gently shut the door behind herself, nervously chewing on her inner lip. She held a clipboard against her chest and swallowed hard. "It looks like neither of the girls was drugged. But …"

"But what?" Constantino asked.

Dr. Lin turned to me. "Laila," she whispered, "you're pregnant."

72

sage

"WH-WHAT?" Laila whispered, confusion etched on her face.

"You're pregnant," Dr. Lin repeated.

Laila collapsed onto her knees and sobbed, shaking her head. "No. No, you're lying."

Constantino crouched next to Laila, his eyes wide. "You're serious?"

When Dr. Lin nodded, Constantino scooped Laila into his strong arms and pulled her into the air. She wrapped her arms around his shoulders and cried into the crook of his neck. I stared at them in awe.

Or at least, I tried.

I opened my mouth and shut it about a million times, attempting to make sense of the words that Dr. Lin had just spoken. Deep down, I wanted to be happy for Laila because she had been trying to carry a child for years now. But I feared what that would mean for us … *for me.*

It was selfish. Extremely selfish.

But now that Laila was pregnant, did they even need me?

How would I add to their relationship? I didn't need to give them another child. I wasn't pregnant yet. What if they just asked me to leave, as I had caused way too many problems and conflict between them?

My stomach twisted into knots, and I found myself leaning against the door and sliding down onto the ground, wrapping my arms around my knees and staring across the room at the bland wall.

I had watched Laila kill Bethany, claiming that she did it for the baby. I had been waterboarded and tortured for the past three hours without knowing if I'd survive the night. And now … Laila was pregnant.

A series of extremely unfortunate events that all screamed that I shouldn't be here. That I wasn't meant to be with Laila and Constantino for the rest of my life. That I should disappear into the New York City streets and let them live their lives by themselves. Alone.

Without me.

"Are you okay?" Constantino asked, glancing over his shoulder yet still by Laila's side.

"Yeah, I'm fine."

And if he kept pushing it, I would probably respond with something like, *Just stressed.*

But he didn't say a word more. Instead, he nodded and turned back to his wife, who was clutching his hand and sobbing about her new baby.

Tears burned my eyes.

I didn't want to be second to Laila or even third to the baby … but here I was, being extremely selfish again. Laila and Constantino deserved this moment together. They had been waiting for it for years now.

Fuck.

After gripping my hair in my fist and talking myself *out* of tugging on it in anger, I stood up and scurried out of the room before Constantino and Laila could notice. I wanted—*needed*—to be alone here and now.

I didn't know for how long. I didn't know if I'd return tonight. The past few days had been nonstop drama, nonstop anxiety. I didn't know if I would live to see the next day, and I feared that if I stayed with Laila and Constantino for too long, I would end up like Bethany.

"Are you okay?" Riccardo asked to my left, standing in the hallway.

Once I took one long look at him, I burst into tears and sprinted down the hallway toward the exit. I didn't want to talk to anyone, didn't want to explain myself, go through the pain of being waterboarded and not having a boyfriend or a girlfriend to comfort me.

I wanted to cry. Hard.

Shoving the doors open, I stepped onto the city streets and ran down the sidewalk. Rain pounded down onto my body, drenching my clothes and matting my hair to my head. But I couldn't get myself to stop, couldn't let myself slip into a building until the storm ended.

The rain didn't help my pain, but it did a hell of a job of hiding my tears.

"Sage!" Riccardo shouted from behind me.

Instead of slowing down for him, I pushed myself faster and harder until I finally slipped in a puddle and tore the skin on my hands and knees. I dropped down into it and curled up into a ball, clutching myself and sobbing hysterically.

Riccardo pulled me into his arms and lifted me into the air.

"Put me down!" I cried.

Yet he didn't.

"Riccardo!"

"I'm sorry," he murmured, walking through the rain back the way we had come. "I should've been protecting you. This is my fault. I'm sorry."

The more he apologized, the more tears streamed down my face. I wanted to go home. I wanted to be alone. But I feared that if I was truly alone, I would break down past the point of no return. I wouldn't be able to function, wouldn't forgive myself for what had happened to me.

So, I clutched on to him as tightly as I could and cried into his shoulder.

Nearly fifty minutes later, Riccardo stepped into the lobby of the apartment building. He ignored all the stares and headed straight for the elevator, not putting me down once. When we made it to my apartment, he walked into it and set me on the couch.

"I'm not going anywhere tonight," he said. "Shower and clean yourself up. I'll be here."

But I could do none of that. Instead, I collapsed into his arms. "They're going to leave me. I am now nothing to them. They have everything they need to finally become a family, and I have no one."

73

laila

"YOU'VE BEEN WORKING on your art gala this week, right?" Constantino asked over the phone while at work. One week had passed since the night that Dr. Lin had told me I was pregnant. "Because I was thinking that we should move it forward."

"Why?" I asked, dressing for the first time in several days.

"You're pregnant, and the cops are on our asses. They don't have much, but we need to keep our name out of any bad business," he said. "Hide our shit behind a charity, and we'll be good."

While I didn't want to move the gala up, we didn't have much of a choice.

"When are you thinking?" I asked.

"Next week."

"Next week?!" I exclaimed, snapping on a necklace.

"Friday night. I've already scheduled the venue," he said.

Someone knocked on our front door, and I hurried out of my closet to answer the door. "Um, sure. Let's talk about it with Sage when you get home tonight. She's here right now, so I have to go."

After saying goodbye, I hung up the phone and opened the door.

Sage had been more than distant lately, though I wasn't sure why. I had tried to talk to her multiple times, but she only came up to the penthouse when I asked, and I couldn't leave my bed that much while I healed my wounds.

Dr. Lin had put me on strict bedrest, especially now that I was pregnant. We had been waiting forever for this moment, and I didn't want to chance anything. But I still wanted to see Sage. I hoped that she didn't think we didn't want her.

"Hi," I said, smiling.

"Did you need me for something?" she asked, stepping into the apartment.

I placed my hand on my stomach and chewed on the inside of my cheek, nervous. "Do you want to shop for baby clothes with me?" I asked. "We can grab lunch afterward and do some shopping for ourselves. My treat."

"Um …" she whispered, not meeting gazes with me. "No thanks."

"Please," I asked, sounding desperate as hell now.

While I could've ordered her to shop with me through our contract, I refused to order Sage to do anything with me anymore. It felt so wrong, so deceitful. I loved her and wanted her to come with me because she wanted to spend time with me. Not because I forced her.

"I'm not really feeling like it," she said, still turned away from me.

My stomach dropped, and I nodded. "Okay."

I wanted to share these special moments with her, but she didn't have any interest.

"Is that all?" she asked.

"Yes …" I whispered, trying not to seem *too* disappointed.

After nodding, she turned back toward the door. But before she could leave, I gently grasped her wrist and tugged her back to me. She sucked in a sharp breath and glanced up at me through her lashes, her brows drawn together. I tucked some hair behind her ear.

"Is something wrong?" I asked.

"No."

"You can tell me," I said, chest tightening. "You've been ignoring me lately. Won't come up and spend time with us like you used to. Nothing has been the same since we came home from Italy."

We'd had such a good time on vacation, and then everything had shattered.

Tears wavered in her eyes. "I'm fine."

"Sage," I whispered, my voice cracking. "Please, talk to me."

I didn't want to cry because I wished to be strong for her, but these hormones had been bad this week. Between the lingering memory that I had killed someone to being waterboarded and beaten to this …

"Sage, please," I repeated.

Yet she gently pulled herself away from me and tore her gaze from mine. "I'm fine."

She wasn't fine, but I didn't want to push her away. I feared that if I asked her too many questions, pushed too hard for an answer, or became too overbearing, then she would leave me. And that was the worst thing that could happen right now.

"If you ever want to talk …" I trailed off because I didn't know what to say.

Grasping the door handle, she lingered by the door, her entire body tense. I wished that she would turn back, tell me everything that was bothering her, but she didn't make a move to do either. Instead, she gave me a small nod and left.

My chest tightened, my stomach in knots. I wanted to hurl again this morning.

Why wouldn't she talk to me? Was it because I had killed someone in front of her? Didn't do more to stop her from being tortured?

Whatever was going on was my fault. And I didn't know how to stop it. I didn't know what to say. Constantino had always been the one who was better at controlling his emotions and thinking about things logically. Better at assessing situations and figuring out solutions.

It was one of the many reasons he and I worked so well. I was a mess, and he wasn't.

But with Sage and me ... it was so much harder.

74

sage

I SAT in my empty apartment with my suitcases packed. They had been packed for three days, but I hadn't had the courage to leave. Honestly, I didn't want to go, but I … needed some time away from the family.

To figure things out.

Was this what I really wanted? Would I ever come first to Laila and Constantino? When the baby finally came in less than nine months now, would I become second to it? Would they have time for me?

Tears streamed down my cheeks. I didn't want to think about it because I didn't want it to be true. I didn't want to go shopping for baby clothes with Laila, knowing that she would ditch me in a few months. I didn't want to attend her art gala and finally be able to go out in public with Laila and Constantino, knowing that they would be too busy for me one day.

But, fuck, I didn't want to leave.

I fucking loved them more than I had loved any man or woman before, even more than most of my family. Yet I couldn't allow myself to get attached more than I already was. I had signed up for a year with them, and that was all.

It had been a month, maybe. Honestly, time was all jumbled for me after everything had happened.

"They don't need me," I repeated to convince myself. "Laila is pregnant."

What use am I now? A fucktoy until … when?

Deciding that I couldn't sit in this room forever in silence with Riccardo, I called Poppy.

"Do you want to go out with me?" I asked as soon as she answered.

"To where?"

"To Italy," I said. "You mentioned that you wanted to go."

"Right now?"

"Yes, right now."

"I, um …" She paused. "Isn't this kinda last minute?"

A sob that I had been biting back escaped my throat. "Please."

"Oh my gosh," Poppy said, worry in her voice. "What's wrong?" She shuffled around in the background, as if she was getting her shoes on and rummaging through her closet. "You know what? You can tell me on the plane ride. I'll be over in twenty minutes."

"Thank you," I whispered.

It was spontaneous, but if I didn't do something, then I would be stuck here forever.

After grabbing the painting I had worked on all night—an exact replica of my digital artwork of Laila—I set it on my dining room table in hopes that Laila would find it when she came looking for me later.

Then, I walked with Riccardo up the stairs to Laila and Constantino's penthouse. I entered the code into their lock and found a slip of paper inside a drawer that I could use to write Laila a note about why I was leaving.

More tears slipped from my eyes, staining the paper. *Fuck, I don't want to do this.*

But I forced myself to finish the note and stuck it right on the counter, where she usually deposited her keys and purse when she returned from shopping. I closed my eyes and vowed not to cry on the flight today with Poppy.

I didn't want her asking questions. I just wanted to be happy again.

And I wouldn't be happy with being second for the rest of my life.

75

laila

WITH MY GUARD holding half my bags, I pushed the front door open and walked into the penthouse. I spent the entire day by myself, shopping for baby clothes and toys and wishing that Sage had come. I had rushed home to spend time with her tonight before Constantino returned from work.

After depositing my bags on the floor, I placed down my keys and purse, noticing a small handwritten note folded up on the counter. Brow furrowed and chest tight, I unfolded it and spotted Sage's handwriting.

Laila,

I'm sorry I haven't been myself lately, but I need a few days alone and away from the family. I wish I could've told you when we spoke earlier, but I didn't want you to be angry with me. I don't know when I'll be back. Riccardo is coming with me for protection.

It might not seem like it, but I'm so happy that you and Constantino finally get to have a baby together. Honestly, I don't want to get in the way anymore of you and him being happy and raising a family together.

I guess what I'm saying is ... I need some time to figure out what I want and what you need because I can't add anything into your life that you don't already have. You're pregnant with an amazing man. You deserve this.

Love,

Sage

P.S. Constantino mentioned that the art gala was moved to next week. I left you a painting that you had asked me for in my apartment. I hope you love it.

"What is it?" my guard asked.

Hands shaking, I dropped to my knees. *Wh-what is this?*

I read the note again and again, my stomach twisting. Bile rose in my throat, but I pushed it back down before I puked again today. *No. This can't be. This … Sage is … she left me? Left us?*

With tears blinding my vision, I sprinted out of the penthouse with the letter and to the staircase. I didn't have time to wait for the elevator. Maybe she was still here. Maybe I could catch her before she skipped town and never came back.

When I reached her apartment, I typed her code on the keypad and pushed the door open. "Sage!" I shouted, running like a madwoman from room to room.

She … she couldn't be gone. Not yet.

"Sage!"

Tears streamed down my cheeks, an ugly sob escaping my mouth. Her note had made it sound like she wasn't planning to return anytime soon, like she might not return at all. She had left me and Constantino after she told me that she loved me.

All of her belongings were gone. The apartment was cleared out of any signs of her even living here.

"No," I repeated, stumbling out into the main living area.

When I spotted the large painting on the dining table, another sob escaped my mouth.

A painting of me. That was all she had left.

76

constantino

STEPPING INTO THE ELEVATOR, I hit the button for Sage's floor and leaned against the metal wall with my hands stuffed into my pants pockets. Laila had officially been relieved from bed rest by Dr. Lin this morning, so I could take both my girls out for dinner tonight.

Sage hadn't been herself since the incident. She had been skipping dinners and cutting visits upstairs short, not wanting to talk for long when I visited her throughout the week. I wanted to give her space to process things, but I also wanted her to know we cared.

That we still wanted this, no matter what.

Tonight, we would make sure she knew.

My lips curled into a soft smile as I thought about how Laila had been so excited to go baby shopping with Sage today. She had been gushing about it all week and nagging Dr. Lin to let her go. I hoped they had bought some clothes and furniture for the nursery today.

When my phone buzzed in my pocket, I pulled it out and pressed it to my ear. "Talk."

"Hello, this is Fluorescence. We're confirming your reservation for tonight at eight."

"We'll be there," I said as the elevator doors opened, and then I clicked off the phone and walked to Sage's apartment at the end of the hallway, excited that shit was finally cooling off and calming down with the FBI.

I paused in front of her door and knocked twice. "Sage!"

No answer, but I heard crying inside the apartment.

The door must've been unlocked because I pushed it right open and stepped into the room, listening to my wife's sobs from the dining area. I sprinted into the next room and stared at Laila, curled up in a ball on the floor, wailing with tears and snot running down her face.

"What happened?" I asked Laila.

She balled my shirt into her fists and buried her face into my chest. "S-S-Sage!"

"Laila, what the fuck is going on?" I asked, scanning the room and noticing that all the decorations were gone, the walls were bare, and Sage's belongings were not here. My chest tightened. "Where is she?"

"G-gone!" Laila cried, barely lifting her finger toward the table. "She's gone!"

While still holding Laila, I reached for the letter in the center of the table that was stained with tears, next to the painting that Sage had done of Laila. I unfolded the note and stared down at Sage's handwriting.

Laila,

I'm sorry I haven't been myself lately, but I need a few days alone and away from the family. I wish I could've told you when we spoke earlier, but I didn't want you to be angry with me. I don't know when I'll be back. Riccardo is coming with me for protection.

Why ... why hadn't she told me this every night I visited her this past week? I would've booked her a spa day, a vacation, and provided her with more protection than just Riccardo. And why was the note only addressed to Laila, not me?

It might not seem like it, but I'm so happy that you and Constantino finally get to have a baby together. Honestly, I don't want to get in the way anymore of you and him being happy and raising a family together.

Hot tears welled up in my eyes, but I pushed them back for Laila. Sage was so fucking wrong. She had never once gotten in the way of our relationship, only made it stronger. And now ... now, she was fucking gone?!

I guess what I'm saying is ... I need some time to figure out what I want and what you need because I can't add anything into your life that you don't already have. You're pregnant with an amazing man. You deserve this.

I balled the note into my fist. Wrong. She was so fucking wrong!

After dropping the crumpled note onto the table, I pulled Laila tighter to my chest and held myself together for her. She continued to sob into my chest, screaming out in pain, like I wanted to do, and fell to her knees.

Why did it sound like Sage wasn't planning on returning? Because if she were, she wouldn't have emptied out her apartment. She had fucking lived with us for so long. I'd thought she was falling for us the way we were with her. How could she get up and leave?

"She's not coming back," Laila cried, grasping on to my thigh from the ground like a child. "I know she's not coming back. Why does everyone I love end up leaving me, Constantino? Why did she leave us?"

Crouching next to her, I picked her up, walked to the couch, and sat down with her in my lap while I desperately tried to gather my thoughts. I didn't have the answers to her questions. This wasn't the Sage we had asked to join our family.

This family had broken her.

We had broken her.

"If she's not coming back," I murmured to my wife, "then we'll bring her back."

She curled up in my arms and continued to cry, cradling her bump with one hand and grasping on to me with the other. Her body trembled uncontrollably, tears streaming down her cheeks and sobs escaping her mouth.

I pulled my phone out of my pocket and dialed Riccardo's number. I was almost immediately sent to voice mail. I left him a message to return my call and let me know his whereabouts as soon as fucking possible.

"What are we going to do?" Laila asked, stress written all over her face. "Sage is gone. The gala is—"

"Fuck the gala," I said. "You and Sage are more important to me than keeping up a good image. We're a family, and families stick together. We'll find her, and we'll get her back, no matter the cost."

Laila stared up at me through heavy tears. "Do you promise?"

"I fucking promise, baby," I said. "Sage is ours."

77

sage

AFTER A MUCH-NEEDED afternoon at the pool, Poppy and I walked back to the hotel room. We weren't staying in a super-luxurious resort or a private villa, like I had with Constantino and Laila, but it was just what I needed.

We had been here for just under a day, and it was drama-free so far. We spent all day relaxing, getting massages together, taking shots of alcohol at the bar while guys flirted with Poppy, but Poppy only flirted with Riccardo.

My little heart was so happy that they were getting along. I really wanted them together.

"I would've appreciated a warning that you two had planned to sneak off," Riccardo said, stepping into the lobby with us.

Dressed in all black, he stuck out like a sore thumb and *definitely didn't*—note the sarcasm—look like he was part of a secret society.

"And I would've appreciated a foot rub at the pool," Poppy teased him.

I nudged her. "He was too busy asking the bartender if they had cookies."

We broke out into a fit of giggles as the elevator doors opened.

Poppy looped her arm around mine and pulled me onto the lift, peering up at Riccardo with a small smile on her face.

The flirting was literally killing me! I needed them in my life.

When the elevator doors closed, I rested my head against hers, my smile slowly fading. While I was having a really great time and much-needed time alone, I really wished that I had come back here with Laila and Constantino.

I had made such a hasty decision, leaving out of nowhere. I should've explained myself.

Being separated from them had really made me realize how much I needed them in my life. I didn't want to be without them, not even for a couple of days.

I'd completely packed up my belongings and left New York City. Which I never should've done.

"Wanna head to dinner at six?" Poppy asked, stealing another peek at Riccardo.

"Yeah, sure," I said with a smile. "You sure you two don't wanna go yourselves?"

"No," Poppy said quickly, looking back at me. "We're here for you."

I bit back a wider grin, and the elevator doors opened. We stepped out of the lift and headed to our hotel room. Riccardo had private quarters, but an attached room. I pushed open our door and walked in with Poppy.

"I'm gonna hop in the shower really quick, and then we can head off to dinner," Poppy said.

She released my arm and headed to the bathroom. I arched a brow at her retreating figure and would bet that she needed to really take care of herself after spending all day at the pool with Riccardo.

I walked to my suitcase and opened my bag, looking for something to wear and deciding on a soft pink sundress that Constantino and Laila had bought for me what seemed like forever ago now. God, I missed them.

"Do you have any bright lipstick?" I asked, standing beside the bathroom door.

"I think it's in my makeup bag!" Poppy called from the shower.

I hurried to her suitcase to find some hot red lipstick that I so desperately wanted to wear tonight. Usually, I wasn't really one to show off or to stand out, but I wanted to feel sexy tonight.

All I needed was some time to myself with friends again.

Dropping to my knees, I unzipped her luggage and rummaged through it in an attempt to find her makeup bag. I swore she hadn't brought it into the bathroom yet. We had gone makeup-free to the pool today.

After unzipping a compartment, I froze and stared at a gun buried in her suitcase. My throat dried as I pulled it out of the compartment and spotted a wallet with it. I took it out, too, and unbuckled it, my hands shaking.

A shiny gold FBI badge sat next to Poppy's picture and the name Elia Johnson.

78

sage

"MY MAKEUP BAG is in here, Sage!" Poppy shouted from the shower.

I snapped my head to the bathroom door, which was ajar, and slowly stood to my feet. Poppy—Elia or whoever the hell she was—had ... betrayed me. She was part of the FBI, only friends with me for information.

What if she had planned for me to be kidnapped? Maybe Laila too. What if she had paid those dirty men to waterboard me and Laila in front of each other so we would break? She had fucking lied to me, tried to get us to turn on each other, had attempted to break us apart.

And she had. She fucking had!

Once I took the gun from her suitcase, I grasped it in my hand, like Laila had when she murdered her best friend. She had done it for her family, for me, and I would do this for mine. I ... I had to. I couldn't give her any time to explain herself.

But my mind was buzzing, thoughts rushing too quickly through my head.

If she really was in the FBI, then I had to be quick. She would have training, be stronger and faster than I was. She could kill me and hide the body with the connections she had, but I had Riccardo in the next room. He would hide her body for me.

Constantino and Laila would too.

"I'll be out in a second!" Poppy called. "And I'll find it for you."

Fuck, I didn't have time to find Riccardo. If I left the room and she got out, she'd realize that I'd rummaged through her stuff. I would put Riccardo's and my lives in danger. This had to be quick, but my hands were trembling around the gun.

I had never killed anyone before, but she was ... threatening to split up my family.

After I pushed away the tears, I walked toward the bathroom without knocking. "Turn away," I called before walking into the room and attempting to keep my voice strong. "I need to use the bathroom."

When I stepped into the bathroom, Poppy stood naked in the shower, facing the wall, her hands in her wet hair while she washed the shampoo out of it. I stood in front of the foggy glass and lifted the gun.

My arms were unsteady, trembling. My heart pounded inside my chest, beating so hard that I thought it would burst straight through my chest. I feared that one bullet wouldn't shatter the glass, that I would miss, that Poppy wouldn't die and would kill me instead.

I feared that I would leave this world without admitting that I loved Constantino and Laila with all my heart, without them really knowing how I truly felt about them and the lengths I would go to in order to protect them, the way that they had protected me.

Tears began streaming down my face, and I attempted to bite back a sob.

"Are you okay?" Poppy asked, her voice so genuine.

Like she actually fucking cared.

And part of me wanted to believe that this was all some sort of mistake, that the gun didn't belong to her and that she really wasn't part of the FBI. I wanted to believe that she had been my friend because she liked me.

Not for information.

"I'm fine. Just ... uncomfortable." *With what I am about to do.*

I aimed the gun at her head and hoped that it was loaded. I wasn't sure how to check, wasn't even sure if the safety was off. I fiddled around with it and did what I had seen Constantino and Riccardo do a couple of times.

Pain shot through my entire body. I steadied my hands.

"I haven't told them yet," she suddenly said.

"Wh-what?" I whispered.

She turned around and continued to shower, staring right at the gun, as if she had known the entire time that I was going to kill her. "I haven't told the FBI and my superiors any of the information that I've learned about your family."

"Liar," I whispered. "You're lying."

"I'm not."

"Yes, you are!" I cried, stepping closer. "You're lying!"

"You're holding a gun to my head. I have no reason to lie to you."

"That gives you an even better reason to lie!" I shouted. "Why?! Why'd you do it?!"

She took the showerhead in her hand and washed the soap off her naked body. "Because it was my job, but I ..." She paused. "I regret ever lying to you. I realize that now, especially because of Ricca—"

I pulled the trigger when she began to say his name. She was using him against me. She knew that I thought she liked him. She was playing into it, and I couldn't let her get inside my head. I wasn't as stupid as she might think.

Glass shattered everywhere, the water from the showerhead spraying into the room. I aimed the gun at her head, standing a few feet away from her, and cried out in emotional pain. I didn't want to do this. Not to her.

"Did you organize the kidnapping?" I asked. "The waterboarding? The torture?"

She paused and swallowed hard, fear crossing her face. "It doesn't matter."

"It does!" I shouted. "Did you do it?"

"Yes, but I—"

Before she could finish her sentence, I pulled the trigger four more times. Bullets whizzed through the air and lodged into her skull. Her corpse smacked against the bathroom floor, her blood mixing with water. And she lay dead in front of me.

79

laila

SEVERAL LOUD BANGS erupted through the air, echoing down into the elevator, where Constantino and I stood after our eight-hour flight from NYC to Italy. It hadn't even been an hour since we had gotten off the private jet.

"What was that?" I shrieked. When the doors opened, I ran toward Room 431, where Riccardo had told us that Sage had been staying with Poppy. I tripped over my own two feet, my eyes swollen from crying all the way here. "Constantino, it sounds like gunshots!"

Constantino picked me up from the floor, his eyes filled with worry, but he didn't say anything. Instead, he set me back on my feet, grabbed my hand, and rushed down the hallway toward the hotel room.

"Constantino," I cried, cradling my small bump in one hand, "I can't lose her."

"I know, doll," Constantino muttered, grasping my hand tighter. "Neither can I."

When we reached Room 431, Constantino banged on the door. "Riccardo!"

There was some shuffling around in the room, accompanied by cursing from Riccardo, and then the door opened wide. I pushed past him and hurried into the hotel room, searching in all the rooms for Sage until I reached the bathroom with Constantino.

Sage stood over Poppy's naked corpse and clutched a gun in her hand.

"I didn't know what else to do," she whispered, her back turned toward us. "Riccardo—"

I lunged forward and wrapped my arms around her waist from behind, tears rolling down my cheeks. I had been worrying all night and morning about her, worried that Riccardo wouldn't be able to protect her alone.

"Thank God you're okay," I cried.

She stiffened and turned. "L-Laila? Constantino? Wh-what are you doing here?"

"Hate us all you want, but we're here for you."

With heavy tears in her eyes, she gazed from me to Constantino, then back. She opened her mouth, then peered at Riccardo, who looked into the bathroom to see Poppy lying in the tub with several bullet holes in her head.

"Fuck," I whispered.

"What happened?" Constantino asked.

Sage tensed even more, the way that I usually did right before I burst into tears. Except she didn't cry, like I'd expected her to, like I would've done. She was stronger than I would've been—than I *had* been—in this type of situation. Someone I could only aspire to be.

A true fucking Mafia boss's wife.

"She had an FBI badge and gun," Sage whispered, handing the gun to Constantino with a shaky hand. She walked out of the bathroom and to the living room, sitting on the very end of the couch, her body pressed against the armrest. "I'm sorry. I should've stayed away from her."

Hesitantly, I followed her into the other room and sat next to her. I had barely seen her all week and had been ruthlessly rejected by her yesterday morning. And she might've hated me, too, but I wanted her to know that I loved her.

That I would be better for her.

That she mattered to us.

"There is shit wrong with this. Shit that doesn't add up, especially her relationship with the FBI," Constantino said, pacing around the room for a couple of moments with his brow furrowed. Then, he paused and gazed over at Sage. He walked over to us and took her chin in his hand. "But that doesn't matter now. What matters is that you're safe and you're coming home with us."

"If that's what you want," I found myself saying.

I didn't want Sage to leave us—I didn't know what the fuck I would do without her—but she had had the hardest few months of her life, living with us and with this family. If she wanted an out, then ... we would have to give her one. We couldn't force her to live like this.

Right? She would end up despising us. And I didn't want that.

"Do you not want me to come home with you, Laila?" she asked through tears. "I just killed one of the only friends that I had in the city for this family, *for you*, and you think that I don't want this?"

"Sage, that's not what I meant," I said.

My words always seemed to come out wrong.

When I had joined the family, I had done so because I loved Constantino. But I hadn't known what the fuck I was getting myself into. I hadn't known that I would have to kill the people that I'd once thought I couldn't live without.

And I didn't want Sage to go through anything like that either. I wanted her to be happy.

"I'm sorry," I whispered. "I—"

"No," she said, and I expected her to continue to scold me. "I'm sorry. I shouldn't have left like I did without warning. I shouldn't have turned down your offers this week to eat dinner with you or to go shopping. I've been having an extremely stressful few weeks, and I needed to talk to someone about it."

"You can talk to us anytime," Constantino said, crouching in front of us.

"But you two have been so happy about your baby," she whispered. "I didn't want to ruin that."

I tucked some hair behind her ear. "You wouldn't have ruined that. You're important to us."

She lifted her gaze to meet mine, the tears in her eyes wavering. "I-I am?"

My heart shattered into a million pieces at the mere sound of her fragile voice. I wrapped my arms around her body and pulled her closer to me, tears welling in my own eyes. "Of course you are, Sage. And I'm so sorry that we made you feel like you weren't."

Sage, who had been holding it all inside her and refusing to shed a tear in front of us, suddenly burst out into tears. She sobbed into the crook of my neck and pulled me tighter.

"You're ours to love, Sage," Constantino said, sitting on the couch next to her and placing his lips on her shoulder. "You're not just some plaything to us anymore. We would do anything for you. We promise."

80

constantino

"ROOM 431," I said to one of my men, handing him the keys to Sage's hotel room. "Clean up the mess. Dispose of the body. Don't make a mistake, or I'll have your fucking head by the time you get back to the city. Understand?"

"Yes, boss."

After watching him drive off from the airport and head back in the direction of the hotel, I boarded the private jet, where Sage slept on Laila's shoulder, her cheeks stained with tears. Laila gently stroked her hair.

"Is everything okay?" she whispered.

"Yes."

"Are *you* okay?"

"I'm fine," I said, but really ... I was still dealing with the fact that Sage hadn't even told me that she had left. No note addressed to me, no call, no text. But I was so fucking torn because she had taken care of Poppy so cleanly, unlike Laila had with Bethany.

Sage was part of this family now and had to deal with the consequences.

Consequences that I should not have allowed her to be part of.

I walked past the girls and sat across from Riccardo near the back of the private jet, not speaking a word to him until Laila passed out, too, and we were in the air.

Riccardo offered a small smile—something he never did.

"What?" I asked.

"You know, she loves you both," Riccardo said, nodding to a stirring Sage. "She needed a break from the family, but she has been asking about you and Laila since we stepped onto the flight to leave New York a couple of nights ago."

"Really?"

He nodded in response.

After dropping my gaze to the ring on my left hand, I frowned. Why hadn't she told me she needed a break? Was it because of the way I'd acted with Laila and Bethany? Did she not trust me anymore? Or maybe she just didn't think it would break me as much as it would break Laila.

But it fucking had. It'd hurt so much to see her apartment completely cleared out.

"I think I'm going to step back before Laila gives birth," I said. "I need to figure shit out with Laila and Sage, especially Sage." I wanted her to trust me again, wanted her to love me, wanted her to know just how much she meant to me.

"From the family?" Riccardo asked.

"From my position, not the family."

"Who will replace you?"

I stayed quiet and raised a brow. *Definitely not my brother.*

When I told him, he would jump at the chance to be boss, but he would get all of us thrown in prison. He was a damn good fighter, but not a leader in the slightest, especially after he had believed Bethany had *any* redeeming qualities.

"You and a couple of my uncles are the only ones I trust not to screw this family up."

"What about Pietro?" Riccardo said.

"What about him?" I asked.

He'd helped me out when I asked him to, but I had gotten him out of more trouble than he even seemed worth sometimes. But if I threw him under the bus, then Laila would really never forgive me.

Riccardo stayed quiet, and I knew that he felt the same way. Pietro wasn't cut out to be a leader of any kind. But … maybe Riccardo could. And if he didn't want it, then one of the uncles that I trusted would happily take the position.

"What about Poppy?" Riccardo asked. "You think she was actually FBI?"

"We don't know enough yet," I said, blowing out a breath. "I can have one of the dirty cops down at the station check it out to see if her badge is real. I'll take care of this particular situation before I step down, but I'm hoping she was lying through it all."

81

laila

"I'M SO HAPPY." I beamed, walking into the cutest damn baby shop in the northeast.

Sage looped her arm around mine, humming and peering at all the baby toys that'd soon be littered around our home. She had moved in last week, and we had started painting the nursery together.

Constantino wheeled a bright red cart through the aisles behind us, then stopped when we reached the cribs. Sage continued toward the baby clothes instead of choosing a crib with Constantino. So, I followed because I liked looking at all the tiny dresses.

She had been quiet today, and I feared that those memories of waterboarding and torture were still weighing on her mind. It had only been a couple of weeks, but she had at least begun to open up to us about it.

Constantino held her every night as she cried in his arms after waking up from nightmares. And then in the mornings, she'd always apologize, as if it were *her* fault, and we'd reassure her that it wasn't and would *never* be.

But this morning, she was quieter than usual.

Once we strolled halfway down the aisle, Sage stopped at the boys clothes and stared down at it with huge eyes. She curled her nude lips into a small smile, then took an outfit from the shelf. "What about this?"

"Sage"—I giggled—"I'm having a girl."

"Yeah, but"—she chewed on the inside of her cheek—"I'm not."

"If I got—what?" I whispered, the world suddenly slowing down as what she had said finally registered. I snapped my gaze to her and beamed, my heart racing and heavy tears welling in my eyes. "No, you're lying."

She smiled softly at me, her cheeks tinting pink, and shook her head.

I stepped back in complete disbelief. "No."

"I found out this morning."

Tears streamed down my cheeks, and I pulled her into a tight hug. "Stop it. I am so happy. God, I'm so fucking happy for you." But then I pulled back slightly and stared into her eyes. "This is what you want, right?"

"To have a family with you and Constantino? Yes."

After pulling her into another tight hug, I wiped my tears before Constantino could spot them from across the store. "Have you told Constantino yet?" I asked, looping my arm around hers and resting my head on her shoulder as we walked down the aisle.

"Not yet."

"You should tell him over dinner," I said. "He's been wanting to talk to you."

"About what?"

"About you being in our family."

She paused and stared up at me in horror. "Does he not want me to—"

"Of course he does!" I exclaimed. "But ever since you left for Italy without telling him, he's been distant. Something has been bothering him. I'm sure you could tell after you moved in with us."

She nodded. "I thought that was how he was to live with."

"No," I said. "So, I conveniently booked some events for the gala that I need to take care of tonight, so you and he can go out to dinner and talk things through. He will be so fucking happy for you too."

"Are you sure?" she asked. "I'm sorta nervous."

When we caught back up to Constantino, who leaned against the cart with his sleeves rolled up his forearms and his phone to his ear, I plucked the device from him, ended the call, and crossed my arms over my belly.

"I forgot to tell you," I said, taking Sage's hand. "You and Sage have to get dinner alone tonight. I have a ... meeting with a couple of people about the gala that we pushed back. You know, important stuff."

"And you had to shut off my call with Riccardo to tell me this?" he asked, brow arched.

"Yes, because you promised that you wouldn't work today," I said.

He brought my hand that held his phone up to his lips and kissed it softly. "Sorry, doll. I have a lot to tie up after Bethany and Poppy."

Sage shyly peered over my shoulder at him. "Sorry about that."

"Don't worry about it, Sage," he said, offering her a small smile.

I nudged her, just wanting her to tell him right now. I couldn't wait to see how excited he would be. But Sage didn't say anything, and I didn't want to force her. It was stressful enough, being in this family.

"Well, come on then," I said, dragging them along. "We have shopping to do."

For *two* babies now.

82

sage

"NO WINE," I said, shaking my head at the waiter who had offered me a glass of Afterglow for the fifth time tonight.

If he kept coming over and I kept refusing, Constantino would know that something was up before I told him.

Laila had ushered us out of the house in a very *obvious* production fifty minutes ago. And while Constantino kept up the nice small talk, he still seemed as distant as he had after we left Italy a couple of weeks ago.

"So," I finally said, nerves bubbling up inside me, "are you excited?"

"About?"

"The baby."

Constantino smiled. "I am."

"I know that Laila wants more kids after this one," I whispered, cutting my steak and avoiding eye contact with him. "But do you? You seemed a bit distracted while we shopped for baby clothes today."

"I've been dealing with family things," he said, drinking a slow sip of his wine and gazing out the large window. When he finally set the glass on the table, he peered over at me and offered a small, almost-shy smile. "But of course I do. I'd love to have them with you too."

"Yeah?"

"Yes," he said, not an ounce of regret on his face.

"Well ..." I whispered, heart racing. My cheeks tingled, and I found myself lost for words as I pulled out a picture of the ultrasound that I'd had this morning before sliding it across the table, hoping for the best.

His eyes widened as he looked at the image and then up at me. "Is this ..."

"Ours? Yes."

"And you want to keep it?"

"Of course I do, Constantino."

An unreadable expression crossed his face, and then ... a tear slipped down his cheek. "You really do? After everything that has happened to you in this family within the last few months, you want to be a family with us? With me?"

I leaned forward to brush the tear off his cheek. It was rare for Constantino to cry and even rarer that it happened in public. But I didn't mind it in the slightest.

"I promise ... you'll never be in danger like that again," he murmured.

"Don't make promises you can't keep," I whispered. "I'll be with you either way."

"I mean it," he said with so much assurance on his face that I couldn't *not* believe him. He sat up a bit taller, as if this was the best decision of his life. "I'm going to step down as boss in a couple of months, before Laila gives birth. I had my doubts about it, but I'm sure now." He gently took my chin in his hand and pulled me closer. "I have a family to protect."

"Goddamn, I love you, Constantino Buratti."

He took my left hand from across the table and drew his thumb across my knuckles. "I want to marry you too," he murmured. "I know Laila would like to have you be part of our family officially, but I don't know how that would look. A traditional wedding? A ceremony for us? Would you like that?"

Tears welled up in my eyes. "Yes," I whispered.

He leaned across the table and brushed the tear off my cheek, like I had just done to him only moments ago. "No tears," he ordered, gently cupping my chin. "You deserve more than we could ever give you. You've made both Laila and me so fucking happy, Sage."

"Sometimes, I … I still worry that I cause more drama than—"

Before I could finish my sentence, he snapped my mouth closed. "Don't even think that." He slowly released his grip on my chin and took my hand again. "Promise me that you won't think that, and if we act that way, then you fucking tell us so we can fix it, okay?"

"Okay," I whispered.

"Promise me."

"I promise."

His lips curled into a soft smile. "And *I* promise that we'll cherish you forever, Sage Stonewell."

Want to read three epilogues for Mafia Toy? Join my newsletter!

Continue reading the Syndicate of Sin with Mafia Betrayal.

also by emilia rose

also by emilia rose

Scan the QR code with your phone to view all of Emilia's books!

about the author

Emilia Rose is a *USA Today* best-selling author of steamy romance. Highly inspired by her study abroad trip to Greece in 2019, Emilia loves to include Greek and Roman mythology in her writing. She graduated from the University of Pittsburgh with a degree in psychology and a minor in creative writing in 2020 and now writes novels as her day job.

With over 18 million combined book views online and a growing presence on reading apps, she hopes to inspire other young novelists with her tales of growth and imagination, so they go on to write the stories that need to be told.

Join Emilia's newsletter for exclusive giveaways, early chapter releases, and more!

acknowledgments

Nicole Bridget-Dallas
El Rivers
Ana Jovel